PENGUIN CRIME FICTION

THIS WAY OUT

Sheila Radley worked at a variety of professional jobs until the 1960s, when she left London to help run a village store and post office. She is the author of *Who Saw Him Die?*, *Fate Worse Than Death*, *The Quiet Road to Death*, *A Talent for Destruction*, and *The Chief Inspector's Daughter*.

This Way Out

→

SHEILA RADLEY

PENGUIN BOOKS
Published by the Penguin Group
Viking Penguin, a division of Penguin Books USA Inc.,
375 Hudson Street, New York, New York 10014, U.S.A.
Penguin Books Ltd, 27 Wrights Lane, London W8 5TZ, England
Penguin Books Australia Ltd, Ringwood, Victoria, Australia
Penguin Books Canada Ltd, 2801 John Street,
Markham, Ontario, Canada L3R 1B4
Penguin Books (N.Z.) Ltd, 182–190 Wairau Road,
Auckland 10, New Zealand

Penguin Books Ltd, Registered Offices:
Harmondsworth, Middlesex, England

First published in Great Britain by Constable & Co. Ltd. 1989
First published in the United States of America by
Charles Scribner's Sons, an imprint of Macmillan Publishing Company, 1989
Published in Penguin Books 1990

10 9 8 7 6 5 4 3 2 1

This is a work of fiction. Names, characters, places, and incidents
either are the product of the author's imagination or are used fictitiously.
Any resemblance to actual events or persons, living or dead, is entirely
coincidental.

LIBRARY OF CONGRESS CATALOGING IN PUBLICATION DATA
Radley, Sheila.
This way out/Sheila Radley.
p.   cm. — (Penguin crime fiction)
ISBN 0 14 01.4453 6
I. Title.
PR6068.O846T4   1990
823'.914—dc20   90–7389

Printed in the United States of America

For T.K.

This Way Out

1

Derek Cartwright had always considered himself to be a decent, honourable man. The thought of doing away with his mother-in-law would never have entered his head, if he had not begun to suffer from bad dreams.

What shamed him most, as he recollected what was to prove only the first of several similar nightmares, was that he had no personal reason for wanting to strangle Christine's mother. Far from hating Enid Long, he rather liked her. It certainly wasn't some festering antagonism that had opened the window on his unconscious, bringing him out of his sleep in a cold sweat to stare with horror in the dark at his rigidly trembling imagined-murderer's hands.

Derek and his mother-in-law had always got on perfectly well together. There was no friction between them, open or concealed. She didn't even irritate him much. He bore no grudge against her, wished for no revenge, had no sordid financial motive for wanting her dead. As he flopped back on his pillow, panting after waking from his third dream-struggle to squeeze the breath out of her, he forced himself at last to analyse their relationship. The conclusion he arrived at, with guilt and further shame, was that he longed to get rid of his mother-in-law simply because she was *there*.

Enid Long was there, living at the Brickyard, the Cartwrights' comfortable Edwardian house in the Suffolk village of Wyveling, entirely by accident.

Until she wrote off her little Fiat by failing to take the 90 degree bend at Wolsey Bridge on the Southwold to Blythburgh road – no other vehicle was involved, but it was a warm summer afternoon and she admitted to a lunch-time gin and tonic and a possible subsequent lapse in concentration – she had been a vigorous and independent widow. Miraculously, considering that the car had landed on its roof in the grazing marshes, her injuries were relatively minor. But she had lain in the wreckage for over an hour before a passing lorry driver saw and rescued her, and she was badly shaken. The accident damaged her body rather less than her confidence.

It was Derek who had suggested to Christine that they ought to ask her mother to come to Wyveling to recuperate after she left hospital, instead of returning immediately to her Southwold flat. He did so primarily in his wife's interests, wanting to save Christine from an indefinite continuation of the long round trips she was making each day to visit her mother. To that extent, he acknowledged, he had only himself to blame for the fact that Enid was still there nearly a year later. But he had never for a moment imagined that Enid would *want* to live with them permanently.

Enid Long was not a sentimental woman. Her relationship with her only daughter had always been one of distant affection. She and her husband Percy (the junior partner in both marriage and business) had owned the guest house – the Glenalmond private hotel – on the North Parade at Southwold where Derek had stayed with his parents for a decade of summers when he was a boy. When he returned, alone, in his late teens for the specific purpose of seeing Christine, Enid had encouraged their friendship and had put no obstacles in the way of their eventual early marriage. And although the couple had never lived more than an hour and a half's drive from Southwold, Enid had made it clear from the start that she was too busy with her own affairs to take more than a detached (though generous) interest in theirs.

Even after Enid was widowed (Percy having departed with a minimum of inconvenience to her, as a junior partner should) she had continued to live her own life. She kept the Glenalmond until she was in her late sixties, then sold it and bought a flat. There she spent each summer, involving herself busily in the life of Southwold; and each winter she took herself off for three or four months to an apartment she had bought as an investment in Majorca, where between summer lets she could warm her own bones in the Mediterranean sun.

The only time she had ever previously stayed with Christine and Derek was in the November before her accident. She had taken them by surprise by inviting herself to Wyveling, at short notice, a few weeks after Laurie's death.

Laurie, the Cartwrights' fourth child, loving and very much loved, was handicapped by Down's syndrome. A happy, boisterously affectionate girl who needed almost constant supervision, she had died suddenly at the age of fifteen from an undiagnosed heart defect, leaving her family—her mother in particular—bereft.

While Laurie was alive, Christine had spent much of her time ferrying her daughter to and from a special day school for the mentally handicapped, thirty miles away in Yarchester. Laurie's death had deprived Christine not only of her youngest child but of occupation and purpose.

Derek, at forty-three the regional marketing manager for a highly rated mutual life assurance society, was out on the road a great deal. Their older children, Tim and Richard and Lyn, were all working or studying away from home. With no one now but the dog for company at the Brickyard, the property they had bought because it was ideal for a large family, Christine had begun to slip into the downward spiral of reactive depression.

Enid's telephone call announcing that she intended to stay with them for a few days had come as a great relief to Derek. Worried about his wife, and coping as best he could with his own grief, he had seen his mother-in-law's impending visit as a sure way of taking Christine's mind off her sorrow. The following day, a cold, dark-clouded Saturday morning in November, he had hurried out with enthusiasm when he saw the Fiat negotiating the open gateway that led from the village street to his long gravelled front yard.

'It's very good of you to offer to come, Enid,' he had said as he lifted her suitcase from the boot of her car. The lowest of the dark clouds had just begun to spit out a shower of hail, and they lingered under the car port – formerly a cart shed, set just inside the gateway and at a right-angle to it – until the precipitation stopped.

9

'It's not "good of me" at all,' his mother-in-law had retorted briskly. 'Sheer self-interest, Derek, I can assure you. I want to get away to Majorca, but I can't enjoy my holiday if I know that Christine's moping about here on her own all day. She can't go on grieving for ever. She needs to find herself a job, and as soon as possible.'

Enid Long was then seventy-five, but she looked ten years younger. Her dark eyes were clear, her cheeks healthily firm. The only indication of her true age was her drooping throat, and she always wore a smartly tied chiffon or silk scarf to retain it.

She was a little overweight, but she had style. Her lower legs were the elegant shape of inverted champagne bottles, her silver hair was bouffant, her discreet make-up was expertly applied. She was accustomed to buy expensive clothes, which she chose in becoming colour combinations of moss-green, cyclamen, grey and violet. Derek had always admired the care his mother-in-law took over her appearance, confident that Christine, who had inherited her mother's dress sense as well as her good features and slim ankles (though fortunately not her bottle calves) would when the time came progress just as smoothly to an ageless old age.

'I could tell from her voice on the telephone,' Enid went on, 'that Christine's making no effort at all to pull herself together. She needs something to galvanize her – and there'll be nothing like having *me* under her feet all day to do that!'

And Derek had laughed, almost for the first time since Laurie's death. His mother-in-law's attitude, as sharply invigorating as the shower of hail, was doing him a power of good already.

'As soon as I've got Christine going again,' Enid had continued vigorously, 'I shall be off. You won't want me hanging about here, especially now you've got your freedom. Because let's face it, Derek—however much you loved Laurie, she was an encumbrance.'

That had stung him, and he answered her with a rare anger: 'She most certainly was not! We *never* thought of her as that.'

'Never?' Enid's eyes were shrewd – a good deal harder than Christine's – but her voice was not unsympathetic.

'You wouldn't be human if you hadn't thought it sometimes,

10

Derek,' she had said. 'If Laurie had been a child of mine, she would have had to go into residential care – but then, I had the Glenalmond to run. Christine's like her father, soft-hearted; but I've always respected you for supporting her. You did what you both thought right, and Laurie turned out to be a lovable girl in spite of everything.

'But did you ever *think through* what you were doing? Did you realize that you were voluntarily tying up your whole future? That's what used to worry me. Between ourselves, I'm thankful for your sakes that Laurie died young. Oh, I don't expect you to agree with me – not at the moment, anyway. And of course I shan't say a word of this to Christine. But it seems to me that now the poor child's gone, the two of you can start living your own lives for a change.'

The hailstorm had stopped as abruptly as it began. Enid clutched her warm coat collar closely about her throat, and set off at a brisk trot up the yard towards the red brick, double-fronted, square bay-windowed house. Derek had followed thoughtfully, his steps obliterating her neat footprints as he crunched the newly fallen hail that temporarily covered the gravel with white icing.

What his mother-in-law had said was so much in character that he thought no worse of her for it. Predominantly, he felt grateful to her for having kept her opinions to herself while Laurie was alive.

There was something more personal that he felt, though; something so unaccustomed that at first he was hard put to identify the sensation that had begun to lift his spirits. It was years – fifteen, to be exact – since he had known what it was to be buoyed by optimism.

Even though he missed and mourned for Laurie he had felt, ever since she had been buried, a lurking sense of relief that the problems she represented had gone with her. At first he had refused to acknowledge the thought. When it persisted he had declined to dwell on it, out of loyalty to his wife and their dead child. But now that Enid, tough old bird that she was, had not shrunk from putting it into words, he was ready to admit to himself what he had denied to her. Yes, Laurie had been a burden.

He had never discussed this burden with his wife. It

11

wouldn't bear discussion. From the moment they were told of the Down's diagnosis, one-day-at-a-time had been their agreed philosophy. But Derek had looked ahead, as any life assurance man does, and had been alarmed by what he saw.

Caring for a mentally handicapped child was demanding enough. The prospect of caring permanently for a mentally handicapped adult was dauntingly different. For himself, it might not have been too difficult because he had his work to take him away from home. But for Christine, a lively and intelligent woman who had once planned to make a career as an interior decorator when their children had grown up, it would have meant a life-sentence of domestic imprisonment.

The thought that she was now freed from that burden gave Derek immense pleasure. There were sure to be some sad months ahead, for all the family. But it was secretly exhilarating to think that, once Christine's paramount grief had eased, the two of them would at last be able to plan an active, interesting future.

With admiration for his mother-in-law's shrewdness and discretion, and with a genuine affection for her, he had welcomed her into his home.

Enid's brisk and unsentimental presence at the Brickyard soon had the desired effect on her daughter. Christine, who found it easier to be fond of her mother in her absence than in her own kitchen, had rapidly decided that it was time she set about finding a job. Satisfied, Enid had repacked her suitcase and buzzed off in her Fiat to Southwold, *en route* for her long winter holiday.

The following summer, having crashed her car, Enid had allowed herself to be taken to the Brickyard to recuperate. A year later she was still there.

Physically, said the doctor, she was in very good condition for her age. But her age was now showing: she was slower of speech, and on her feet; her hairstyle was deflated, her lipstick was shakily applied. Worse – despite having been persuaded by her daughter and son-in-law to spend the winter in Majorca as usual, though in a hotel rather than the apartment – she had never regained her confidence.

When Enid was active, she had rarely bothered to read the

newspapers. Now she bought them in quantity, with a preference for the easy-to-read and the sensational. The newspapers told her that violent crime, particularly against the elderly, was rapidly increasing. Nervous since her accident, Enid began to regard herself as a member of an endangered species.

Despite the fact that she knew Southwold to be one of the quietest and most respectable of seaside towns, and that she was not personally acquainted with anyone who had been burgled, let alone attacked, she convinced herself that it would be the height of folly to return there to live alone. She was afraid that she would be mugged while she was doing her shopping, or – more probably and – that she would be murdered in her bed by a burglar.

Derek said everything he could to reassure her. In actuarial terms, he told her, she was every bit as safe on her own in Southwold as she was with them in Wyveling. As soon as she was back in her own flat, among her friends, she would wonder why she had been worried. Why didn't she try it?

His mother-in-law, now comfortably ensconced at the Brickyard with all her clothes and the most treasured of her possessions, didn't think she could take that risk; at least, not until she felt her usual self. 'Next week, perhaps – ' she would say.

But next week never showed any sign of coming.

Enid was now seventy-six years old. Derek knew that a woman of that age, in average health, has a further life expectancy of eleven years. What depressed him more was that her true life expectancy was probably a good deal longer than that.

Enid knew it, too. She included the local weekly newspaper in her reading, and on several occasions she had commented on the fact that it had become almost commonplace for elderly people – women in particular – to celebrate their centenaries.

'And here's another one,' she had said cheerfully to her daughter and son-in-law one evening, as she showed them the newspaper photograph of a very lively looking birthday girl. 'I only hope *I'm* as good as that when I reach a hundred!'

It was during the course of that night that Derek had the first of his bad dreams.

2

'You're chasing rabbits again.'

'*Uhh*?'

Derek struggled into consciousness. His heart was pounding, his lips were drawn back in a snarl, his throat was so dry that it hurt him to swallow. Sweat stood cold on his forehead. His stomach seemed to be undulating, moving in panicky corrugations as he fought his way out of yet another homicidal dream.

Christine's bedside light was on. Propped on her left elbow, half-turned towards him, her own face in shadow, she was watching him. Instinctively he covered his face with his hands. For a guilty moment he thought that she had been a spectator at his dream; that she had seen – could still see – him as a murderer.

'Chasing rabbits,' she repeated. And now he realized thankfully that there was nothing but affection in her voice. 'You've been twitching and panting, just as Sam does in his sleep.'

Sam was their soppy old beagle.

Derek groaned with relief, though he tried to disguise it as a yawn. Untangling himself from the duvet, he staggered to the bathroom – but quietly, so as not to wake his mother-in-law – and sluiced his face. His heart was still thumping abnormally, and there was a foul taste in his mouth. His cheeks, reflected in the mirror, were sickly pale under the stubble, and his bloodshot eyes had an alarming residual stare.

How could Christine *not* know what he'd just been doing in his sleep? He had shouted aloud as he tightened his grip on Enid's throat. Pliable as putty, it had offered no resistance to his squeezing hands. His thumbs could find no windpipe to crush, and he had shouted in panic because the old woman refused to die. Surely Christine must have heard him?

He rinsed his mouth, and padded back to the bedroom. His wife, still propped in the same position, smiled at him.

'Did you catch it?' she asked.

He kept his eyes averted, and slid back into bed. 'Catch what?'

'The rabbit you were chasing. You've been after it three or four times during the past few weeks.'

Sitting up beside her, his head deliberately higher than hers so that she couldn't see his face, Derek tried to laugh the subject away. *His* rabbit was an elusive major client, he told her. But it worried him that she knew he'd had the dream more than once before.

'I haven't been talking in my sleep, have I? Don't want to start giving away details of a client's finances!'

'Not talking, no. Whimpering a bit, sometimes – just like Sam . . .'

Whimpering? For a moment, Derek felt almost offended. His dream-experience had shocked him with its ferocity. How could such a brutal act – committed only in the imagination, true, but with such intensity that it had left his arm and stomach muscles aching – have been expressed in reality by nothing more than a twitch and a whimper?

But thank God Christine suspected nothing.

He eased down in the bed, stretched his right arm across the pillows, and gathered his wife to him. Christine rested her head on his shoulder, and gave a half-suppressed sigh.

Derek kissed her forehead. 'Sorry I woke you, darling.' Her skin was dry under his lips, and unduly – slightly feverishly – warm. He stroked her hair: once so thick and glossy, it had lost some of its life since her operation.

'I was awake anyway.'

He paused in mid-caress, anxiously alert. 'Are you feeling ill?'

'Not really. I just couldn't sleep.'

'I'll make you some tea.' He started to get out of bed, but she drew him back.

'Don't bother,' she said. 'Not unless we have to for Mum.'

Derek made no attempt to suppress his sigh. With tender care, he folded his wife in his arms. Bleakly – because of course he wouldn't murder Enid in real life; morality apart, he knew that he could never bring himself to attempt it, except in those savage dreams – he contemplated the unhopeful future.

There had seemed to be so much to hope for, once Enid had got them both going again after Laurie's death.

Christine had still needed time to mourn, of course. The first Christmas after bereavement is difficult for any family, and Derek had dreaded it on his wife's behalf because the season had always given Laurie such particular delight.

But their older children had rallied round magnificently. They had come home from their respective occupations (Tim, massively bearded, from his job as assistant warden of a nature reserve; Richard, in collar and tie, from a polytechnic course in business management; Lyn, as tough and style-conscious as her grandmother, from medical school) to fill the house with so much noise and clutter, and to make so many deliberately outrageous demands on the time and energy of their parents that however many private tears were shed, collective sorrow never got a look-in.

Immediately after their children scattered again, Derek had booked a holiday for Christine and himself. They hadn't been abroad for years. Laurie had suffered from travel sickness, and while she was alive they had been restricted to the holidays that suited her best, in self-catering seaside cottages not too far from home.

The travel brochures had provided hours of family entertainment over Christmas. Their offspring had insisted that they ought to go somewhere *different*: on the Trans-Siberian railway, or a ninety-mile walking tour in the Apennines, or a tent-trek across the Sahara. But Christine had eventually decided that what she really wanted to do was to learn to ski, and so Derek had booked a late-February winter sports holiday in the Austrian Tyrol.

By the time their holiday came, Christine was beginning to look much better. By the time they returned to Wyveling, with Alpine sun-tans and an exhilarating sense of achievement, she

16

was once again as vivacious as she had been in the early years of their marriage. Derek was delighted for her.

Delighted by her, too. He was proud of his wife, and of the fact that – while some couples they knew had been divorced or were contemplating it – he and Christine were still friends and lovers after twenty-three years of marriage. He attributed this, partly, to natural reticence. Having known each other since they were children, they instinctively respected each other's areas of privacy. As adults, they had never discussed their inmost thoughts. Their unspoken agreement was not to probe.

He had never questioned Christine about her feelings over Laurie's death, just as he had never revealed his own – or her mother's – to her. After their skiing holiday they had rarely talked about Laurie. Christine seemed to be reconciled to their child's death, and eager to begin a new phase of her own life.

Having studied fabric design at art school in her youth, and subsequently done all her own home decorating and curtain-making, she had found a job with a friend, the wife of an architect, who had recently opened an interior design consultancy in Breckham Market. Christine loved the job. She did it well, and her friend had offered her the prospect of becoming a partner in the business.

But that was before her mother had had her accident.

Naturally, Christine had taken leave from work so that she could make the long daily trip to the hospital to visit her mother. Derek had thought it would be a good idea to bring Enid to the Brickyard for her convalescence, simply because it would enable Christine to return to work. His wife, although eager to get back to her job, had not been enthusiastic about having her mother to stay; and when Enid showed no inclination to leave, Christine had become tight-lipped.

Derek had never enquired into the relationshp between mother and daughter. That was another of the areas he had preferred not to probe. He had always known that they got on better on the telephone than they did in the flesh, and gradually he began to realize why.

Even after all those years of independent living, the two women were unable to see each other as people. When they were together, they reverted to their original roles. Enid – over-compensating, perhaps, for her loss of confidence after her accident – played the authoritative mother; Christine's response was instinctively adolescent. The atmosphere between them was one of hardly suppressed impatience, erupting every so often in bursts of exasperation.

Finally, Christine had said to her husband: 'It's no good, Derek – she'll have to go. I know it's undutiful of me, but I can't stand having her here any longer. I will *not* be treated like an irresponsible teenager in my own home. But if I try to be firm with her we shall end up having an almighty row, and I don't want that. You've always been her blue-eyed boy – *you* tell her.'

At the time, Derek was under considerable pressure at work. He would have objected to being dragged in to resolve Christine's difficulties with her mother, were it not that his wife was looking unusually tired.

His solution to Christine's problem was to book an immediate long-stay holiday for Enid at a hotel near her apartment in Majorca. His mother-in-law had objected: it was too early in the season, she didn't know whether she felt up to the journey, she didn't want to spend so much money, she needed time to make up her own mind. Derek ignored her protests. He drove her to Heathrow and told her firmly that when she returned, fit and well, he would be there to meet her and take her straight to her own flat in Southwold.

Shortly after his mother-in-law's departure, Derek made a discovery that explained Christine's tiredness. He persuaded his wife to see her doctor for the first time in years, and she was almost immediately called into hospital for an operation.

To his great relief Christine was home again within a fortnight, although she needed some further out-patient treatment. They had agreed not to let Enid know about the operation; no point in worrying the old girl, and the last thing they wanted was to encourage her to think that her daughter might need her. By the time Enid was due to return, Christine would be – in the event was – making a satisfactory recovery.

But Derek's plan for taking his mother-in-law straight back to Southwold was never put into practice. Enid appeared to be in excellent health; a bit shaky, still, but obviously capable of living on her own. Christine, however, had thought that they ought to invite her mother to return to Wyveling for one night at least to rest after the journey, and Enid had accepted.

Derek never knew what passed between mother and daughter that evening. But on the following morning Christine had said to him, 'Mum is going to stay with us a bit longer, if that's all right with you.'

What could he say? It was Christine who had been adamant that her mother must go. He didn't *want* to have Enid there, for heaven's sake; but he worked such long hours that her presence didn't particularly bother him. Enid usually kept to her own sitting-room – Laurie's former playroom – when he was at home, and he felt that he could put up with her if Christine could.

How Christine could put up with her, though, was a mystery to him. The relationship between the two women almost immediately resumed its former irritability; more so, because Christine was not yet fit to return to full-time work and they spent longer in each other's company. In the weeks that followed, Derek kept expecting his wife to announce, as before, that she couldn't stand Enid's presence any longer. But all she did was to tighten her lips and bear it.

Concerned for Christine's health, Derek had begun to urge her to get rid of her mother. Christine refused; and refused to discuss the subject. Enid stayed on. And Derek, baffled by his wife's obstinacy but loving her too compassionately to be angry with her, found himself dreaming of taking the problem into his own hands and providing a fearful, final solution.

The Cartwrights had been accustomed throughout their marriage to compose themselves for sleep in a particular way, both lying on their right sides with Christine fitting snugly against Derek, as though she were sitting on his knee. Since her operation, she had adopted a position that retained their closeness but helped to ease the discomfort of her weakened arm. Now, after Derek had recovered from his nightmare, they settled down again: he on his right side as usual, Christine on her back. As usual he put his left arm round her, slipping his hand inside her nightdress.

He had always been attracted to her breasts. It had been the

19

fevered adolescent recollection of those soft twin cones, each with its delicate central eruption outlined by the cling of her clothes, that had first sent him bicycling crazily from Chelmsford to Southwold to renew his holiday acquaintance with Mrs Long's daughter.

Childbearing had of course changed the shape of Christine's breasts, and maturity had rounded them, but their attraction for him had remained constant. Always, he had settled himself for sleep with his left hand cupping her right breast in an attitude of love.

Now, as always, he slid his hand across her left breast, caressing its fullness in passing. As always, he opened his hand to encompass her right breast. Tenderly, but without pause – because to pause would be to betray his wife, allowing her to think that he felt the revulsion he denied – he placed his hand on the alien skin, part flat, part hollowed, part ridged with a long horizontal scar, that covered the place where her breast had once been.

'Darling,' he whispered. 'Chrissie darling ...'

Christine murmured something that he couldn't hear. They lay in silence for several minutes, both of them mourning their loss. He felt her body stiffen against his, and knew that she was trying not to weep.

He kissed her hair and whispered once again what he hoped would reassure her: that no one could tell from her appearance that she had had the operation, that her femininity was still complete, that dressed or undressed she attracted him as much as ever. But about their deeper cause for depression, the fear that she might die, there was nothing he could say.

Christine's surgeon had told them that the cancer might never recur, especially after the post-operational radiotherapy treatment; and indeed Derek's cousin's wife had had a mastectomy six years before, and was now leading a normal, active life. But then again, Christine had had a friend –

The fear was always there, though they tried not to dwell on it. One-day-at-a-time was the way they had lived while Laurie was alive, and that was how they lived now. The exciting glimpse they had once had of a long and interesting future had after all been nothing but fantasy.

What seemed to him particularly cruel about the drastic

curtailment of Christine's life expectancy was that she had already foregone so much for Laurie's sake. And now their handicapped child's bedroom was occupied by another dependant who, having accurately identified poor Laurie as a burden, was unable (or unwilling) to conceive that she herself might be an encumbrance.

Derek felt no personal animosity towards Enid. That was probably why he never saw her face in his dreams. But on the rare occasions when he allowed himself to dwell on the fact that his mother-in-law would probably outlive his wife, he was filled with impotent anger.

He was still raging inside his head when the sound came from what he thought of as Laurie's room. It was soft at first, the mewling cry of a small baby with nothing in particular to grumble about. He held his breath, as he had done when their children were babies, willing it not to recur.

Then it came again, louder, a rising wail that – like a demanding child's – could penetrate the deepest sleep. Christine woke, and groaned. They held each other for a few moments, hoping that this would be one of the nights when the noise suddenly stopped. Instead it increased in volume, a prolonged eerie cry of *oh oh oh ... oh oh oh ...*

Like Derek, Enid had begun to suffer from occasional bad dreams. Fortunately for his conscience – since she insisted on relating them in detail as soon as she was woken – they were usually of non-violent burglaries of her flat. Unfortunately for his peace of mind, they reinforced her disinclination to return to it.

He rolled reluctantly out of bed. Christine was already up and putting on her dressing gown. 'Don't you come, love,' she said. 'You've already had a bad night, and I know you've got an important meeting tomorrow. She isn't your responsibility.'

'It's not *her* sake I'm coming for.'

They followed their routine, Christine going to rouse her mother from her uneasy sleep, Derek going downstairs to make a pot of tea. He carried it up on a tray, with cups for all of them.

Christine met him at the door of her mother's room. It was

on occasions like this, when his wife was without her brave daytime camouflage, that he grieved for her most. Her eyes were hugely weary in her pale face. Loosened from its pleat, her once-lovely dark hair hung as though it too was exhausted. In the absence of the prosthesis that she wore in the cup of her bra, the empty right side of her dressing gown sagged against her mutilated body.

'I *must* go to the loo,' she said. 'Be a love and take in Mum's tea. She's perfectly all right – she just needs someone to talk at.'

Enid was sitting up in bed, capped by a mauve sleeping net, flushed and cheerfully garrulous. Derek put the cup on her bedside table and let her talk on. His attention was concentrated on her throat. Now that he could see it properly, scarless, drooping against the lacy plunge-neck of her nightgown, he knew that it was not the same throat that he squeezed in his dreams. That was inert, a column of putty. This was a warm trembling dewlap – something that he would be even less able in reality to bring himself to grasp.

Enid lay back against her pillows. Having related every inconsequential detail of her dream, she allowed her eyelids to droop. In that moment it came to Derek that his fixation on strangling was as unnecessary as it was fearful. There would be a much less distasteful method of killing his mother-in-law.

He had no need to touch her slack flesh at all. He could simply snatch up a pillow and press it over her face.

It would be so simple, so merciful, such an easy way out. Not now, this moment, of course; but when he'd had time to get it all planned.

Except that he wouldn't ever be able to do it.

He knew quite well that he couldn't use the pillow method, any more than strangulation. It was a matter not of technique, nor of the fear of discovery, but of morality. He looked at his mother-in-law, now fully recovered and happily sipping tea. However much he longed, for Christine's sake, to remove the old woman permanently from their home, he couldn't possibly take her life. His respectable background, his Sunday school and Scout upbringing, his own sense of values would always stay his hand.

For a decent, honourable man, there was no way out.

3

Lieutenant Colonel Hugh Rowland Lumsden, OBE, MC, late the Suffolk Regiment, was dead and buried but by no means forgotten.

Born and educated in Yarchester, he had dedicated his life since his retirement from the army to the service of the cathedral city. As a boy he had been a chorister in the cathedral. Latterly – until shortly before his death – he had been honorary secretary of the Friends of Yarchester Cathedral, the volunteer fund-raising organization that kept the fabric of the great building in good repair. It was therefore entirely appropriate that, some weeks after his death, a thanksgiving service in his memory was held in the cathedral he had loved.

The service, on a bright cold morning in March, was well attended. Colonel Lumsden had been involved in many local organizations and he had a large number of friends, regimental and civilian, who were glad to take the opportunity to honour his life and work. His relatives, though – Hugh Lumsden was a bachelor – scarcely filled a pew.

None of them now lived in Yarchester. His dowager sister, Helen Cunningham, had driven from Worcestershire the previous day and had stayed at the Duke's Head. It was a comfortable timber-framed hotel, conveniently situated just opposite the main gateway to the cathedral close, and Mrs Cunningham had arranged for refreshments to be available there for members of the family immediately after the service. She had ordered champagne and smoked salmon sandwiches. As she said to the oldest of her cousins, Godfrey Lumsden, who had also stayed overnight: 'Might as well see the dear man off in style.'

The rest of the family – mostly cousins, middle-aged or elderly – drifted into the hotel after the service exchanging news as they came. The last to arrive were also the youngest: an uneasily matched couple.

The man was in his middle thirties, short, with handsome swarthy features, dark curly hair, and a touch of the dandy in his dress. The girl was some twelve or thirteen years younger, and taller by half a head.

She was almost a beauty, the physical type the pre-Raphaelite painters sought as their mistress-model-wives: well-built, full-bosomed, with a magnificently curved throat, strong symmetrical features, large heavy-lidded eyes. But nature had unkindly deprived her of some of the essential Rosettian details. Her skin, instead of being creamy, was almost transparently thin. Her hair, instead of being heavy and richly auburn, was fair, straight and wispily fine. Her eyes were a watery, beseeching blue.

She was obviously embarrassed by the fact that she was altogether larger than her escort; she wore clothes that could have been chosen only for their inconspicuousness, and she walked with her head shyly lowered. But she watched him all the time.

Although there were no more than eight of the family present when the couple arrived, the lounge of the Duke's Head seemed to be full of Lumsdens. They were all tall, clear-voiced, self-confident. One end of the room had been reserved for them, with sofas and armchairs arranged round low tables decorated with bowls of yellow and white flowers. Two champagne bottles stood in an ice bucket, and an assistant manager hovered, waiting to do the uncorking, but most of the Lumsdens were too busy greeting each other in the middle of the room to think of sitting down.

'We shouldn't have come, Hugh,' whispered the girl, hanging back. 'It's just for the family—they're not expecting us to join them.'

'Oh, shut up,' said her companion through his teeth. '*I* count as family too, on this occasion, and I'm not going to let them pretend I don't exist. The old boy sitting down must be cousin Godfrey. Come on, we'll start with him.'

He gripped her arm just above the elbow and pushed her

ahead of him through the assembly, rather as though he were a tugboat controlling a liner. And like a tug's, his relative size belied his strength. The girl winced with the pain of his grip, but said nothing. When they reached their destination she allowed herself to be put aside.

'How do you do, sir.' Her escort thrust out his hand to the elderly man who had just limped over to a chair and taken his weight off his lame leg. 'I'm Hugh Packer – Colonel Hugh's godson.'

'What?' Godfrey Lumsden, long-faced, grizzle-haired and with somewhat raffishly distinguished outcrops of additional grizzle high on either cheek, had been clutching his knee and grimacing. Surprised by a stranger, he peered suspiciously at the young man. Then, 'Oh – oh yes, come to think of it I did hear there was a godson.' He gave the proffered hand a brief, firm shake. 'How d'ye do.'

'And this is my fiancée, Belinda Brown.' Hugh Packer pulled her forward. 'Sadly, Belinda never had a chance to meet my godfather. I was going to take her to see him just at the time he fell ill. But I've told her so much about Colonel Hugh that she feels she knew him, and of course she wanted to join me at the thanksgiving service. And naturally I couldn't attend the service without paying my respects to the Colonel's family afterwards ... Belinda, this is Mr Godfrey Lumsden – I think I've got that right, sir?'

'Quite right, m'boy.' Godfrey Lumsden, having already appraised the girl's figure, heaved himself to his feet and took her hand, holding it rather longer than was strictly necessary. 'Delighted, Miss -er-.'

Belinda blushed. 'Please don't get up, Mr Lumsden,' she said. She sat down quickly, rather clumsily, partly to encourage him to resume his seat, and partly because she was suffering from the onset of particularly horrendous stomach cramps. She longed to disappear in search of the ladies' room, but Hugh hadn't given her an opportunity.

Her fiancé sat on the arm of her chair, his back half-turned to her, his hands spread confidently on his short muscular thighs. He had comparatively large hands, well-shaped and well-kept, with a gold signet ring on his right little finger. His wrists sprouted black hairs, some of which curled back against his white shirt cuffs, some of which advanced along the outer edges of his hands and reappeared on the backs of his fingers. The hands were conspicuous against the dark grey flannel of his suit, and Belinda sat staring at them as he talked to his godfather's cousin.

'My late father had the honour of serving under Colonel Hugh's command in the first battalion of the regiment,' he said. 'That was just after the war, when they were in the Middle East. In fact my father saved the Colonel's life on one occasion.'

'*Did* he? Did he indeed? Splendid chap!'

'I'm not clear about the details – my father was always very modest about it. I believe he said they were in Palestine at the time, being bombed and sniped at by terrorists. He wanted no recognition for what he'd done, of course, but he had such respect and admiration for the Colonel that when I was born he asked him to be my godfather. Hence my name – ' Hugh Packer gave an unexpectedly delightful smile and his fiancée smiled to see it, as though her personal sun had just put in an appearance at the end of a long hard winter.

'Splendid! Very glad to meet you both.' Godfrey Lumsden beckoned a waiter who was offering filled glasses from a tray. 'Now, you must have some champagne.'

Belinda tried to refuse. She suspected – correctly, Mrs Cunningham having worked on the principle that while one bottle for eight people would be mean, three would be an unnecessary extravagance – that if she and Hugh accepted drinks, someone in the family would have to go short. But Godfrey Lumsden insisted on her having a glass, and Hugh needed no persuasion.

'Let me wish you both a very happy marriage,' said the old man. 'I say, Helen – ' he called to his cousin, 'I expect you know your brother's godson? He's just been telling me that his father was in Hugh's regiment. Saved his life on one occasion, too. And this is his fiancée, Miss-er-' Godfrey Lumsden's voice wavered as he contemplated the generous swell of Belinda's bosom.

The rest of the Lumsden family had fallen silent, turning to look as the uninvited guests rose to their feet, Belinda guiltily, Packer easily and with an engaging smile. He put out his hand. 'How do you do, Mrs Cunningham? I don't know whether you remember me – Hugh Packer. We last met about ten years ago, when I was spending a weekend with Colonel Hugh.'

Helen Cunningham stood eye to eye with her brother's godson and looked at him with stately, ill-concealed disdain. 'I don't think I recall it.'

Packer kept smiling, though more widely and with visible effort. His teeth were large and white and almost perfectly even, with the exception of one canine which – when, as now, he drew back his lips – was seen to be narrow and sharp as a fang.

'May I introduce my fiancée, Belinda Brown,' he persisted. 'She came with me to the service, of course. I'm sure my godfather – '

'My brother Hugh,' Mrs Cunningham interrupted, 'is alas dead. Thank you both for coming to the service, as so many others did – but *this*, as you see, is purely a family occasion. Good afternoon, Miss Brown. Good-*bye*, Mr Packer.'

His facial muscles tightened. He glowered, then drained his champagne glass and swaggered off to the bar. Belinda, hot with embarrassment and tormented by a relentless grinding in the region of her pelvis, stumbled away in search of refuge and relief.

For the past two weeks Belinda Brown had been desperate with anxiety. Her period was very late, and she was convinced that she was pregnant.

Her present pain should have been reassuring. It wasn't, because it was different from her usual period pains both in kind and in intensity. And so far, there was nothing to show for it. Sitting hunched in one of the bleak cubicles in the ladies' room of the Duke's Head hotel, she longed for her own warm bathroom, for the privacy of her single bed, and for the comfort of a hot-water bottle clutched to her stomach.

She really didn't want a baby, not yet anyway. Plenty of time to think about it ... And with things as they were at home – Dad incapacitated by a stroke, and needing full-time attendance from herself or the nurse she employed when she needed a few hours off – she didn't want another helpless member of the family to look after.

And Hugh would be furious. That was her real fear. She hadn't been able to share her anxiety with him because he had been furious enough with her already, having only recently learned that she wasn't financially independent of her father. In fact until ten minutes ago, when he'd smiled and introduced her to Godfrey Lumsden as his fiancée, she hadn't been at all sure that Hugh wasn't about to break off their engagement. Telling him that she was going to have a baby might be just the thing to make him leave her; and she loved him too much to provoke a parting.

At least, she supposed it was love. It wasn't at all what she had thought love would be, in the days when she was the largest and dreamiest pupil at an expensive girls' boarding school, where she was unmercifully teased for her size, her common accent, and for having spots on her face. But then, Hugh was not the type of man who had featured in those old romantic dreams.

His comparative shortness was only a minor disadvantage. What made her unhappy was his attitude towards her.

Belinda had hoped to be wooed by a man at once kind and ardent. For someone who, while giving her the security of affection, the hugs and cuddles she had been deprived of by her mother's early death, would also provide the mysterious extra ingredient she had so often read about in romantic fiction: the special something that would make her heart beat so deliciously fast that she would know without doubt she was in love.

The churning emotion Hugh Packer aroused in her was quite different, a mixture of fascination and fear. He was inconsiderate, frequently off-hand, often verbally cruel and sometimes physically so. But Belinda couldn't bring herself to break their relationship because she had never recovered the self-confidence she lost at school. The fact that she had since got rid of her spots and practised to acquire a conventional accent, and that many men – older men in particular – now looked at her figure with admiration, had not been enough to revitalize her self-esteem.

Belinda felt grateful to Hugh for choosing her. He was so good-looking, so well-mannered and amusing in company. ('There's exactly the same difference in age between myself and

Belinda as there is between Prince Charles and Diana,' he liked to say, adding with a grin, 'and as you see, exactly the same difference in height.') And because he was the only suitor she had ever had, and she was urgently in need of a husband's companionship and support, she was terrified of losing him.

She just wished that she wasn't, at the same time, scared by the thought of being married to him. She had tried to resist his pre-marital demands but Hugh had refused to be denied, and all she ever experienced in the process was shame and discomfort and anxiety.

Belinda dreaded the prospect of having to submit to Hugh whenever and wherever and however he chose. She was disturbed by his hairiness, and alarmed by the way his lips drew back to reveal his one sharp tooth as he scrutinized her naked body before swarming over her like a perverted ape, biting her tender flesh and prying into every orifice. Surely, she thought, making love ought to be *nicer* than this?

She hugged her stomach and moaned softly, partly from unhappiness, partly from pain. And then, thankfully, she discovered that her flow had started.

The couple left the Duke's Head and went to lunch at a spaghetti house further down the road. Hugh was self-employed, with more spare time than money, and Belinda's allowance from her father, though originally generous and still more than enough for her own needs, did not run to expensive meals.

Hugh was surprisingly cheerful. '*Snobs*,' he had snarled dismissively of his godfather's relatives; but that was all.

Belinda knew what he meant. She had had to dodge back into the ladies' room cubicle at the Duke's Head in order to avoid an embarrassing re-encounter with Mrs Cunningham and another female member of the family, and had overheard them discussing her fiancé. Happy not to be pregnant, and to be out of pain, she had felt defensive on Hugh's behalf when she heard him described as 'that *odious* little man.'

'So pretentious,' Belinda had heard Mrs Cunningham's voice continue. 'He left Godfrey with the impression that his father was one of my brother's company commanders, instead of merely his soldier servant! And as for having saved his life . . . '

'Not true?'

'*I* don't know. My brother never talked about such things. But I simply don't believe a word that upstart says.'

Belinda couldn't see that Hugh's father's army rank mattered a scrap. Her own father had been a corporal or something in the war, but who cared about that kind of thing now? She too had been prepared to dismiss the women's attitude as snobbery; but then Mrs Cunningham, raising her voice above the splashing of the washbasin taps, had given her something to worry about.

'The man's a thief. My brother encouraged him to join the Army, in the hope of establishing him in a career, but he was cashiered for misappropriation of Mess funds. He used to visit Hugh regularly until about ten years ago, and apparently there was always something missing after his visits – loose cash, or anything that was easily pocketable and saleable. Eventually my brother caught him at it, though he refused to prefer a charge against his godson. He did ban Master Hugh from his house, though, and I'd hoped we'd seen the last of him.'

'What colossal cheek, then, to come here today!'

'Exactly. No doubt the little horror was sniffing round in the hope that he'd been left something in my brother's will, but as you know Hugh divided what he had between the family and the Cathedral.'

'Quite right too. It would be wasted on that godson.'

'And *what* a mistake his unhappy fiancée is making!'

'Yes indeed.' The cousin's voice had become distorted, as women's voices do when they apply lipstick while they're talking. 'No doubt he's marrying her for her money—her father's Sidney Brown, who became notorious in the eastern counties thirty years ago for having made a quick fortune out of surplus army equipment. He then set himself up as a racehorse owner, with considerable success ... Oh yes, Master Hugh would have known what he was doing when he became engaged to Brown's only child!'

The women's conversation had distressed Belinda. Not the bit about Hugh wanting her for her father's money, because she had assumed it from the first – why else should such a good-looking man have sought her out? But she had never imagined that Hugh was a thief. The revelation had come as a

30

shock to her. Almost as much of a shock, she supposed, as Hugh himself must have had when she'd confessed to him a week or two ago that she hadn't a penny of her own apart from her annual allowance; and that because of her father's incapacity, she could expect nothing more within his lifetime.

But now, as they ate spaghetti bolognese, Hugh seemed to have got over his resentful ill-humour about her lack of money. He was smiling at her again, and Belinda thought she had better try to forget about the theft. After all, the woman had said it was a long time ago.

'I've decided,' said Hugh, twirling a practised fork, 'that we might as well get married as soon as possible. I had thought, you see, that we'd be able to park your old man in a nursing-home and buy a house of our own near Yarchester, and it was a bit of a shock to find that you had no financial freedom. I certainly hadn't contemplated living with the two of you in that back-of-beyond place near Newmarket. But if the household bills really are all dealt with by the accountant . . . ?'

'Oh yes,' said Belinda. 'And garage bills too. It really wouldn't matter about our not having much actual cash.'

He frowned. 'It may not matter to begin with, but I don't intend to put up with it for very long. It's ridiculous for you to be expected to wait for your father to die before you can get hold of any capital. Once we're married, we shall have to set up a more satisfactory arrangement.'

'I don't think', said Belinda, 'that Dad's solicitors would allow it.'

'There are always Ways and Means,' said Hugh significantly.

He put down his fork, and looked at his watch. 'I've got to see a man at four . . . Come on, we'll go to my place for a screw, and then you can push off home.'

Belinda flinched. She hated it when he used such casually coarse expressions, the more so because she knew that he did it quite deliberately. It was one of his little cruelties, perpetrated precisely because he knew that it offended her. But today, at least, she had a valid reason to deny him any physical satisfaction. She leaned across the table and whispered it to him.

Hugh simply gave her a grin. She saw the sharpness of it and accepted with a downcast heart that she was engaged to a man who would always find ways and means of getting what he wanted.

'Come on,' he said, rising. And Belinda picked up the bill.

4

On an unusually warm Friday afternoon in April, two heavy vehicles collided at a junction on the main Cambridge to Saintsbury road not far from Newmarket. One of the vehicles was a fuel tanker. Although the collision was relatively minor it left the damaged tanker slewed across both carriageways, spraying diesel over the tarmac and making the junction impassable for hours.

A massive traffic jam ensued. Before the police could set up official route diversions, some approaching drivers saw the congestion ahead, did U-turns and went off to find their own alternative routes. Among them was Derek Cartwright in his company top-of-the-range Ford Sierra.

He was well acquainted with the area, and knew exactly where he was going when he turned off the main road and almost immediately took a left fork in the general direction of Saintsbury, but it was obvious that the driver who was following him was lost. No one who knew that particular by-road, which crossed a grass upland between chalky banks that soon narrowed it to a single carriageway with occasional passing-places, would have attempted to drive along it in a vintage Rolls-Royce.

Even Derek cursed himself for a fool when he realized how many other motorists had decided to use the road. Whether they had taken it by design or in blind hope, the result was the same. He rounded a clump of Scots pine that crowned an ancient tumulus, saw the sun glinting on stationary traffic on the rising ground half a mile ahead, and knew that they were all stuck.

He groaned, but philosophically, knowing that there was

nothing he could do but join the queue and wait. With the plum-coloured Rolls filling his rear-view mirror, he drew up behind a VW Golf, switched off his engine and got out to stretch his legs.

Many of the drivers ahead – male, one to a car; business executives or sales reps, shirt-sleeved in the unusually warm sun – were doing the same thing. One or two thrusters hurried up and down the line of vehicles courting early heart attacks in their attempts to get something or someone sorted out, but most drivers had resigned themselves to the wait and were passing the time by chatting to each other. Derek took off his jacket, leaned back against his car, folded his arms, and sunned his face while he mentally rearranged the remainder of his working day.

'*Now* what?' The shirt-sleeved driver of the Rolls, a short, swarthy, good-looking man, approached him indignantly. 'I thought you knew where you were going.'

Derek shrugged. 'I know *where*,' he said. 'It's *when* that's going to be the problem.'

'But we can't just stay here waiting for something to happen! I've got my old father-in-law with me – I'm trying to hurry him home from a hospital appointment.'

Derek straightened, concerned. He looked towards the back seat of the massive car, where an elderly man appeared to be half-supported by a young woman. 'Is he ill?' he asked.

'No, not exactly *ill*,' said the driver of the Rolls impatiently. 'Things would be a lot simpler if he were, then we'd know that he was either going to get better or peg out. As it is, he's more or less a cabbage as a result of a stroke. He had a fall this morning and hurt his good wrist, so I've just taken him to hospital for an X-ray.'

'Any damage?'

'Only a sprain, but even so he's going to be more helpless than ever until it heals.' The man – in view of his small size and their nearness to Newmarket, Derek took him for a successful jockey – ran his hands despairingly through his curly black hair. 'I've only been married a couple of weeks and I had no idea what a hell of a responsibility I was taking on.'

Derek gave a short, grim laugh. 'Have any of us, with elderly relatives?' he said. 'I'm lumbered with a mother-in-law ...'

'Lumbered' was not an expression he would normally allow himself to use of Enid. On the rare occasions when he spoke of her to friends or colleagues, it was always in terms of loyalty. She was wonderful for her age, he told them cheerfully; no trouble at all. But out here, at least forty miles from Wyveling and in the fortuitous company of a complete stranger who was similarly lumbered, he found it a relief to be able to uncurb his tongue.

'Is your mother-in-law decrepit, too?' asked the man.

'Far from it. Strong as a horse, and planning to live to a hundred.'

'God, I hope we get rid of Sidney long before then! Not to mention getting him home this afternoon before he starts to stink.' The man fidgeted up and down, and cursed the traffic ahead. '*Move*, can't you!'

Derek, preferring to avoid stress where he could, was admiring the Rolls, though he was careful not to infringe the privacy of the occupants by looking towards the interior. 'That's magnificent,' he said. 'I don't think I've ever seen one except in old films. What year is it?'

'A 1959 Silver Cloud. It's my father-in-law's bus, not mine. If I had this sort of money I'd get something racier. Sidney bought it new and still loves to be driven in it, according to my wife. Though God knows how she can tell,' the man added savagely, 'because the noises he makes are unintelligible. Take my word for it, if your mother-in-law's articulate and able-bodied, you've got no problems worth mentioning.'

'I have, you know!' Derek had worried in secret for so long that he was thankful for this opportunity to unburden himself verbally. 'My wife has had a cancer operation. They say she's clear now, but we know it could attack her again at any time. That's what I'm desperately afraid of, and why I resent our being lumbered with her mother. But there's absolutely nothing I can do about it – short of knocking my mother-in-law on the head.'

The man gave a sympathetic grimace, drawing back his lips to expose one narrow canine tooth. 'There's always that solution,' he agreed with a laugh.

'Don't think I haven't contemplated it,' said Derek bitterly. He pushed his hands into his trouser pockets and stared at the line of stationary cars far ahead. Sunlight struck glass and chrome; hot air shimmered over radiators, distorting the figures of the drivers as they moved round their cars in boredom or impatience. He felt totally frustrated by his domestic situation. He was immobilized by it, as incapable of getting rid of Enid as he was of unjamming the traffic ...

'Well, I'm damned if *I*'m going to hang about indefinitely waiting for something to happen,' said the driver of the Rolls. 'This is bloody ridiculous! I'm going to find out why we're not moving.'

He set off abruptly, jog-trotting up the road without so much as a glance at his passengers. Derek, thinking that it was a charmless way for a newly married man to behave, looked back at the Silver Cloud. The pale-haired young woman was gazing worriedly through the open window after her husband, and Derek felt that the least he could do was to give her a nod and half a smile. Surprised, she coloured a little and smiled shyly in return.

He reopened his own car door. The interior was unbearably stuffy. He opened all the windows and then, while he stood waiting for the temperature inside the car to drop, he stretched and took a few deep breaths of sunwarmed air.

It was oddly peaceful on the by-road, now that the engines of the nose-to-tail cars had all stopped and the forceful stranger had jockeyed off. The sun was so warm that a tall hawthorn bush growing singly on the roadside bank was not merely coming into leaf but erupting almost as Derek watched. Celandines and dandelions made cheerful blobs of yellow on the grass, a blackbird sang, and for a few unthinking moments he felt his spirits rise.

Then he remembered: Christine's cancer; his mother-in-law.

Ineluctably burdened, he sighed, hitched his waistband, settled himself in his seat, opened his briefcase and made a start on the day's paperwork.

'Excuse me – '

The young woman from the Rolls had come to speak to him through his open window. As she leaned forward her straight fair hair swung across her face, and she drew it away from her mouth as she spoke. Her flushed skin looked almost transparent, her large pale eyes were anxious, her voice was breathy. 'Did my husband by any chance tell you where he was going?'

'Not exactly, no.' Derek looked at his watch and found that twenty minutes had elapsed. 'I expect he's talking to someone further ahead. He went off to find out why we're not moving.'

The woman sighed. 'He can't bear having to wait for anything,' she said. She straightened to look up the road, and Derek realized that she was a good deal larger than her husband; a magnificent figure like hers, he couldn't help thinking, was surely wasted on that man.

'Is anything wrong?' he asked. 'Your husband told me about your father. I know you're anxious to get him home as quickly as possible.'

'It's Dad I'm worried about,' she agreed. 'He's distressed by the heat in the car, and I'd like to get him outside. I've set up his folding chair in the shade of that hawthorn – he'll be able to walk those few steps. But now that his left arm's temporarily as useless as his right, I don't think I can get him on his feet by myself.'

Derek put aside his calculator and papers and, as he would have done for anyone, offered to help. Now that they were both standing, he realized that the young woman – to think of anyone so statuesque as a 'girl' would be entirely inappropriate – was not far short of his own five-eleven height. And she, evidently conscious of the difference in size between him and the man she had married, added defensively, 'My husband's very strong. He's a great help to me with Dad.'

Dad – heavy, balding, his left arm strapped and in a sling – sat and perspired in the back seat of the Rolls surrounded by a litter of tissues and white terry towels. His daughter had already eased off his jacket, loosened his tie and unbuttoned the collar of his shirt. The car's built-in cocktail cabinet was open, but empty apart from a bottle of diabetic orange juice and a plastic non-spill cup.

The need for the cup was all too evident. Derek, who had never before made contact with the victim of a severe stroke, was disturbed and repelled by its visible effects on the right side of the man's body: the fallen eyelid, the slack arm and hand, the twisted mouth from which emerged an occasional gobble of words.

He felt pity for the old man, of course; but even more for the daughter. God knew how she coped, but her calmness and patience were admirable. She was so evidently expert at moving her father, and the Rolls was so roomy that between them they had comparatively little trouble in getting the old man out, and on to the chair she had set for him in the shade.

Derek felt almost ashamed when she thanked him for the little he had done. As he watched her position the old man's limbs, wipe his chin and mop his forehead, talking positively to him all the time, he realized that her husband had been right: by comparison, thank God, his mother-in-law was no problem at all.

'If there's nothing else I can do – ?' he said, beginning a thankful retreat to his car. He was conscious of a patch of damp on the front of his shirt where the old man's head had lolled, but courtesy prevented him from wiping it in their view.

The woman looked up with a distracted smile. 'Well, I *would* be grateful if you'd be kind enough to stay with Dad for a moment, while I fetch him his drink. The chair's unstable on grass, and I'd hate him to have another fall.'

'Of course.' Derek lowered himself to his haunches, the better to steady the arm and the back of the chair, and found that for the first time he was on the old man's good left side. It seemed unmannerly not to attempt some kind of friendly communication, and so he smiled and nodded. 'Feeling better?' he asked, realizing too late that the question was fatuous.

The afflicted man looked at him with his one good eye.

Derek was an old-film buff. He knew instantly that he had seen such an eye, such a look, on celluloid, and after a moment's thought he identified the actor: Charles Laughton as Quasimodo in the late 1930s version of *The Hunchback of Notre-Dame*. The rest of Laughton's face had been made so hideously immobile that he could act only through that single eye, and its eloquence was masterly.

And now here was this old man producing just as much of a *tour de force*. There was no mistaking the anguish and frustration that his one eye conveyed – but then, of course, he wasn't acting.

Shaken, Derek rose rather too abruptly to his feet. The chair lurched sideways. The young woman, approaching with the lidded cup, sprang forward just as he grabbed the chair again, and the two of them collided.

They backed apart immediately, laughing their apologies. Derek relinquished his infinitesimal responsibility, brushed aside her thanks, and strode back to his car. The whole encounter had been so casual, so brief, that there was no need to say good-bye.

But as he sat in his seat and looked through his papers again, he felt too disturbed to concentrate on his work. He was strangely conscious of his upper arm. Wondering why – rerunning the encounter as though it were a film – he recalled the moment of the collision, when her hair had flown across his face and his arm had been pressed against her body.

Specifically, against her full, soft, warm right breast; against what she, the lucky stranger, had, and his Christine had lost.

His pity for the father and daughter evaporated. Yes, it was tough for both of them. But when the old man died, as he might at any time of a merciful second stroke, his daughter would still be young, still whole. Whereas in Derek's family, it was Christine who was likely to die while her healthy old mother went on for ever . . .

Gripping the steering wheel with his strong hands, he felt all the frustration and anguish that he had seen in the old man's single eye. Felt, too, a mounting bitterness as he contemplated the fact that his own impotence was entirely self-imposed.

'We should get going in about ten minutes.'

The driver of the Rolls had come hurrying back down the long line of stationary traffic, as satisfied with his news as though he personally had sorted out the jam. Derek nodded an acknowledgement and began to stow his work into his briefcase. He didn't want to re-open a conversation, but for some reason the man lingered beside the open door of the car, peering at the printed heading on his papers.

'In insurance, are you?'

Derek wanted to get rid of him. He felt guilty that he had confided, even to a stranger, his fantasy of doing away with his mother-in-law.

'Life assurance,' he said, knowing that it was a social turn-off. Most people, hearing the words, would have backed away hurriedly, expecting a sales pitch to follow. Maddeningly, the Rolls driver looked pleased.

'*There's* a coincidence!' he said. 'I was thinking only this morning that now I'm a married man I really must get some life insurance. Let me have your card, and we'll do business.'

'It's assurance, not insurance,' Derek said stiffly. 'There's no insurance against death. That's the one thing that's certain.'

The man scratched his dark curly hair. 'Well, whatever,' he said cheerfully. 'I'd like to buy some, and you might as well have the commission as anyone else. Let's have your card.'

Derek felt a growing dislike for him. 'My company doesn't work on a commission basis,' he said, 'and I don't deal with individual clients.'

But he was too good a salesman to let a prospect slip. He got out of his car, made himself more agreeable, and produced his card with the regional office address and telephone number. Before handing it over, he crossed out his own name and substituted a junior colleague's. As an afterthought, he obliterated his private number and address.

The driver of the Rolls thanked him with unnecessary warmth. They both looked up the road. There was still no sign that the traffic was about to move, but Derek prepared to return to his car. The man detained him.

'By the way – do you often watch old films on television? You mentioned something about seeing vintage cars on film.'

'Yes, I sometimes watch them. Why do you ask?'

'I wondered if you saw last week's late-night thriller. The one about two men who meet by chance on a railway journey.'

'*Strangers on a Train*? I have seen it, of course, but not recently. What about it?'

The man was looking at him with a smile. 'I just wondered what you thought of it.'

Derek shrugged. 'It's not one of Hitchcock's best, in my opinion. It certainly doesn't do justice to Patricia Highsmith's novel.'

'But what about the theme, eh?' His smile widened as he spoke, but his dark eyes watched Derek closely. 'Two strangers, discovering that they have similar problems and agreeing to provide a solution for each other ... It's an interesting thought, isn't it?'

Derek stared at him in amazement. Good God, surely the man wasn't suggesting that they should commit murder on each other's behalf?

It was outrageously unbelievable. And yet there was something about the driver of the Rolls – the gleam of spittle on his sharp tooth as he drew back his lips – that gave him an alarmingly wolfish look.

Yes, quite possibly he *was* crazy enough to mean it. But whether or not, there was only one effective reply. Derek drew himself up to his full height, and glowered down at the man. 'Sod off,' he said contemptuously.

He got into his car, slammed the door shut and wound up the window. How the man reacted, he didn't know; he didn't deign to look. But as he sat gripping the wheel, willing the traffic to start moving, he found that he was sweating even more than the stuffy warmth in the car warranted.

His hands were shaking. He felt sick. He was appalled. But what appalled him was not so much the enormity of the man's proposition as his own instinctive reaction to it. Because for a moment – just for one moment, before his sense of morality took over – he had felt a *frisson* of excitement as he realized that here was a practicable solution to the problem of getting rid of his mother-in-law.

5

Honourably, Derek put the proposition out of his mind. But he regretted that he had given the driver of the Rolls his card.

True, he had taken the precaution of obliterating his home address and number. But though he had also deleted his name it was probably still legible, which meant that he could be traced through the telephone directory.

Derek sweated for a few days, afraid that the man might ring him at home, or even turn up at the Brickyard, with his wolfish grin and a renewal of his monstrous suggestion. But nothing like that happened, and by the end of the following week Derek was too much occupied with his work to concern himself any further.

His current preoccupation was with a presentation he was due to make at an investment conference in the west of his region, near Peterborough. The conference was being held at an old country hotel where he and Christine had spent the first night of their honeymoon, the Haywain at Nenford. They had returned for a happy weekend when Christine was carrying Laurie, and had said then that they must go there more often; but the birth of their handicapped daughter and the continuing responsibility of caring for her had made further self-indulgence impossible.

Christine's eyes had brightened when Derek told her that this conference was being held at the Haywain. He had thought immediately that they might reactivate the plan for their long-postponed weekend, but he said nothing because he was afraid that the small village with its cottages of local stone, once an important river crossing and a staging post on the old Great North Road, might have been spoiled by modern development. But as soon as he turned off the busy by-pass that had left the village backwatered, he saw that everything was still as he remembered it.

The hotel itself, a handsome stone-built early eighteenth-century coaching inn, high-gabled and high-chimneyed, looked just the same on the outside. But the interior that had creaked at its dusty joints sixteen years earlier had been discreetly renovated. It was now distinctly upmarket. Checking the tariff, Derek saw that a double room with antique furniture and a four-poster bed would cost a lot more than he'd expected. But hang the expense, Christine would love it. Come the summer, he determined, he would bring her here for a second honeymoon.

Always providing, of course, that she was well enough when the time came. And that her mother didn't make such an issue of being left on her own that Christine would decide that it wasn't worth the hassle.

Derek had made a point of arriving at the hotel early on the evening before the conference began, so that he could look round before the place became crowded. Having bought a drink at the bar, he carried it out into the garden. The previous week's warm weather had gone as suddenly as it came and this evening was back to normal for late April, long and light but sunless and too chilly to enjoy. Even so, Derek retraced the paths he and Christine had taken on their summer honeymoon, drawn irresistibly to the far end of the walled gardens by the smell and the slap of river water.

It was just the same now as it had been then. Or it would be, when the sun shone, and narcissi and tulips gave way to delphiniums and roses, and the riverside vegetation grew tall. Parking his glass, he leaned his elbows on the wall overlooking the river and smiled to himself as he saw again the old stone bridge with the nine or ten arches that carried the road across the water, recollecting how, newly married, he had run the length of the parapet, leaping across from cut-water to cut-water, showing off in front of Christine.

And she had shown off too, posing on the parapet while he took a photograph of her wearing the mini-skirt that was then the fashion and demonstrating that she had a very fine pair of legs.

Not that he had ever been a dedicated leg-man. For young hopefuls of his generation there had been legs wherever you looked, some of them decidedly unalluring. But though girls in those days had displayed their legs – in tights, of course – almost all the way, toplessness hadn't been invented. Perhaps, he meditated, that was why he had always found the female bosom so mysteriously attractive; and why Christine's loss had devastated him almost as much as it had her.

'Small world!' said a friendly voice behind him.

Derek turned, expecting to renew a business acquaintance, and found himself looking at the jockey of a man who had been at the wheel of the 1959 Rolls-Royce in the traffic jam near Newmarket.

The moral guilt he had felt immediately after their encounter came flooding back, making him belligerent. 'What the hell are you doing here?' he demanded.

The man took no offence. 'Thought I recognized your back view as you left the bar,' he said. 'I've stopped for a break on my way home from a car auction at Retford. I'm in the trade, didn't I tell you? I suppose you're here on business – I gather there's a conference tomorrow. To tell you the truth I haven't got round to doing anything about my life insurance – ' he corrected himself with a chuckle: 'life *assurance* I mean – yet. But I certainly intend to. Look, I've still got your card.'

He plucked it from the top pocket of his navy blue blazer. 'Derek Cartwright,' he read out, apparently deciphering the deleted name for the first time. He smiled, offering friendship. 'My name's Packer.'

Derek instantly turned aside and took a long slow swig from his glass, so that if the man held out his hand he wouldn't see it. He didn't want to talk to Packer, and he certainly didn't want to get to know him. But he realized, now they were at closer quarters, that his guess about occupation had been well off course. Packer was insufficiently weathered for a jockey; his face and his hands were too smooth. A used-car salesman sounded much more likely.

'I suppose you drive a company car,' the man went on amiably. 'But have you ever thought of getting a runabout for your wife? I've got an option on a very clean little – '

He stopped abruptly and slapped his curly head in dismay.

'Oh, I'm *sorry* – what must you think of me? You told me your wife has cancer. How *is* she?'

'Improving, thank you,' said Derek stiffly. 'And she already has her own car. Excuse me, I'm going in for dinner.'

Packer didn't move. With or without intent he was standing immediately in front of Derek, blocking the garden path.

The man was younger than him, and well-muscled. But Derek was fit; a former hockey-player of county standard, he still took part in the game as a referee. He had a considerable height and weight advantage over Packer, and he would have no trouble at all in shoving him out of his way.

On the other hand, decent men don't use physical violence, particularly against those smaller than themselves.

'Excuse me,' he repeated loudly. Packer, affecting not to hear, continued the one-sided conversation.

'Glad about your wife ... I only wish I could say the same about my father-in-law.' Horizontal furrows ploughed deeply across the man's forehead. 'It's grim, for a person to be in Sidney's condition without any hope of improvement. You saw him, didn't you? My wife told me that you helped her move him. What did you think of the old fellow?'

At their previous encounter, Packer's attitude towards his wife's father had seemed to be one of dislike and dismissal. Now, he sounded so genuinely concerned that Derek began to wonder whether he had mistaken the man.

Surely no one who had proposed setting up a conspiracy to murder could behave as calmly as Packer was behaving today? So perhaps he hadn't meant it at all. Perhaps, thought Derek uneasily, the idea had sprung from the dark workings of his own unconscious. What he had instinctively interpreted as a serious proposition might well have been put forward by Packer as nothing more than a slightly off joke.

Not that the old man's stroke was a joking matter. But then again, anyone faced with the kind of burden that Packer had taken on when he married might find that sour laughter was the only possible alternative to despair. Acknowledging it, Derek felt obliged to be more civil. He relaxed his get-out-of-my-way stance and turned aside to rest an elbow on the wall while he finished his drink.

'I was shattered when I saw the state your father-in-law is

45

in,' he admitted. 'I'd had no idea what a stroke could mean. It's the fact that he *knows* how helpless he is that's so desperate.'

'D'you think he does know?'

'Certain of it. You can see the terrible frustration in his eye, poor devil. God, what an existence . . .'

Packer came to stand beside him and they both leaned on the stone wall, silent for a few moments, looking down at the river. The thick green water, unable to catch any light from the overcast sky, was darkly uninviting. A cold breath rose from its depths as it went slopping past. Derek, absorbed in the imagined horror of being left helpless by a stroke yet fully aware of his condition, found himself shrugging to ward off a shiver.

'If I were in poor old Sidney's state,' said Packer at his shoulder, 'I'd rather be dead.'

'Much rather,' Derek agreed fervently.

'Ironic, isn't it?' said Packer. 'If we were to let an old animal suffer like that, we'd have the RSPCA after us. But then, we wouldn't let it suffer, would we? I wouldn't, and I bet you wouldn't either. We'd do the merciful thing, and put it out of its misery.'

Derek didn't answer. He was watching something half-floating in the water about fifteen yards downstream, something pale and inflated, wedged among the burgeoning rushes. Nothing significant; rural litter, possibly a plastic fertilizer sack.

But it had revived a childhood memory. When he was twelve or thirteen, he and his friend Mike had set out on their bicycles from Chelmsford with the intention of tracing the river Chelmer to its source in deepest rural Essex. They never got there, because they were easily distracted. And one of the distractions on their route that summer's day had been a mill pond, somewhere near Felsted.

As they'd mucked about, over the tops of their shoes in water and mud, they noticed something bobbing among the waterlilies on the other side of the pond. They couldn't reach it. Curious to know what it was – much bigger than a football, and greyish in colour; floating like a ball and yet so elongated that one end was submerged – they had begun to fling stones at it.

It was just about at the limit of their throw, and most of their shots simply made waves. The thing lurched and swung with the movement of the water, but it remained in the same position, as though the submerged end was anchored. When they did score a direct hit, the stone struck with a dull thump and bounced off.

Unwilling simply to abandon their find, they agreed without discussion that if they couldn't retrieve it they would sink it. Whooping and shouting, they rushed about the thistly field looking for larger, more effective stones.

It was Derek who found the half-brick, beside the five-barred gate in the hedgerow where they had propped their bicycles. Kicking off his muddy shoes and rolling up his splashed trousers, he had waded out among the reeds until he was nearly up to his knees in water. He could recall, even now, the foetid warmth of the mud that squished up between his toes as, swinging his arm to increase the momentum, he had hurled the missile across the pond with all his strength.

The brick fell with a mightly splash. It was such a near miss, and it made the thing shift so violently, that Derek knew he must have scored an underwater hit. Both boys had jumped and cheered, thinking he had freed it, because the floating end immediately reared up out of the water, fully into their view.

What he had seen, then, was that the thing had appendages. They looked incongruously small on that bloated body, but they were unmistakable: a stump of a tail and two stiff legs, the hindquarters of a dead dog, anchored in the shallow water by whatever weight had been attached to its collar before it was thrown into the mill pond to drown.

Perhaps it was an old dog that had been 'put out of its misery' by someone unable or unwilling to afford a vet. Or possibly just an unwanted dog, callously disposed of. Recalling the whole incident – the thud of their stones on the drum-tight skin, followed by the rearing-up of that obscenely gaseous body, the sight of those pathetic paws, the stench of decay that had momentarily corrupted the breeze – Derek felt his stomach lurch; just as it had done on that long-ago morning when, half-sobbing with the pity and the horror of it, he had jammed on his shoes, and he and Mike had jumped on their bicycles and fled.

Now, leaning over another river in the unsought company of

47

this man whose smile would widen from amiable to unpleasant, Derek fancied that he could catch again that same rotten-sweet smell. This time, a whiff of contagion.

He stood up abruptly. 'If you're trying to put a proposition to me,' he said, tight-voiced with anger, 'the answer is most emphatically *no*.'

Packer looked reproachful. 'Not even to help a man in poor old Sidney's condition?'

'You're not talking about help, you're talking about murder. And I am having nothing to do with it – or with you. If you feel so strongly about ending your father-in-law's life, do it yourself. But don't try to involve *me*.'

Derek elbowed the smaller man aside and began to stride back through the darkening gardens, where narcissi gleamed white beside the stone-paved paths. The lights were on in the hotel; bank managers and stockbrokers and solicitors and accountants would be assembling for tomorrow's conference, and he had never before felt so eager for their company.

He thought he had shaken Packer off. But the man had simply dodged round a yellow forsythia and was now blocking the way again.

'I can't risk doing it myself, Derek,' he protested, low-voiced. 'You know that. The police would suspect me straight away. Just as they'd suspect *you* if you killed your mother-in-law.'

'I have no intention of killing her.'

'You've thought about it, though. You told me so.'

Derek cursed himself for having been so unguarded. 'I was joking,' he said.

'Come off it!' said Packer. 'Of course you've thought about getting rid of your mother-in-law. Who hasn't, at one time or another?'

'What if I have? I wouldn't ever do anything about it. I couldn't. I couldn't bring myself to do it.'

'But that's what makes this system so brilliant! Don't you see? You don't *have* to do anything to your mother-in-law. You just arrange to be somewhere else at a certain time, and then leave the job to me.'

'As simple as that?' said Derek with heavy sarcasm. 'Or would there be a little matter of my being expected to kill your father-in-law for you in return?'

'Well yes. Naturally.' Packer seemed impervious to sarcasm. 'But I'd fix it up for you, I'd make all the arrangements – '

Derek turned away in disgust. 'You're *mad*,' he said.

'I'm not, you know. *You'll* be the one who's mad. Mad with yourself for not having jumped at this offer, if your poor wife dies young and leaves you lumbered with her old Ma for the next twenty-five years –

'Damn you,' said Derek, slowly and quietly, though rage was swelling inside him until he felt that his ribs would crack. 'Get out of my way – get out and stay out, you little *turd*.'

What happened next was entirely unpremeditated. Afterwards, as Derek held his throbbing right hand under the cold tap in his hotel bathroom, he acknowledged that effective action is much more difficult to take in real life than old films had led him to believe. What he had so instinctively launched had not been a clean, straight-to-the-jaw punch, but a hopelessly inexpert haymaker that felled Packer only because it caught him off balance. It had, he suspected, done more harm to his own hand than to the side of Packer's head.

Even so, Derek felt a considerable satisfaction. It was good, very good, to recall the man's look of pained surprise as he sprawled on his back in a flowerbed. Well worth a badly bruised hand.

Yes, he felt pleased with what he'd done. Greatly relieved, too, by the knowledge that the conspiracy to murder hadn't after all been his own idea. It wasn't his unconscious that had put forward the proposition, it was that evil little bastard Packer. If ever a man deserved to be knocked down, it was him.

It wasn't until after midnight, when he lay sleepless, that Derek realized that he had just abandoned the inhibitions of a decent, honourable lifetime. He had used – and justified the use of – violence against someone smaller than himself.

He had no sympathy for his victim. Far from it. With renewed unease he began to consider the possibility that the man, though comparatively small, couldn't be written off as proportionately weak.

Couldn't be written off at all.

Worrying about it through the early hours, Derek felt sure that he hadn't seen the last of Packer. He sensed, obscurely, that the man had somehow tricked him; had gained an advantage by deliberately tempting him to make that unprecedented physical assault.

Though it seemed that he had won this particular encounter, Derek had a guilty premonition that if the attack on his principles were to be renewed, he might yet succumb to the ultimate temptation.

6

'In here, Dee.'

Stretching a smile over his dark thoughts, Derek followed the sound of his wife's voice and found her in her work-room. It was officially the dining-room, but except for major family gatherings they always ate in the kitchen, and the large dining-table was an ideal place for Christine to spread her furnishing fabrics.

Like the other main rooms in the Edwardian-built Brickyard this was large and light, with a squared bay window occupying one wall. The room was at the back of the house, facing west over the modest dip in the landscape that was the valley of the Wash brook.

Although the long gravelled yard at the front of the house abutted on the village street, with its dwellings and shops and comings and goings, from the back windows there wasn't a building to be seen within half a mile. This duality was one of the features of the Brickyard that had particularly attracted the Cartwrights when they first saw the property. They enjoyed being a part of the community, and yet they valued the privacy the house gave them.

They also enjoyed the view. The back windows overlooked a down-sloping lawn where, at this season, clumps of daffodils blew beneath a pear tree in full blossom. The lawn was bounded by a tall old hedge, bustling with birds, and in the hedge was their private gate leading to a field path where they walked the dog.

Overtopping the hedge were the chestnut trees that stood in a group in the meadow beyond, their candles still yellowy-green but promising an outburst of white. Further away, lower in the dip, were the greyer-green tops of the willows that grew beside the brook. Then the land rose again, vivid with winter barley, towards a pink-washed farmhouse backed by late-leafing oak trees on the far side of the little valley. Further still, the flint tower of Doddenham church stood up against the wide East Anglian sky.

It was a pleasant outlook. Unspectacular, quintessentially rural, utterly peaceful. The only movement—apart from wind-blow, the darting birds, clouds skittering across the sky, and Sam the beagle scouring the hedge-bottom for rabbits – came from infrequent local traffic on the minor road that crossed the far slope on its way between Wyveling and Doddenham.

Today, though, the view from the tall window was partly obscured by a swathe of fabric in a swirling, leafy design of blues and greens and lilacs that complemented the plain blue-grey of the wallpaper. Christine, balanced on a stepladder, her prosthesis riding higher under her blouse than her remaining breast, was stretching up to hang a curtain.

'For heaven's *sake*!' Derek protested, hurrying forward. 'My love, what are you *doing*?'

'Exactly what it looks like,' said his wife cheerfully. 'I finished making these new curtains this morning and I wanted to get them hung before you came back from the conference. Do you like the colour?'

'Yes, it's fine ... but why on earth couldn't you have waited for me to hang them? Come down this minute, Chrissie, and let me finish the job. You'll hurt yourself if you stretch up like that.'

'No I shan't. I have to do stretching exercises to strengthen my shoulder, so I might as well be productive about it. If you want to help, you can put the hooks in that other curtain for me.'

Derek had always reckoned to do his fair share of the routine household work. He'd had plenty of practice during the long years when they were training Laurie to feed and dress herself, and again since Christine's operation. But putting hooks in curtains had never before come into his province, and he hated jobs that were self-evidently fiddling. Besides, he wasn't sure how the hooks fitted into the tape, and masculine pride

52

inhibited him from asking for instructions. And anyway, his right hand was still painful.

'Sorry, darling. I'll have to leave that to you, my fingers are a bit swollen. I managed to shut my hand in a door.'

'Honestly, Dee ... ' Christine scolded him affectionately, leaving the curtain half-hung while she sat down on the steps to take a rest. She looked tired, as she so often did now, but unusually cheerful. 'How did the conference go?'

'Fine,' he said brightly.

'And how was the hotel? The Haywain?'

Derek assured her that the hotel had been fine, too. He couldn't hope to put the place and its alarming new associations out of his mind, but he had no intention of talking to her about it. 'And how have *you* been, my love?'

'Oh, such a wonderful thing has happened!' Christine's news was obviously of more interest to her than the hotel. 'I've met someone else in the village who's had a mastectomy. I don't suppose you know her – Sylvia Collins from that thatched house on Church Hill. I only knew her by sight, and I had no idea she'd had the operation. But we started chatting yesterday morning while we were waiting for the library van, and then she invited me to tea.'

'That's good,' said Derek, genuinely pleased for his wife but finding it difficult to sound enthusiastic when his own new acquaintance was so alarmingly on his mind. 'Nice for you to make a friend who's in the same situation.'

'It's more than just "nice"!' Christine's eyes were brighter than he had seen them for months. 'I can't tell you what a relief it is to be able to talk to someone who knows all about it. Sylvia had her operation two years ago, and she's feeling really well now. She's encouraged me to join the Mastectomy Association – I was given all the leaflets about it before I left hospital, but I just didn't want to know at the time – and we're going to work together to raise funds for the Yarchester Hospital scanner appeal. Oh, you can't imagine how wonderful it is not to feel isolated any more! Not to feel desperate about being a lop-sided freak ... '

Derek reached up to her. 'My dear stupid girl – come on down from those steps, you've done quite enough for today.'

He caught her carefully in his arms and held her close;

deliberately close, so that she couldn't see his expression. Absurdly, perhaps, he felt injured by what she had just said. It was the first time, in the whole of their married life, that Christine had suggested that they were not an emotionally self-sufficient couple.

He was well aware that it was only the warmth of his wife's affection that had kept him going, through the daunting years when they were bringing up their handicapped child. In loving return, he had done and said all he could to help Christine come to terms with her mastectomy. With a marriage bond as strong as theirs, he had thought that it was his support that sustained her; that he was giving her all the reassurance that was necessary. But apparently not.

'*Of course* you're not a freak,' he protested. 'Haven't I made that clear to you? God knows I've tried.'

She smiled at him and stroked his face. 'You've been marvellous, Dee. And that's something else that's cheered me up – realizing that I'm so lucky to have you as my husband.'

Partially appeased, Derek rubbed his cheek against the warmth of her hand and kissed her palm.

'Poor Sylvia didn't just have cancer to cope with,' Christine went on. 'She had an unfaithful husband as well. She's divorced now, but I suspect that money's a problem. All the same, she's so positive and amusing and encouraging that she's made me feel ashamed of my miseries. The way she tells it, every other woman in Suffolk is walking round with only one boob!'

Unbidden, the recollection of the magnificently whole young woman who had pressed accidentally against his arm on the day of the traffic jam surfaced in Derek's consciousness. A faithful husband in thought as well as deed, he dismissed it immediately and concentrated on what his wife was saying.

'So I'm determined that I'm going to be positive too. I'm going to beat this cancer, and you and I are going to live to a ripe old age together. Aren't we?'

'We most certainly are.'

It was mutual bravado, of course. For his part, Derek was still entirely pessimistic about Christine's life expectancy. But at least he felt reassured that they were still the same invincibly bonded couple. It was not they who had changed, but their domestic circumstances. If something had come between the two of them during the past few months, worrying and frustrating him to such an extent that he had given Christine the impression that he didn't understand how desperate she felt, he knew exactly what it was.

Or rather, who.

He could hear his mother-in-law now: moving about their house, destroying their privacy, consuming what little might remain of their life together ...

'Is everything all right, Dee? Your eyes look very heavy, and your breath's slightly off.'

'I'm fine.' Unable to face her scrutiny, and unwilling to offend her with his breath, Derek let go of her and turned away to pick up his briefcase. 'My hand's been painful, that's all.'

'Oh, and I'd forgotten about it! Let me see.'

'No, it's all *right*.' He tried not to sound irritable. 'I'll hang those curtains for you later. I'm going to change, and then take Sam for a walk.'

His wife sat down at the table and began to fix the hooks on the other curtain. 'You'd better work up a good appetite,' she said. 'Mother's cooking supper.'

Derek's stomach contracted, as it had been doing at intervals all afternoon; ever since he'd been called to the telephone during lunch at the Haywain, and heard Hugh Packer at the other end of the line.

'No hard feelings, Derek,' Packer had said cheerfully. 'Just wanted to let you know that I'll keep in touch. I'm ringing from your part of the world, by the way: Breckham Market. Happened to be coming in this direction this morning, and what should I see but a signpost to Wyveling, so I took a small detour.

'Nice village you live in, Derek. Very nice-looking property you've got. It's vulnerable, though – you know that, of course. A prospective burglar, say, could approach it from the back along the field path and get into the house and out again without being seen. I think we ought to do something about that as soon as possible, don't you? We must meet within the next day or two and make arrangements.'

Derek had told him to go to hell.

'Don't be like that!' Packer had said. 'You've got a problem, and I'm offering to solve it for you. All you have to do is stay out of the way for an hour or two while I do it. What could be simpler? Don't worry about a thing. I'll be in touch.'

No wonder, Derek thought, that his breath was bad. What was stirring his gut and sending a sour taste up into his mouth was panic.

'I don't *want* one of your mother's heavy meals,' he burst out, hearing – without being able to control it – the crack of anger in his voice. 'I can't eat it, not after a conference lunch. Why the hell can't she stay in her own room and leave us alone?'

Christine stared at him over an armful of curtain. 'All right, Derek,' she said, audibly controlling her own irritation. 'No need to make a major issue out of a chicken and apricot casserole. If you don't want to eat it, don't. I didn't ask Mum to cook it – she insisted, and I'm not going to waste my energy arguing with her. After all, she's only trying to help.'

'Help be damned,' said Derek bitterly. 'If she really wanted to help, she'd – '

He stopped in mid-sentence, irradiated with unaccustomed hope. Of course! He drew a deep breath and then let it out slowly, feeling his tensed-up muscles relax. There was no need for him to go on agitating about his mother-in-law. Enid had just been made redundant.

Derek supposed – he could only suppose, since she had never offered him an explanation – that when Christine had allowed her mother to stay on at the Brickyard it was because she was in need of feminine moral support after her operation. That was why he had felt unable to refuse Enid house-room. Now, though, the situation had changed.

While he was away at the conference, being pressured by Hugh Packer into imagining that the only way of getting rid of his mother-in-law was by conspiring to have her murdered, Christine had been making a new local friend. A friend, what's more, who'd had the same operation, and would therefore be able to support her far more effectively than her mother ever could.

Enid was no longer needed! She could start packing her bags right away, and he would take her back to Southwold on Sunday. *End of problem*, thank God.

End of nightmares; end of the evil persuasions of that bastard Packer. Oh, thank God. Thank God!

But when Derek seized his wife's hand and made the eager suggestion Christine turned away from him immediately, and all she said was, 'No.'

7

'*Why*, Christine? Just tell me why!'

Set-faced, his wife fixed another hook in the curtain tape. 'She's my mother, isn't she?'

'What's that got to do with it? It's not as if she's ancient, or incapable. She doesn't need you. And now you're feeling so much better, and you've found a new friend, you don't need her either. It's not even as if you enjoy each other's company. You don't get on with her as well as I do.'

'If you get on with her so well,' Christine retorted, 'why are you so anxious to push her out?'

What could he say? *Because I'm desperately afraid that you're not going to live much longer? Because I want us to be alone together during what little time we've got left?*

He drew a steadying breath, and tried to be patient. 'My love, I know how fractious you and your mother get with each other. I want to save you from stress, so you can concentrate on getting well – that's all.'

'Thank you, Derek,' said Christine composedly, 'but I don't need that kind of help.'

'Oh for God's *sake*.' His veneer of patience had cracked. If he hissed his exasperation, rather than shouting it, it was only because he was ashamed to be rowing with Christine and didn't want her mother to hear. 'Can't you understand? All right, it's not you I'm thinking of, it's me. I resent the fact that our lives are no longer our own, and I want to get rid of your mother because I'm sick of having her in the house. So now you know.'

His wife looked up from the curtain. Her eyes were troubled but her chin was firm.

'I'm sorry you feel like that. You've always been so nice to her that I hadn't realized . . . But it doesn't change my mind. I'll tell Mum to keep well out of your way in future, but I'm not going to ask her to leave the house. And it is, after all,' she reminded him, standing up, 'as much mine as it's yours.'

They stared at each other, breathing anger. 'If that woman stays,' Derek threatened, 'I won't be responsible for the consequences.'

'What do you mean?'

'What I said. I won't be responsible for – for whatever might happen.'

Christine's look of anger changed to something verging on contempt. 'Don't be silly,' she said, turning away to fold the finished curtain.

'I mean it.'

He longed to be able to unburden himself to her: to tell her what a mess he'd got into with Packer, to ask for her help in extricating himself from the man's influence. But that would be to admit a weakness, and what would Christine think of him if he revealed that to her? Besides, he could hardly expect her to go on loving him if she knew that he had even trifled with the idea of killing her mother.

No, confession was out. It would ruin his relationship with Christine. And their happy marriage – what few years, or months, of it might remain – was after all the most important thing in his life.

The only way he could save himself from Packer was by removing Enid from the house. It was such a simple solution to the whole problem that it ought to be easy enough to accomplish. But Christine had a mind and a will of her own. He knew that confrontation was useless.

'Please,' he coaxed, trying the alternative tactic. 'I want to live with *you*, not with your mother. Is that so strange? Isn't it what you want too? She can always come and visit us – but please, Chrissie, make her go back and live in her own home.'

His wife refused.

Derek slammed out of the house and took long savage strides down the back lawn and through the picket gate in the hedge.

Then he paused for a moment, screwing his eyes against the concentrated final rays of the sun. The grazing field that sloped away in front of him to the Wash brook was brilliantly green under a rain-dark evening sky. An earlier shower had brought out the smells of pushing vegetation, and of the mud that oozed from the beaten earth of the field path he was standing on.

He was, he realized, still wearing his grey flannel suit and black shoes. After the row with Christine he hadn't thought of stopping to change, and he certainly wasn't going to go back to do so now. He reached behind him to slam the garden gate shut, felt an obstruction, and heard an anguished howl.

'Oh, *Sam*, you stupid old mutt. All right, I didn't mean to squash you. Come on then, if you must.'

Better to take the dog anyway. That was what he had planned, on the drive home, so as to have a credible reason for covering the ground where Packer had been that morning.

He turned to the right, with Sam lolloping ahead of him, tongue out, stern happily high. Derek hadn't been along the field path for some considerable time. The beagle had been Laurie's pet – hence its tartan collar, unsuitable for a hound, but her own choice – and walking it had never been his responsibility.

He felt deeply ashamed of the row with Christine, their first since her illness. Theirs had always been a perfectly normal happy marriage, enlivened by arguments and the odd shouting match, and enriched by reconciliations; but when Christine's cancer was diagnosed he had believed that if only she were spared he could never be angry with her again.

He still felt angry, despite the shame. How could she be so obdurate? Even though she had no idea that her mother's life was on the line, surely she could see that her attitude was affecting their marriage?

Or didn't she value his love any more?

They hadn't actually made love since her operation. At first, of course, she had been too unwell; later she had felt sore, and inclined to nausea. Now, although her chest was no longer tender, she felt too weary. Derek prided himself on being a considerate husband and lover, and he had no intention of trying to rush his wife. He was quite prepared to be continent until she regained her interest in sex. All the same, it was galling that she didn't appear to realize the additional tension that this generated in him. If Christine were really considerate of his needs, surely she would understand that the least she could do for him would be to relieve him of the presence of her mother.

But if she wouldn't, she wouldn't. Derek knew his wife too well to imagine that he could make her change her mind. And if she wouldn't –

He felt choked with anxiety as he remembered that Hugh Packer must have walked that same path a few hours earlier: invading his territory, spying on his domain, probing his defences.

Packer was prepared to carry out the proposition, there was no doubt about it. Derek could of course refuse to co-operate; he *intended* to refuse ... but he wasn't sure how long he could hold out against so great a temptation.

Besides, he felt sure that Packer wouldn't accept a refusal. The man would keep on at him, on and on until the pressures became insupportable. Unless he could get Packer off his back, he would almost certainly be driven to connive at his mother-in-law's murder.

That was why ridding himself of Packer had now become Derek's first priority, and why he had come out on this walk. Surely, unbalanced though the man undoubtedly was, Packer had enough sense of self-preservation to realize that his scheme would have to be abandoned if anyone had seen him in the village that morning. And surely he must have been seen?

Derek's address – *The Brickyard, Wyveling, Breckham Market, Suffolk* – gave no clue to the house's whereabouts in the village. The name, in iron letters screwed on to a plaque on one of the brick gateposts at the entrance to the yard, was not conspicuous. Hopeful that Packer had blown his own scheme by asking for directions, Derek had made casual inquiries on his way home. A colleague, he invented, had promised to leave some documents at the Brickyard but hadn't done so. Had a stranger by any chance stopped to ask the way to his house from the garage? From the post office? From the newsagent's? From the village shop? From the Five Bells?

Apparently not.

Instinctively, Derek had avoided describing the stranger to anyone. He couldn't bring himself to analyse this wariness, but something in the unexplored darkness at the back of his mind prompted him not to give anyone an opportunity to associate him with Packer.

Just in case.

Derek had decided to walk in the field path because it was far more likely that a stranger would have been noticed there than in the village itself. The path passed the end of a dozen other gardens as well as his own, and he hoped to see at least one of the other residents, either gardening or dog-walking, and introduce the subject of strangers into a casual, neighbourly conversation. But there seemed to be no one about at all.

He paused, frustrated, at a fork in the path. Ahead of him was the churchyard wall, cushioned at its foot by mounds of celandines and overhung by lime trees whose new leaves were bursting out of their pink scales. Above and beyond the trees, the clock on the flint tower of the church showed eleven twenty-seven, as it had done ever since the Cartwrights first arrived in Wyveling; but in fact it was past seven o'clock, and the sun had set. Presumably most people were eating supper or watching television. He and Sam had the path to themselves.

Sam ...

Derek looked round, his anxiety abruptly changing course. The sturdy little tri-coloured dog, treasured by Christine as a living link with their dead daughter, was nowhere to be seen.

Panicking, not knowing which fork of the path to take, Derek called and whistled and called again. He knew that he ought to have brought the dog out on a lead, because it had no road sense at all. Oh God – it if had gone to the right, out into the village street ... or to the left, down through a spinney and out beside the Five Bells on to the Doddenham road, and had been killed, Christine would never forgive him.

He began to run. First along the short path to the streeet, then back to the fork and down through the spinney, his light shoes sliding on mud, his hands – bruised or not – grabbing at saplings to keep his balance.

There was no sign of the dog on either road. He scrambled up the bank again and ran back the way he had come. 'Sam ... Sam!'

Then he saw the beagle. Evidently it had picked up a scent: nose to the ground, tail up, it was working its way down the field towards the distant brook. Derek swore with relief, and skidded to a halt.

If he'd thought before he started running, he might have known where to find the animal. When he and Christine had bought the beagle for Laurie they had thought of it simply as a Snoopy dog, the live counterpart of the endearing cartoon character that their daughter had learned to identify. But it was of course a hound, a hunter. It was now too elderly and cosseted to catch anything faster than a baby rabbit, but while it was on a scent he might as well give up calling because it wouldn't take a blind bit of notice of him. Its hunting instinct was too strong.

Field sports had never appealed to Derek. His natural sympathies were with the hunted. He had read somewhere that hares, the quarry of beagle packs, are so fast and elusive that they have a greater-than-even chance of escape; but as he watched his sturdy, persistent hound, he couldn't believe it.

Beagles, he recalled, are bred for stamina. Moreover they hunt in packs. It seemed to him that the odds must always be against the lone quarry and on the hounds, backed up as they were by an organization of huntsmen.

Just as, when a murder was committed, the odds were that the police, with all their resources, would eventually hunt down the murderer.

Shaken by the analogy, Derek came to a decision. It was crazy of Packer to think that he could kill Enid Long and get away with it. He would have to be stopped. And the only way Derek could feel sure of stopping him was by turning Enid out of the Brickyard whether Christine agreed to it or not.

He shouted angrily for Sam through the gathering dusk. The beagle, having lost the scent, came trundling back up the field panting and grinning unrepentantly. Derek slipped his belt through its collar and hauled it back to the Brickyard, intent on a confrontation with his wife that he knew he had to win.

*

'I want a private word with you, Christine.'

He had found her and her mother in the kitchen, having one of their spats of irritability over the supper table. As he stood in the doorway of the room, momentarily dazzled by the lights, he felt as verbally reckless as though he were drunk. Fear of Packer's influence, and of his own powerlessness against it, had eroded his behaviour. He didn't speak the words, he snarled them, and he took a grim satisfaction in the look of shock on the women's faces as he did so.

The air in the kitchen seemed to be impregnated with the alien richness of the casserole Enid had cooked. Its thick spicy smell nauseated him; it was, he convinced himself, the final provocation.

'Now,' he heard himself shout, glaring at his astonished mother-in-law and jerking his thumb at the door. And after a moment's hesitation, Enid went.

'Derek!' Christine protested. She rose to face him. On the table between them, the remains of her mother's casserole began to congeal on the plates. 'What's wrong?'

There was a strange, heated, prickling sensation on the top of his head, as though his fermenting emotions were trying to burst through his skull. 'You *know* what's wrong. That bloody woman. I've had enough of her, do you hear? She is not going to go on living in this house any longer.'

'It's as much – '

'I'm not arguing with you about it, and I'm not begging for your co-operation, either. I've gone past that. She can start packing her bags, because I'm going to drive her back to Southwold first thing on Saturday morning – whether you like it, madam, or whether you don't.'

The insulting tone of his voice appalled him, but he knew that it was fear that was putting the words into his mouth. If he couldn't get her mother out of the house, he dreaded what would have to happen.

'Yes, I know what you're going to say,' he went on with a sneer. 'This is your house just as much as it's mine. Good old Percy, for leaving you enough money to go halves when we bought it. But halves means *equal* rights, and you've already had more than your fair share. I've been pandering to you because of your operation, but now you're well again we're going to do what *I* want for a change. Enid is out.'

Christine's face was white. She looked scared. 'I *can't* tell her to go, Derek. Please don't ask me.'

'I'm not asking you, I'm telling you. If you won't shift her, I'll do it myself. I've always been nice to your mother, right? Well, that's finished. I'm sick of being Mr Nice. From now on I'm going to make her life so bloody unpleasant that she'll be only too thankful to clear off. Is that the way you want it?'

For a few seconds they glared at each other. Then, with a sob, Christine dodged round the kitchen table and fled out into the hallway and up the stairs. Derek raced after her, putting his shoulder against the bathroom door just as she was about to bolt it against him.

'Well?' he demanded fiercely, switching on the light. But her stricken face filled him with remorse. He hesitated for a moment, then stumbled towards her holding out his arms.

'Oh my love – I'm sorry, I'm sorry ... '

Her body was tense, unresponsive. Her forehead was hot against his cheek. 'If only you'd tell me *why*, Chrissie,' he groaned, stroking her hair. 'If only you'd talk to me about it.'

He guided her to the edge of the bath and sat beside her, one arm across her rigid shoulders. She kept her eyelids lowered and said nothing. She had stopped crying, but her tears had left snail-tracks of dampness on her face.

Despairing of helping her in any other way, Derek reached for a tissue from the box. As he tenderly wiped her cheeks he said, in the affectionate half-scolding, half-joking tone he had always used to Laurie when she had a runny nose: 'Where's that girl's hanky?'

Christine lifted her head immediately. Her eyes seemed to be the very dark blue of an infant's, unfocused and unfathomable.

'You do still think of her?' she said.

'Think of her? Of *course* I do.' Derek sought for something to say that would ease his wife's tension. 'That's what I was doing this evening, when I was out with Sam. Who else but our Laurie would have insisted on putting a beagle in a tartan collar!'

His wife was frowning. 'Yes – but *how* do you think of her?'

'With tremendous affection. You know that. You know how cut-up I was when she died.'

'Yes . . . But afterwards, Dee – when you'd got over the shock – were you secretly glad?'

So this was the key to Christine's problem. She suspected him of being thankful that Laurie had died, and so she had been using her mother as a way of punishing him. Relieved that he now understood, Derek tried to find an answer that would satisfy his wife without actually letting her know that she was right.

'I do feel, with hindsight, that her death was probably best for Laurie's own sake,' he said carefully. 'She'd be seventeen now, if she'd lived. Physically a woman, but mentally always a child. I was worried about her long-term future, Chrissie, about what would happen to her if she were to outlive us. So I can't honestly say that I wish she were still alive – but for heaven's sake, I wasn't *glad* that she died. How could you think that of me?'

Christine rose to her feet and walked slowly over to the washbasin. 'I didn't really think it,' she said in an expressionless voice. 'You're a good man, Derek, I know that. *I'm* the one who's guilty. I'm the one who was glad when Laurie died.'

She picked up the cleaning cloth and the bottle of Ajax, and began to work on the basin.

'When Laurie was a baby, and the doctor confirmed the Down's diagnosis, I prayed that she wouldn't survive. I used to go to her cot when she was quiet, hoping to find that my prayers had been answered and she'd died in her sleep. But then I gradually realized that her handicap was my own fault. I'd brought her into the world damaged, so I owed it to her to love and look after her. And that's what I did – and intended to go on doing.

'When she died so unexpectedly, it came as a terrible shock. I certainly wasn't glad at the time, because I felt as though the purpose of my life had been taken away. It was a long while before I could get used to being without her. But then we went for that lovely skiing holiday – '

Christine's busy cloth slowed. She lifted her head, and Derek saw in the mirror that her eyes were closed. Her tone grew lighter.

'It's all so vivid, still. There I was, skiing confidently down a mountain slope ... warm sun, crisp snow, the scent of the pines ... and I was completely happy. I felt young again, and carefree for the first time in fifteen long years. I'd got my freedom at last! I can remember shouting my relief aloud: *Thank God. Thank God she's dead.*'

Christine paused. 'And that,' she continued in a matter-of-fact voice, resuming her burnishing of the taps, 'is what accounts for my cancer. They say it's a stress-related disease, and I'm sure they're right. I know quite well that mine was brought on by the guilt I felt because of being glad that my daughter had died.'

Derek started to protest against such unscientific thinking, but his wife seemed not to hear.

'That's why I won't send Mum back to Southwold. Goodness knows I don't *want* her to stay here – she irritates me beyond measure. But this is my way of trying to atone for my wickedness.

'I'm terrified of secondary tumours, you see. I'm terrified that the cancer is spreading silently inside me, and that I'm going to die. But I truly believe that as long as I go on punishing myself by giving up my freedom for Mum's sake, then I've got a hope of surviving.'

She put down the cleaning cloth, turned, and looked compassionately at Derek. 'Don't think I don't know how hard it is on you, Dee. It seems so unfair to punish you as well. But what I tell myself is that it might be even harder for you if I were to die ... '

Anguished, he reached out to her. Christine put up a hand to ward him off.

'You do understand?'

He nodded.

'And you'll support me? Please? After all, Mum can't live for ever. She's noticeably frailer, and at her age she could be carried off quite quickly by a heart attack or something. I don't want to sound callous but I hope she will be, for her own sake as much as ours. She's always been so independent and active. She must secretly dread the thought of deteriorating into a helpless old age, and I hope she doesn't. But please, Dee – promise you'll help me by letting her stay with us for the rest of her life?'

Derek promised.

8

'Small world!'

Derek had half-feared, half-wanted to hear that voice again; but not so soon, not the following day.

He had forced himself to blank off his personal problems while he kept an appointment with the manager of the Saintsbury branch of Lloyd's Bank to discuss life-assurance-linked mortgage options, though a knot of anxiety in his stomach had prevented him from accepting an invitation to lunch. He had walked out of the bank, briefcase in hand, thinking of nothing but the administrative follow-up to his visit. But as soon as he saw Packer standing on the pavement grinning at him, his fears broke through to the forefront of his mind.

He wanted to ask for more time: it was too soon, he hadn't made a decision, there were so many things to be considered; not yet, not just yet. But he couldn't bring himself to beg.

'Surprise, surprise. Fancy seeing you here, Derek! How are you?' The man's swarthy grin was replaced by a look of spurious concern, and a tone of voice to match: 'And how's your wife?'

The pavements were crowded. It was Friday, market day, as warm and sunny as when they had first met, and half the population of west Suffolk seemed to have converged on the town. For the sake of public decency, Derek suppressed the retort he would have liked to make. 'Get lost!' he said instead, through his teeth.

With one last burst of independent energy he elbowed the smaller man aside. Abandoning considerate behaviour – and why not, when his sense of morality was already half way down the drain? – he barged through the crowds of shoppers in the Butter Market, pushed past a stallholder's rails of spring dresses, dived into the County hotel, shouldered his way among the customers thronging the bar, and emerged from the back door into Tanner Street. A quick glance round confirmed that he had shaken Packer off.

He had parked his car on Angel Hill, two minutes' walk away. As soon as he reached it, he could have jumped in and driven off. He knew, when he thought about it later, that he ought to have done so. But what he did instead, without consciously considering what he was doing or why, was to take his time.

He removed his suit jacket, and folded it neatly before putting it beside his briefcase on the back seat. He wiped his forehead, acknowledging wryly – since he prided himself on being fit – that the beads of sweat were the result of anxiety rather than exertion. He settled in the driver's seat, clipped on his seat belt, and turned the ignition key. He was in process of adjusting the rear-view mirror to his complete satisfaction when Packer came sauntering up to the open window and bent to speak to him.

'Stop playing silly buggers, Derek. I know where you live, and where your office is, and I can always follow your car. That's what I did when you went to your conference. That's what I did this morning.' He jerked his thumb. 'Mine's the Toyota parked in the row behind.'

Derek turned his head.

'Don't waste your time trying to identify it,' said Packer. 'It isn't my personal car – I'm in the trade, remember? I can follow you for weeks if I have to, using a different one every time. So no more games of hide-and-seek, eh? You've got a problem, I've got a problem, and together we've come up with the perfect solution. The sooner we get the jobs done, the better.'

Compact as it was, Packer's body seemed to be blocking the sun. Derek suppressed a shiver. He despised himself for being influenced by the man, but there was someting about Packer's one-fanged tooth – its gleaming sharpness, the beaded line of spittle that linked it to his full lower lip – that held him mesmerized.

'Switch off your engine,' said Packer.

70

Derek switched off his engine.

Packer walked round to the passenger door. Derek leaned across to unlock it, but having done so he made a final verbal attempt to break free. The idea had come to him in the early hours of the morning, and it was only by clutching it to him that he had at last managed to fall asleep.

'The whole thing's off,' he announced, trying to deny Packer's ascendancy by keeping his eyes on the car parked immediately ahead. 'And it's your own fault for going snooping round my place yesterday. You were noticed, and by more than one person. If a crime is committed' – he couldn't bring himself to say anything about his mother-in-law being murdered – 'the police will start hunting for someone of your description right away. You blew it, you idiot.'

Packer was sitting sideways in the passenger seat, looking directly at Derek from very close quarters. His dark-browed face was smoothly shaven, and he had brought into the car with him a hint of masculine toilet water. He wore a natty blazer with two vents and crested gilt buttons, well-pressed grey flannel trousers, a fashionably striped shirt and a club tie. The combination was just a bit over the top, almost a caricature, and it made him seem charmingly untrustworthy; a rogue, but essentially a harmless one.

Derek knew better. And now that they were in such close proximity, it seemed to him that Packer exuded the latent strength of some half-tamed animal. Glancing at the small man's comparatively large hands, and at the unusually thick growth of hair that crawled from under his shirt cuffs and along the backs of his fingers, Derek felt a moment's revulsion on behalf of the magnificent young woman Packer had married. No wonder she had looked unhappy. God, if only he could escape the man's influence and go straight home to his own wife –

But if he did so, he'd be back to square one. And having come so far, mentally and emotionally, could he really bear to give up this opportunity to get rid of his mother-in-law? He tightened his grip on the steering wheel, trying to steady himself while conflicting wishes see-sawed in his mind.

'I blew it, did I?' the man was saying in an interested voice.

71

'How did that happen?' His tone changed: 'Who saw me, and where?'

It had seemed such a good idea, at two a.m. Derek had reasoned that the fact that he hadn't met anyone on the field path didn't mean that no one had seen Packer earlier in the day. The man could well have been spotted without knowing it. He certainly couldn't disprove that he had been seen. *Got him*, Derek had thought.

But now, as he explained that two of his neighbours had noticed a short, dark, curly-haired stranger walking along the path at the far end of their gardens, he felt less sure. Packer continued his cross-examination.

'Short, dark, and curly-haired, eh? Was that how you described me to them, when you asked them if they'd seen me?'

Derek scorned the trap. 'Of course I didn't ask them! It was my neighbours who mentioned you to me, precisely because it's so unusual to see any stranger walking along the path. They both described you, wondering if I knew you – and of course I said I didn't. But you must realize that this makes the whole thing impossible.'

Packer was looking at him with what seemed like unqualified approval. 'Well, well . . . I took you for an honest man, Derek – and here you are, lying with the best of us! That's good. I wouldn't work with you if you couldn't think on your feet. But – ' His expression hardened as he jabbed his forefinger viciously into Derek's ribs, making him wince ' – I won't work, either, with any man who's fool enough to underestimate me. If you want my help – and you do – *don't ever call me an idiot again.*'

Despite the fact that the window was half open, Derek felt a build-up of heat and tension inside the car. He wiped his forehead with the back of his hand. 'But you can't possibly be sure you weren't seen, either on the path or somewhere else in the village,' he argued. 'How can we risk it?'

'I'm sure,' said Packer, 'because I didn't go anywhere near the path. I didn't need to. I used to be in the Army – and after spending four years of my life training infantrymen, I should know how to use an Ordnance Survey map. I've studied – and since dumped – a large-scale map showing every detail of your village, including the footpaths. It also named larger properties such as the Brickyard. I drove along the main street just once yesterday morning, so that I could get a quick look at your house. Then I parked the car down by the bridge on the road to Doddenham, and used binoculars to check the route of the lane and identify your back garden gate.'

'You must have been seen while you were doing that,' insisted Derek. 'It's a quiet road, and the traffic is local. Somebody would have noticed you.'

'They did. Two cars, one butcher's van and a tractor crossed the bridge while I was there, and all the drivers gave me a glance. But shall I tell you what they saw? An old Ford Fiesta, with number plates that I've since changed; and a scruffy man hung about with binoculars and a camera, wearing a weatherproof jacket and a woolly hat. They saw a bird-watcher – satisfied?'

Derek was silenced. His head ached with conflict. Part of his brain was still trying to escape Packer, but another – perhaps the greater part – was beginning to respect the man's cunning.

'Don't think I don't know you're trying to wriggle out of it,' went on Packer. 'But I'm not forcing you to stay parked here, am I? You're a free agent. If you don't want to co-operate, you can say so and drive off.

'But you could have done that ten minutes ago, couldn't you? I gave you the opportunity when you bolted. You didn't take it, though. You deliberately sat here and let me come to you. Why? *Because you know you need me.*'

Acknowledging it, Derek lowered his head and abandoned the conflict.

When Packer spoke again, he sounded almost benevolent. 'You're a lucky man, Derek, d'you know that? I mean, to have met me.

'True, it wouldn't have been difficult for you to find someone else who shared your problem. There must be an army of middle-aged people out there, seething with frustration and resentment because they're hog-tied by ancient dependants. Medical science has got a hell of a lot to answer for, in my opinion. Where's the sense in old people being kept alive at the expense of younger people's freedom?

'All the same, your chances of finding a fellow-sufferer who

73

had the guts to do something about it would have been pretty small. And even if you'd found somebody, the pair of you would almost certainly have botched it. An operation like this needs meticulous planning – and luckily for you I'm a professional.

'I've already planned both phases of the operation. All you have to do is exactly what I tell you. Oh – and remember this: the Army taught me how to plan, and it also taught me how to be a bastard to anyone who doesn't give me one hundred per cent support. If you let me down, in any way, the rest of your life won't be worth living. Understood?'

The knot in Derek's stomach tightened. He sat rigid behind the steering wheel, staring straight ahead. The situation was unreal. He couldn't believe that he was actually there, in his own car, on the familiar open space of Angel Hill between the creeper-covered Georgian façade of the Angel hotel and the Great Gate of the former Abbey, with cars neatly parked all round him and an ice-cream van doing a sunny day's trade ten yards away, allowing this poisonous little man to talk him into committing murder.

Whatever Packer said, Derek knew that he couldn't do it.

It wasn't any longer a question of trying to wriggle out of the conspiracy. The conflict in his mind had resolved itself in Packer's favour. But the actual commission of murder was another matter, one that he'd already contemplated and dismissed.

'I can't,' he said. 'It's no good – I know I can't.'

'Can't what? I'm not asking you to do anything, initially, except keep out of the way. Where's the problem?'

'I'm talking about . . . the other end of the operation. I couldn't bring myself to kill anybody. I certainly couldn't touch that old man.'

'You don't need to touch him,' said Packer, benevolent again. 'I knew I couldn't rely on you for that, so I've made your job as simple as possible. Sidney's a diabetic, and he's going to slip into a coma one day when my wife and I are out and there's only an untrained minder with him. I'll explain the details when you need to know them. Basically – to set your mind at rest – all you'll have to do is switch his plastic beaker of orange juice for one laced with insulin. Easy. No problem.'

As far as he could recollect, Derek had never before in his life bitten his fingernails. He wouldn't have known how to go about it. Now, deprived of both willpower and initiative, he found himself instinctively trying to cram the nails of all four fingers of his right hand between his clenched teeth. He removed them long enough to say, 'Yes, but – '

'Look,' said Packer: 'there's nothing *selfish* about what we're planning, is there? We're not doing this for our own benefit. Poor old Sidney's a burden to himself as well as to my wife. You said yourself how wretched he looks.

'And as for your mother-in-law – she's already lived out her own life. It's not right that she should be battening on the two of you in her old age, when your wife is fighting against cancer. Any loving husband would put his wife first in those circumstances. Just remember that you're doing it for *her* sake.'

Packer got out of the car and went round to the driver's side.

'I'm going for a walk,' he said, jerking his thumb towards the Abbey gardens that lay beyond the Great Gate. 'Come on if you're coming.'

As he watched the man strut off, conspicuously dapper among the lunch-time ice-cream lickers, Derek was aware that he was being given one final chance of escape. All he had to do was to switch on the ignition and drive away.

But that would require an act of will that he no longer possessed. With a numbing sense of inevitability, he got out of his car, locked it and followed.

9

Five minutes later Derek was sitting on a bench in the Abbey gardens, with a note pad and pencil provided by Packer, making sketch plans of the interior of the Brickyard. Packer himself, at the other end of the bench, was engrossed in the financial pages of the *Daily Telegraph*.

Derek found it almost impossible to draw the lines straight. His hands were shaking, and they left dark smudges of sweat on the paper. But he concentrated fiercely on doing the job he had been given, leaving himself no room to think about its true purpose.

Operation Brickyard, as Packer had briefly referred to it, was planned to look like a burglary gone wrong. Derek was to give himself an alibi by going out for an evening with his wife. Packer would then break in, and take some of the Cartwrights' valuables. At the subsequent investigation, the police would believe that Mrs Cartwright's mother had met her end because she had disturbed the intruder. There would, Packer said, be no reason for the police to look for any other motive; nor would there be any possibility of their tracing the burglary back to him. And Derek would of course be completely beyond suspicion.

It sounded watertight. Professional, as Packer had promised. Derek felt an unwilling admiration for the man. He was thankful that Packer had taken charge, and that he himself had been relegated to the role of burglar's accomplice.

Ordinarily, of course – in his former decent honourable life, Before Packer – Derek would never have given anyone the plans of his house. The Brickyard was his and Christine's sanctuary. He would have been appalled by the thought of an imminent burglary, not so much because of the loss it would entail – he was, after all, comprehensively insured – but because it would invade their privacy. Any suggestion that he would one day facilitate a break-in would have seemed to him outrageous beyond belief.

But their privacy had already been invaded, even before Packer. Their domestic life had been disrupted by Christine's mother. Having their house burgled was, it seemed to Derek, a small price to pay for a restoration of their former state.

What would happen to his mother-in-law in the process was something he tried not to think about. It was, thankfully, out of his hands.

He made no attempt to ease his conscience with a spurious justification for Enid Long's murder. Only a thoroughgoing bastard such as Packer would suggest that the end could possibly justify the means. It was precisely because Derek knew in his heart the enormity of what he was doing that he was now co-operating so willingly with Packer, offering up the plans of his home, and his possessions, as a form of expiation.

His sense of unreality persisted. There were dozens of people strolling past within a few feet of their bench, laughing and talking, carefree, but Derek felt as isolated from them as though he and Packer were still behind the windscreen of his car. He could see smiles and birds and flowers and sunlight, but he seemed unable to distinguish the voices or hear the birdsong or catch the scent of the hyacinths or feel the warmth of the sun.

At the same time he felt oddly distanced from himself. He watched and listened from somewhere above his head as he explained the sketch plans to Packer, and as he did so he mentally congratulated himself on the clarity of his exposition, and on the coolness with which the two of them were discussing the operation in a public place.

'Any alarms?' asked Packer.

'No, we're in a low-risk area. We're very security-conscious, though. The doors are solid, with bolts and chains and mortice locks. The windows are all of the sash type. The large ones have secondary double-glazing, and all the catches have locks on them. I go round last thing at night to check that everything's secure.'

'What about when you go out for an evening? Do you check all the windows then?'

'We hardly ever do go out, what with one thing and another. But as long as we weren't leaving the house empty, and I knew that all the downstairs windows were closed, I could overlook the fact that one of them wasn't locked.'

'Which one?'

Derek pointed on the plan to a small room on the north side of the ground floor. 'The pantry.'

'How big is the window? If a burglar were to smash the glass, undo the catch and push up the sash, could he get through?'

'A burglar your size, yes.'

Packer asked for details: of the fastening on the gate that led from the field path to the garden, of the ground between the gate and the house, of the composition of the paths round the house and the ground immediately below the pantry window; of the interior of the pantry, of the door handles, of the floor-covering of the passages, the hall, the stairs.

'And when I'm in, what am I looking for? What have you got that would interest a burglar?'

'The usual, I suppose.' Derek began to offer the items that he knew were prime targets because they were easily saleable, but Packer cut him short.

'Have some sense! How d'you expect me to haul a video recorder and a hi-fi along the field path? I want the small stuff – silver, jewellery, pocket antiques.'

Derek took a rapid mental inventory. The family had acquired all kinds of decorative and collectable bits and pieces over the years, as every family does, but little of it was of any intrinsic value. The best things belonged to Christine, and for her their value was predominantly sentimental.

No, he wasn't going to have her deprived of them. It wouldn't be fair. Any personal loss must be his; and so he told Packer where he kept the two small silver cups he had won for athletics when he was at college, his gold cufflinks, the silver cigarette case that had belonged to his father, and the camera his children had given him on his fortieth birthday.

'What else?' said Packer.

'Isn't that enough?'

'Not nearly enough to murder for.'

Suddenly angry, not with Packer but with himself, Derek sprang to his feet and strode away from the people and the flowerbeds towards the Abbey ruins. How could he have been so thoughtless as to support the plan for a burglary!

He had been in favour simply because he hadn't, until now, considered what a real burglary would entail. Worse, he hadn't taken into account the effect it would have on his wife.

He wasn't closely acquainted with anyone who had ever been burgled, but he had of course read about it, and seen the *Crimewatch* programmes. And Packer was right. An opportunist burglar who was so wound up as to kill anyone who disturbed him would ransack the house, not search considerately for a few insignificant items. But if the burglary were to be made realistic, Christine would be horrified by the violation of their home.

How could he do this to her, poor girl, after all she had been through? Slowing his pace, he stared bleakly at some fragments of monastic stonework that poked out of the grass like ancient fangs and molars. God, what a mess he was making of his attempts to help the wife he loved ...

He turned on Packer as the smaller man caught him up. 'I won't have Christine upset, she's suffered enough. Don't you bloody *dare* take her treasures and wreck our home!'

Packer eyed him coldly. 'You're talking like a sentimental fool. If I don't do a proper job, the police'll be suspicious.'

'I don't see why.' Calmer after his outburst, Derek was thinking on his feet again. 'You want to leave the impression that you were disturbed on the job, right? That somebody called out from upstairs ... So why couldn't that have happened before you had time to get very far? If you start by searching the hall cupboard – '

'Hall cupboards aren't worth searching.'

'This one will be, I guarantee. And there's another thing: the police aren't to know that you're on foot, are they? You've no need to pull the living-room apart because there's about two thousand quid's-worth of video and audio equipment in there, all immediately get-at-able. If you shift it out into the hall, the police'll assume you were intending to load it in a vehicle. That should convince them – and confuse them as well.'

Packer thought for a moment or two, then nodded. 'Not a

bad idea. Anyway, I don't want to stay in the house any longer than I have to, so pulling it apart would be a waste of time. All right, I'll leave most of it untouched.'

Derek felt so relieved that he found himself thanking the man.

They walked on. 'What time does the old woman go to bed?' said Packer.

As if watching from a distance, Derek saw the two of them pass between a double row of cherry trees, treading on a path carpeted brownish-white by fallen blossom. He heard his calm reply: 'She usually goes up to her room about ten, then watches television in bed.'

'But if you and your wife are out, is she likely to stay up until you come home?'

'I really don't know. We haven't ever left her alone in the house for a whole evening.'

'Then it's time you did. Try to persuade her to go upstairs as usual. It'll be simpler if she's in bed.'

Derek's stomach lurched, bringing him back to reality. He stood still. This was it. He could no longer ignore the purpose of the operation.

'How—' Something seemed to be rising in his throat, thickening his voice. 'How are you going to ... to do it?'

Packer was looking at him with mild interest. 'How did *you* do it?' he said. 'In your dreams, I mean.'

'By str – '

Derek turned abruptly away. Coincidentally, perhaps, he hadn't had one of his terrible dream-struggles to squeeze the breath out of Enid since his first meeting with Packer. Now, the recollection of his dream – of his hands frantically kneading that nightmare throat, pliable, putty-like – brought a resurgence of panic.

His stomach contracted again, and his knees felt weak. He clutched at the varnished trunk of a cherry tree to steady himself. Screwing up his eyes in his efforts to control the nausea, he found that he could now visualize his mother-in-law's throat as it was in actuality, as he'd seen it on his visit to her bedroom. The remembrance of her slack, withered, trembling flesh, so vulnerably exposed by the lacy plunge-neck of her nightgown, filled him with compassion. How could he bring himself to conspire to kill poor old Enid?

But then the image faded, to be replaced by one that was far more vivid and painful and urgent: by Christine's desirable body, and her surgically mutilated breast.

His moment of weakness passed. He swallowed hard, spat the bitter taste out of his mouth, and rejoined Packer.

'I dreamed I was suffocating the old woman,' he said.

Derek wanted Enid's death to be made as merciful as possible, not only for her own sake but for his wife's. The death of her mother was bound to come as a shock to Christine, however thankful she might privately be. The least he could do for her in the circumstances was to lessen the shock as much as he could.

He explained to Packer that he was anxious for there to be no sign of violence. 'I don't want her shot, or stabbed.'

'Guns make too much noise,' said Packer, 'and knives make too much mess. Anyway, I don't possess either.'

'I'd prefer you to use a pillow,' said Derek. 'It'll be kindest for her, and simplest for you.'

Packer promised to bear it in mind. Then he laughed.

'As a matter of fact, I've never killed anyone before. All that time in the Army, and I never had a chance to put my training to the test! P'rhaps, when it comes to the point, I shan't have the guts. P'rhaps tomorrow, when you and your wife get home after your evening out, you'll find the old woman still alive and kicking.'

'Tomorrow?'

Derek was shaken. Tomorrow was much too soon. He wanted to stammer out protests and excuses, but he forced himself to stay outwardly calm. There was, after all, a lot to be said for getting the operation over and done with.

'Any reason why not?' said Packer. 'Have you made any other arrangement?'

'No – '

'Then tomorrow, Saturday. Two good reasons. First, there'll be a moon, so I'll be able to travel fast along the field path. Second, according to a poster in the window of the Five Bells, 'Saturday night is music night, eight 'til late.' That must mean they've got an extension until eleven-thirty or twelve and there'll be strangers about. I can park outside the pub between ten forty-five and eleven-thirty and never be noticed. Good, eh?' Packer grinned: 'It says on the poster, RABBIT PIE. D'you suppose that's the name of the group, or the menu?'

They had begun to walk back the way they had come. Derek put one foot in front of the other, feeling as numbed as when he had followed the man into the Abbey gardens.

'I don't see how Christine and I can stay out that late, especially at such short notice. The Five Bells fills up with drunken yobs on Saturday nights, I wouldn't dream of taking her there. And we don't belong to any clubs – '

'Don't worry. I told you, I've got it all arranged. The important thing is for you to establish your alibi, so I've provisionally booked a table for two in your name for dinner tomorrow night at the Angel, here in Saintsbury. You'll find it pricey, but I hear the food's very good. I'll ring them later today to confirm.

'I've booked your table for nine o'clock. It'll probably be at least ten-thirty by the time you've finished eating, and then you can sit for another hour over coffee and liqueurs. By the time you've driven back to Wyveling it'll be well after midnight. And if you get done by the traffic cops on the way home for driving under the influence, so much the better for your alibi! Any questions?'

Derek could think of nothing at all. He felt as though his mind had been anaesthetized. He walked to his car, and opened the door.

'Easy, eh?' said Packer encouragingly. He grinned: 'Dead easy, I'd say. There's just one important thing for you to remember: before you go out, *make sure you leave the pantry window unlocked*. After that, all you have to do is relax and enjoy yourselves. All right?'

Derek nodded. He started to get into the driving seat but Packer moved even faster, slamming the door on his shin and trapping his leg against the sill.

'*Christ*,' Derek gasped. 'What d'you think you're *doing*?'

'Making sure I've got your attention,' said Packer grimly. He eased the pressure a little. 'I said, "All right?" and I want to hear your answer. I'm doing all this in *your* interest, remember. If you let me down – '

Grimacing with pain, Derek promised to carry out the man's instructions. Packer let go of the door. Derek retrieved his leg, rubbed it gingerly, closed the door and fastened his seat belt. He was feeling sick again. He longed to get home; but on the other hand he couldn't imagine how he was going to face Christine. Or her mother.

A peremptory rap came on the window. Derek wound it down and Packer's curly head and sharp tooth appeared. 'Nearly forgot: have you got a dog?'

'Yes, an old beagle.'

'You'll have to take it out with you, then.'

'I can't do that – Christine would think it very odd.'

'Well, you can't leave it at home to raise an alarm. You'll have to get rid of it some other way.'

10

As he drove away from Saintsbury, Derek realized that he wouldn't be able to go home that night. How could he hope to behave normally towards Christine and her mother when he knew what was going to happen the following evening?

And if he didn't behave normally, his wife would be sure to remember, afterwards, that something had been wrong. He had been so vehement about getting rid of Enid that Christine might even begin to wonder whether he knew anything about her death.

Not, of course, that she'd ever say so to the police. The bond between them was too strong, thank God, for him to have any worries on that score. He wanted to give her no cause for suspicion simply because he loved her. It was important to him to retain not merely her loyalty but her affection and trust.

Derek supposed that he still had an afternoon's work to do, but he couldn't possibly give his mind to it. He drove to Colchester and back just to fill in the time, then returned to the office after the rest of the staff had left. He shrugged and tore up an urgent memo about an appointment he had forgotten to keep – too late to do anything about it now – signed his letters, and then telephoned Christine.

To explain his overnight absence from home on a Friday, he invented a colleague's retirement party for that evening, and an end-of-season hockey match he wanted to watch in Cambridge the following morning. He might as well enjoy the party, he said, and spend the night at a small private hotel he sometimes used, just round the corner from the office.

'Not sure what time I'll be home tomorrow,' he concluded. 'I'm bound to meet people I know at the match, and there'll be a get-together afterwards. Anyway, you're driving your mother over to Southwold for lunch with her friends, aren't you? If I'm not at home when you return, it'll be because I've taken Sam for a walk – I promised him a good long one this weekend. You all right, sweetheart? Drive very carefully. Love you. 'Bye.'

Derek had intended, when he dialled their number, to tell Christine that he would be taking her out to dinner the following evening. He hadn't forgotten. Something had made him hold back.

Now, with the working week over and all the offices empty except for the cleaners, he sat at his monitor staring blankly at the figures on the screen. He had thought he could use the evening profitably by writing an article on personal pension plans, to be distributed to major businesses in the region for publication in their house magazines. But the comparative tables of past and projected retirement benefits on a with-profits policy for an annual premium of £500, which showed that his own company's projections were based on an enviable track record, failed to hold his attention. His brief conversation with his wife had opened the floodgates in his mind, and anxiety had come pouring in.

To hell with Packer and his arrangements for an alibi! Derek realized that he couldn't possibly go out for a meal with Christine tomorrow evening, knowing that in their absence her mother was being suffocated. The food would choke him. Packer himself might be – was – evil enough to do such a thing; Derek wasn't.

That didn't mean the operation was off. Derek had no intention, now, of trying to back out. He was glad it was going to happen, eager to get it over. But he knew his own capabilities and he reserved the right to do things his own way.

He accepted that he had to find an alternative method of getting himself and Christine out of the Brickyard for the evening, and of establishing their presence elsewhere. It was *where* that was the problem. The Suffolk countryside offered little in the way of evening diversions, other than eating out.

True, there were cinemas in Yarchester and Ipswich, theatres in Yarchester and Saintsbury, and the concert hall at Aldeburgh. But since their marriage, the Cartwrights had gone to none of them. What with the distance and the winding

Suffolk roads, their young family, and then of course the Laurie years, they had never considered the possibility of going out for an evening's entertainment. Christine would think it very strange if he were suddenly to suggest driving miles to see a film or a play about which they knew nothing. She would almost certainly refuse to go.

They could perhaps call on some friends ... but that wouldn't work because he would still have the problem of making cheerful conversation while Christine's mother was being murdered.

No, a social evening of any kind was out of the question. He would be sure to betray his anxiety, and Christine wouldn't fail to notice it. Besides, his conscience wouldn't let him do anything that he would normally find enjoyable.

What was going to happen tomorrow evening was unequivocally wrong, and he didn't know how to live with himself through the hours leading up to it. He had thought that offering that bastard Packer the run of his home, and his prized possessions, would be sufficient in the way of expiation; but of course it wasn't.

He had come to realize that whatever he did to provide himself with an alibi would have to be unpleasant. The only way he could cope with the knowledge of Operation Brickyard was by putting himself through some form of punishment.

Derek switched off his monitor, locked up the office, and drove out of Cambridge through the April dusk. His company had block membership of the health and fitness club at the Post House hotel on the Histon road, but because he lived elsewhere and his job involved so much travelling he couldn't use it as often as he would like. Winter weekend hockey-refereeing helped to keep him fit, but tonight's stay in the city would for once give him an opportunity not just to swim but to make full use of the club's power-sport equipment.

Changing into the kit that he carried in the car on the off-chance, he began his work-out gradually. He warmed up on the exercise bicycle, then stepped on to the power jog, moving comfortably to begin with. As the speed increased he strode out, pounding grimly on and on until his chest hurt and his

86

knees weakened and a stitch in his side brought him to a doubled-up, gasping stop.

Next, to the sit-up board. Lie down, feet higher than head; hook feet under padded bar, link hands at back of neck. Sit up. *Sit up*? God, easier said than done, at forty-four . . . *Try* to sit up, woofing at the ferocious pull on hamstrings and stomach muscles . . . Lie back and pant. Then gulp, take deep breath, grit teeth and try again. Sit . . . up, up, grunting with the effort. Collapse and gasp for mercy.

But give yourself none. *Think* why you're doing this. Think of Enid Long, whose coming death this is all about, and stop groaning over a bit of pain. Sit up – down – up – down until your body no longer responds to your will.

And then to the weight-lifting machine. Brace yourself, take the strain on biceps and shoulders and . . . lift. Yes of course it's torture. That's the idea. Keep going: lift, grunt, heave, sweat. Don't merely endure the pain, *welcome* it. Think of your involvement in Enid's murder, and don't let up until you're too exhausted to remember what you're punishing yourself for.

11

Derek slept that night as though he were dead.

When he woke, abruptly, in a cramped hotel bedroom, he wondered for a few moments which part of the region he was in, and what appointments he had that day. Then the ache in his body – just the one monstrous ache, in every muscle – reminded him what he had been doing the previous evening. And why.

He limped to the window, pulled back the curtains and looked out at the traffic moving along the glistening surface of the Chesterton Road, and at the willow-swept, rain-pocked river beyond. A wet Saturday morning. Enid's last.

The thought of her coming murder no longer had any capacity to move him. All his attention was concentrated on his arrangements for the day. He made a cup of instant coffee in his room, gulped it down black while he dressed, then left, scrupulously paying the bill with his personal credit card rather than his company charge card.

First, to get himself going again, he crossed the river by the footbridge and walked on Midsummer Common in the rain. Then he collected his car from outside the office, drove back to the Post House, and spent the morning at the health club. Not overdoing the exercises, because he needed to be fit for the day ahead, but putting himself through grim tests of will-power and endurance on the treadmill and in the swimming pool.

The only relaxation he allowed himself was for the benefit of his muscles. He spent five blank-minded minutes sitting up to his chin in the foaming grey water of the jacuzzi, while jets of water massaged his aching body. Then he showered, dressed, lunched sparely on a salad sandwich and a glass of Perrier, and left Cambridge for home.

He had timed his journey so as to be sure that Christine and her mother would have set off for Southwold before he returned. They had left the house in Sam's charge and when Derek opened the door the beagle, who hated to be alone, wriggled and barked and waved his rudder in an enthusiastic greeting.

While the dog, liberated, ran snuffling round the wet garden, Derek consulted the yellow page section of the telephone directory and made a few notes. Then he took Sam's lead and tartan collar from the coat-rack in the kitchen passage, locked up the house again, and called to the beagle. 'Big walk, old boy?' he said, and the dog jumped eagerly into the car.

The Cartwrights' usual routes from Wyveling were south to Breckham Market, east to Yarchester, west to Saintsbury and Cambridge. On this occasion Derek took the minor road northwards, in the direction of the area of heath and forest where they had often taken Laurie for long walks with her dog.

Packer's cold instruction to 'get rid' of the beagle had made sense; but how could you temporarily get rid of a pet without arousing your wife's suspicion? Fortunately, Derek had thought overnight of a solution that would not only keep Sam safely out of the way, but also occupy his own time until mid-evening – and, what's more, provide a good reason for any agitation he might show as the time for Enid's death drew near.

What he intended was simply to put the beagle in a boarding kennels for twenty-four hours. Not in a local one, of course, where he might be known by sight to one of the staff or another customer, but somewhere at least twenty miles away. Then, late in the afternoon, he could telephone Christine from a call-box saying he'd taken the dog for a walk in the forest and it had run off. He could then stay away from the Brickyard until after dark on the pretext of searching for Sam, and go out again next day to 'find' him.

Christine would be upset, of course. Derek was sorry about that, but he saw no alternative. She wouldn't have long to dwell on the loss of the dog, though – the other events of the evening would soon take her mind off it. And when he 'found'

Sam for her, the relief would go some way towards helping her through the aftermath of her mother's death.

That aftermath was something Derek had made a point of not thinking about. What he was doing was entirely for Christine's benefit, and he preferred not to dwell on the fact that its immediate effect on her was bound to be shattering.

But, he argued in his head, it would be the unexpectedness of it that would shock her, not the death itself. After all, only a couple of days ago she had said that with a bit of luck her mother would be carried off quickly by a heart attack. Well, perhaps she hadn't actually said 'with a bit of luck', but that was certainly what she'd implied.

Enid couldn't live for ever, Christine had definitely said that. And, surely, for an old woman to be smothered with a pillow as she slept – unknowingly, painlessly – would be an even more merciful way to go than a heart attack? He was confident, he told himself, that Christine would agree with him once she got over the initial shock.

He drove quickly along the narrow country roads, with Sam alert on the seat beside him, searching for the first address on his list. The rain, which had eased off in mid-morning, was now coming down seriously, hampering his search. But after an enquiry at a filling station and some splashy backing and turning, he found a roadside notice saying *Barn Farm Boarding Kennels and Cattery.*

An arrow pointed up a pot-holed track, with a thorn hedge on one side and a field of winter barley on the other, towards an isolated farmhouse. Yellowish surface water running off the field was using the track as a ditch. In other circumstances Derek would have taken one look and driven on, but today he saw the unprepossessing access to the farm as an advantage. The kennels were most unlikely to be full.

Hedged in at the end of the track was the former farmyard. Many of the outbuildings seemed to be tumbledown, and the yard itself was a wasteland of mud and knee-high nettles traversed by a concrete path splattered with poultry droppings. Wherever there was shelter, assorted poultry stood huddled against the driving rain. On the far side of the yard was the farmhouse, a bleak box of grey brick lidded with blue slate. All its doors and windows looked to be in need of a coat of paint.

Derek felt a moment's misgiving, on Sam's behalf. The beagle was old, and accustomed to every home comfort; he'd never been in a kennels in his life. Would he be properly looked after, in a run-down place like this? Would he be secure?

But it was only for one night. The dog had to be kept out of the way while Operation Brickyard was in progress, and Derek felt too keyed-up to go searching the countryside for a five-star boarding kennels. This would have to do.

At the entrance to the yard was a farm gate (*Please keep this gate shut*) between two still-leafless ash trees. Derek parked on a cinder patch just outside the gate. *Please leave your pet in the car until you have booked in* advised another notice, pointing to a small wooden hut just inside the gate labelled *Reception. Please Ring*, said a notice on the hut, indicating the whereabouts of the bell.

Derek rang. And rang again, impatiently. He was still wearing yesterday's fine-day business suit, and he was getting wet.

At the third ring, a slight female figure in an over-large dark-green waxed cotton jacket, a jungle hat, shabby cords and dirty wellington boots emerged from one of the outbuildings and came splodging down the yard.

'Sorry!' she called breathlessly as she approached the reception hut. She was in her mid-thirties, with an air of harassment, a tangle of brown hair and delicate features that were thickened – as was her pleasant voice – by a streaming cold.

'Frightfully sorry to keep you waiting. I was making up the feeds and I'm single-handed – my husband's had to take to his bed with 'flu. Do come in.'

The hut contained the bare essentials of an office. On the wall opposite the door was a large notice, artistically hand-painted: *Barn Farm Boarding Kennels and Cattery – John and Rachel Dean.* Beside it was pinned a newspaper photograph of a young couple surrounded by domestic pets. The clipping, yellowed by a year or two's exposure, carried a story headed *Ex-teachers' rural venture.*

'My dog's in the car,' said Derek abruptly. In his former life, Before Packer, he would – as a matter of normal civilized

91

consideration for a person who was having problems – have commiserated with her before telling her what he wanted. But now there was too much on his mind for such courtesies. 'Can I leave him with you?'

'Gladly.' Looking more cheerful, Rachel Dean pushed back the sleeves of her jacket with small, grubby, weather-reddened hands and opened a register. 'How long would you like us to keep him?'

'Just the one night.'

Her disappointment was obvious, but she made an effort at concealment. 'Fine. Would you like to see the accommodation? We're rather proud of it.' Her voice began to sound as though she had a peg on her nose. Pausing to blow, and draw breath, she began a muzzy recitation: 'Each dog has its own brick-built and tiled kennel, with a covered outdoor run. The kennels can be heated individually, but I'm afraid we do have to charge extra for that.'

It sounded a better place than Derek had thought. He declined the tour (there were hours to be got through before he could return home, but the build-up of anxiety made him feel that he was in a hurry) and agreed to pay for a heated kennel. Might as well make the old dog as comfortable as possible.

Rachel Dean sat at the table and began to fill in the register, breathing through her mouth and wearily ignoring the drops of rain that rolled off the brim of her hat and plopped on to the page. There had been very few entries, Derek noticed as she wrote the date, since the beginning of the year.

She sneezed, mopped her nose, and held the handkerchief ready for further use. 'Could I have your name and address, please?'

He had come prepared for the question. 'David Carter,' he said, 'Flint Cottage, Fodderstone.' Fodderstone was the name of a village he had passed through on his way to the kennels, and several of its old buildings were faced with flint.

'We usually ask for the name and address of your own vet,' she said as she wrote, 'but as it's only for one night there's no need. You have a current vaccination certificate for the dog, of course?'

'Of course.'

She looked up at him, bleary-eyed but expectant. Uncomprehending, he looked blankly down at her.

'With you, I mean,' she said. 'You've brought the vaccination certificate with you?'

'No – no, I haven't.'

'You do need to, I'm afraid. It's a precaution we have to take for the sake of the other dogs.'

Derek frowned. 'I didn't know that – we've never boarded him before. Well, I can assure you that he's had whatever jabs are necessary. We've got the certificate somewhere at home.'

'Yes, I'm sure you have. But I do need to see it.' She sneezed again. 'It's not that I doubt you, Mr Carter, but unless you produce the certificate I'm afraid we can't accept your dog. I know it's an awful nuisance, but would you mind fetching it?'

'*Fetching* it?'

The tension had been gathering hot and tight inside his chest; now, suddenly, it rose in his throat like a noxious vapour. Its only way out was through his mouth. Decent, honourable men don't resort to verbal aggression, but Derek's inhibitions were no longer functioning. He began to shout, his anger fuelled by fear of the events that were to come.

'This is *stupid*. I've never *heard* of anything so bloody stupid! Do you seriously expect me to go all the way home just to fetch some ridiculous piece of paper for you to look at? For God's sake – '

Rachel Dean stood up, a tiny person swamped by her wet-weather clothes and exhausted by her cold. They were standing so close together that she had to pull off her hat and tilt back her head in order to be able to look up at his face. Her eyes were watering, her cheeks were as pink as her swollen nose, and she had to dash away a drip before she spoke, but she gave him her answer with dignity.

'What you do is entirely up to you, Mr Carter. But if you want us to take your dog, yes, I *am* asking you to fetch the certificate. After all, Fodderstone's not more than five miles away, is it?'

Baulked, Derek fumed for a moment in silence. It would take him a good three-quarters of an hour to drive back to Wyveling. By the time he got there Christine and her mother would probably have returned, and that would put an end to his chances of getting the dog out of the way. And even if they weren't back, he wouldn't know where to begin to look for the wretched vaccination certificate.

But he wasn't going to have his plans frustrated. Shouting at the woman had been counter-productive, but at least it had relieved his tension sufficiently to get him thinking on his feet again. His best move, he decided, would be to appeal to her sympathy with a story that was sufficiently near the truth to account for his anxiety.

'Mrs Dean – ' he began apologetically.

He understood the importance of body language. Had there been a visitor's chair he would have sat on it, in order to stop towering over her. Unable to sit, he changed his upright stance to a careworn slump.

'Mrs Dean – that is right, isn't it? I don't know what you must think of me after that outburst. I do apologize, most sincerely. The fact is ... The fact is, I didn't want to bother you with my own problems when your husband is ill and you're not at all well yourself. I do sympathize believe me. I'd never have shouted like that if I hadn't been so desperately worried. This is a family emergency, you see. I'm trying to get to Peterborough as quickly as possible. It's my wife's mother ... she isn't expected to live through the night.'

Rachel Dean began to sympathize, but Derek cut her short.

'That's why I'm in such a hurry, I'm afraid. I told my wife I'd find somewhere to leave the dog while she went on ahead, and naturally I want to follow her as quickly as possible. The dog's hers, and even if I were to dash back home I wouldn't know where she keeps his vaccination certificate. But we do have a current one, I promise you. *Please*, Mrs Dean – even if you can't forgive me – won't you be kind enough to look after my wife's dog without seeing the certificate, just for this one important night?'

The young woman was biting her lower lip, wavering. 'It's always been one of our basic principles, you see,' she said unhappily.

He pressed in for the close. 'I understand that, Mrs Dean, and in normal circumstances I'd respect you for sticking to it. But this is an *emergency*. Surely you can overlook a principle when you're asked to help in a matter of life or death?'

She was bemused. She looked as though she was running a temperature. Derek was confident that he had won, if only because she was in no fit state to continue the argument.

Greatly relieved, he took time to feel sorry for her and her husband, and their rural venture that had so evidently turned into a financial flop. 'Look,' he said, with impulsive generosity, 'I'll pay-you in advance, of course – ' he pulled his wallet from his hip pocket ' – and I'd like to make up for my rudeness by giving you the money for a week rather than for one night. A full week, plus a week's heating charge. How much will that be?'

It hadn't occurred to him that she might interpret his offer as a bribe, until he saw her affronted look and the patchy flush of crimson on her face.

'Nothing,' she said breathlessly. 'Nothing at all, because I'm not going to take your dog. No reputable kennel would do so without evidence that it's been vaccinated. We may not have many customers, but they know they can leave their pets here without fear of infection, and I'm not prepared to take any chances. I'm sorry, truly sorry, about your wife's mother – but, as I see it a principle's a principle.'

'What am I do with the dog, then?' he protested.

She sneezed, and sneezed again. 'That's your problem, isn't it, Mr Carter?'

12

'Shut up, Sam! For God's sake shut up and let me think – '

The beagle, unused to being spoken to so savagely, stopped whining and gave his master a reproachful look. 'You stupid old fool,' said Derek, this time with more exasperation than anger. He was driving fast, now the rainstorm was over, but getting nowhere. 'What the hell am I going to do with you?'

There was no point in trying another boarding kennel. He couldn't go through all that business about the vaccination certificate again. The alternative seemed to be to find somewhere secure – an empty shed, that kind of thing – where he could shut the dog up overnight.

But sheds are only to be found in populated places. Supposing someone saw him bundling the dog inside? Or discovered Sam, and remembered having seen his car?

No, much too risky. Whoever-it-was might tell the police, and that would either foil the whole operation or put his alibi under suspicion. Any kind of shutting-up was definitely out. What, then? *What?*

It was no use being sentimental. The dog had to be got rid of somehow, and before very much longer. Derek looked at his watch. It was nearly five o'clock; Christine and her mother would have been home for an hour or more, and she would be starting to wonder where he was. He would have to telephone soon to tell her that Sam was lost.

The beagle was whining again. No wonder, when it was past his meal time. Whatever else happened – and Derek had more or less made up his mind what it would have to be – the animal needed to be fed.

They were still in the forest area, and the villages were miles apart. In the first they came to, the only shop was shut. The second village, however, had a Georgian house whose ground floor had been gutted and turned into a self-service general stores, and it offered a wide choice of dog food. Derek picked up a can of Pedigree Chum with rabbit, Sam's favourite, and then went to the hardware section.

He saw what he wanted almost immediately, an old-fashioned metal can-opener, one of a bunch hanging on a string from a shelf bracket. Realizing that he would have to turn the meat out of the can on to something, he settled hurriedly for a left-over packet of waxed paper plates with a children's Christmas party design. And then he found the other things he was going to need: a nylon-covered clothes line, and some black plastic dustbin bags.

He paid and drove on, taking the narrow roads that led well away from habitation and into the deepest part of the forest.

On a fine early spring evening there would have been other dog-owners about, leaving their cars parked under the oak and sweet chestnut trees that bordered the roads and walking, by courtesy of the Forestry Commission, along the grassy rides between the pine plantations. But today's heavy rain and the threat of more had evidently been a deterrent. He and Sam had the forest to themselves.

The rides were blocked to cars by larch pole barriers, but Derek backed off the road as far as he could. 'There you go,' he said, letting the beagle out. Sam doused the roots of the nearest tree, barked vigorously, shook himself, and snuffled about for a few minutes. Then he came running back to the car, stern waving, ears flapping, with an enquiry about supper.

Derek collected his purchases, together with the piece of old sacking that he kept with his tool kit. 'Come on, then,' he said. 'You're going to have a picnic.'

He walked rapidly through the wet grass, up the dim, silent aisle between two mature larch plantations. The trees were so tall and dense that even on a bright day they would have excluded the light. The air was filled with the pungency of damp resin. Not a bird sang. The atmosphere was so strangely oppressive that even Sam seemed subdued, and trotted silently to heel.

After about a hundred yards, Derek plunged into the outer fringe of trees. The ground, covered with fallen conifer needles, was fairly dry. Squatting on his haunches, he quickly opened the can of Chum at both ends and pushed the meat out on to a waxed plate. The rich gooey smell of the dog food almost turned his stomach, but he forced himself to break it up into bite-sized chunks with the handle of the can opener. Sam looked on, whining softly, eager for his meal but unmistakably puzzled.

'Go on,' said Derek, pushing the plate towards him. 'This is what you've been wanting, isn't it? Eat it, you great silly. Make the most of it.'

While the dog scoffed its food, Derek flattened the empty can with his heel. He had always been conscientious about the disposal of picnic litter, but this was one occasion when he didn't propose to take it home. He shoved both can and opener into a convenient hole under the roots of a tree, added the unused party plates, and kicked a covering of pine needles over the lot. Then he unravelled the clothes line. He looped it round the trunk of another tree, and approached the beagle with the spare end in his hand. 'Good boy,' he said. 'Good old boy. Let's have you.'

Sam, having finished eating, had been about to set off and explore. Still licking his chops, he submitted to having the line fastened to his tartan collar. Expecting to be taken for a walk, he looked up and wagged his rudder.

Derek ignored him. If he took too much notice of the dog he would never be able to go through with his plan. He collected some dead branches and hurriedly constructed a rough shelter, made it more or less watertight with dustbin bags, concealed them with newly green larch fronds, and spread another plastic bag and the piece of sacking on the floor. Then he picked up Sam's empty plate, crushed it, and added it to his rubbish dump.

The sturdy tri-coloured beagle stood watching, a worried look on his domed forehead.

'You're camping out tonight,' Derek told him. 'You'll be safe enough here.' Satisfied that he had done the best he could in the circumstances he took a moment to crouch down and make much of the dog, rubbing its broad chest and fondling its flop-ears. 'Now, you be a good boy, and Dad'll come and fetch you tomorrow. All right?'

He produced from his pocket the last of his purchases, a bone-shaped chewing bar, and pushed it into the dog's mouth. 'That's a good boy. Now, stay! Stay.'

He stood, one admonishing finger upraised. But it seemed that he had communicated anxiety rather than reassurance, because the dog had begun to shiver. Sam remained obediently where he was, but his jaws opened in dismay and the chew fell to the ground. He began to whine, and then to bark.

Derek turned away. Slipping on the wet grass, he ran towards his car.

What else could he do but leave the dog? What alternative was there? Sam was safely tied, that was the important thing. If the old fool insisted on barking, well, he'd simply have to bark himself into exhaustion. At least there was no one to hear.

But as soon as Derek reached the point where he was out of sight of the dog, the barking stopped. Thankfully, he slowed. There was a brief pause. The silence of the forest closed about him.

And then another noise began, one so unfamiliar that he couldn't at first believe that it was issuing from his own domestic pet. It was penetratingly loud, both mournful and alarming: not an ordinary dog's howl, but the deep baying cry of a hunting hound in distress. Hearing it, feeling it almost, as though cold fingers were saxophoning low on his spine, Derek was suddenly afraid.

Idiot! Of course he couldn't leave the beagle tied up in the forest. There was no one about this evening, but tomorrow morning – Sunday – there would be people walking their dogs, whatever the weather. If Sam went on kicking up a row like that, someone would be sure to find him: *complete with his tartan collar on which was a brass tag engraved with the name Cartwright and their telephone number.*

And if anyone were to report his tied-up dog, what would the police make of that? Particularly on the day after his mother-in-law, left alone in the house, was found suffocated . . .

Thankful that he had realized his near-blunder Derek ran back the way he had come, following the sound of the baying.

Sam stood rigid under the trees, straining the clothes line to its furthest extent; head thrown back, eyes rolled up and showing their whites, he was voicing his desolation with such intensity that he wasn't at first aware that Derek had returned for him.

'All right – *all right*, you stupid old mutt . . .' Derek crouched to comfort the dog, keeping his balance with difficulty as it launched itself ecstatically at him. 'Of course I won't leave you tied up – here, let's get rid of that bad old line.'

He released the line, looped it up quickly and slung it out of the way on the broken lower branch of a larch tree. Sam, still shivering, pressed close against his legs. Derek bent to pat the dog, at the same time unfastening the tartan collar and pushing it into his pocket. 'Where's your chew?' he said. 'Good boy – let's see if we can find your chew.'

He searched for and found the bone-shaped comforter, and teased the dog with it as they hurried together towards the car. Sam, his terror forgotten in the joy of going home, leaped eagerly for the chew.

'Here then, fetch it!' said Derek, throwing it back towards the trees. And as the dog went chasing off he sprinted the final ten yards, wrenched open the car door, slammed it behind him, started the engine and tried to roar away.

The car shot forward a couple of yards on the rough ground, and then jolted as the front offside wheel hit an obstruction. The engine stalled.

Derek swore. He was aware that the beagle had followed and was running anxiously round the car, asking to be let in. Concentrating on restarting the engine, he ignored the imploring barks, the frantic leaps, the scrabbling claws against his door and window. He opened the throttle wide, felt the rear of the car skid sideways on the wet grass, then bumped it off the verge and began to gather speed on the deserted forest road.

He prayed that Sam hadn't been hit by the skid, but he couldn't bring himself to stop and find out. When he heard the barks that told him that the dog was racing alongside, he was at first almost relieved; but then Sam's persistence began to torment him. 'Get off the road!' he shouted, as though the beagle could hear. 'Stay where you are! I'll come for you tomorrow – '

He changed up and accelerated away. No longer able to hear the barking he exhaled with relief, until he looked in his mirror and saw behind him the long straight road, and the little dog still running.

13

The news that Sam was lost affected Christine more strongly than Derek had bargained for. She wasn't merely upset, she was distraught.

He had tried to prepare her by telephoning from a call-box, but his necessary assurances that he was still looking for the dog had given her too much hope. When he finally returned to the Brickyard, after dark, she came hurrying out to the car port, splashing through the puddles that had been left on the gravel by the afternoon's downpour.

'Have you – ?'

'Sorry. My love, I'm sorry.'

She gave a cry of distress, half-stifling it with her fingers. Derek tried to put his arms round her but she pushed him distractedly away, grieving over Laurie's pet as though her husband's loss of the dog was a betrayal of her dead child.

Eventually Derek managed to lead her back to the house, saying what he could to comfort both her and himself. He had no need to simulate anxiety, because he felt it; he couldn't rid his memory of the frantic scrabbling of the beagle's claws against the car, of its imploring eyes.

At least Sam would take no harm in the open at this time of year, he argued aloud, secretly thankful that he'd given the dog a meal. First thing tomorrow, he said – swallowing hard as another image, that of Enid who would by then be lying suffocated in her bed, intervened – he'd go out looking for Sam. And find him, he was sure.

'But I simply don't understand what you took him out *for*.' They had entered the lighted hall and Christine turned on Derek, her eyes angry, strands of dark hair escaping wildly from her French pleat. 'You hardly ever take Sam for a walk. What on earth possessed you to go as far as the forest on a pouring wet afternoon?'

'It wasn't raining when we set out,' said Derek, wearily reasonable. 'I'd enjoyed our walk the other afternoon, and I wanted to do it more often, that's all.'

'But why the forest?'

'Because I'd been thinking of Laurie, and the walks we used to have with her.'

'Not in weather like this! We never went to the forest on wet days. I simply can't understand ... Where did you go, anyway? Whereabouts did you lose him?'

'At our old picnic place, by the sweet chestnut trees in Two Mile Bottom.'

'Was there anyone else about?'

'Not that I saw.'

'I'm not surprised, in all that rain! Oh Derek, how could you? How *could* you?'

'But I didn't *mean* to lose the dog,' he protested. 'Anyone would think from the way you're going on that I set out with that intention! I'm every bit as cut up about it as you are.'

Christine's anger began to subside. She sighed, and touched his hand. 'Yes, I know ... '

Glimpsing herself in the looking glass on the massive Edwardian hallstand, she raised her arms to tidy her hair. As she did so, her one breast lifted independently of the prosthesis on the other side. She set her chin determinedly: 'Well, I won't give up hope. I haven't given it up for myself, and I'm not going to give it up for Sam. I'll come out to Two Mile Bottom with you, first thing tomorrow morning, and between us we're sure to find him.'

'Yes ... only – '

For a moment Derek floundered. He hadn't bargained on Christine wanting to go with him. Guilt over what he had done to Sam made him desperately anxious to find the dog as soon as possible, but the place where he'd abandoned him was nowhere near Two Mile Bottom. He tried to think of some way of deterring her.

But then he remembered what was going to happen between now and first thing tomorrow morning. With her mother lying murdered upstairs, Christine would hardly want to go out looking for the dog.

'I'm going to call the police,' she said suddenly.

'*What?*'

He began to panic, thinking that he must have spoken his thoughts aloud.

'To report that Sam's lost. That's what we ought to do, isn't it?'

'Well, yes. But there's no point in doing it now, is there?' The last thing he wanted was for the attention of the police to be drawn to his household before the murder took place. 'No one's going to find him tonight, are they?'

'They might. Someone might drive past the picnic place, see him by the roadside and be kind enough to pick him up.'

Christine hurried towards the alcove where they kept the telephone. Then she stopped with it in her hand, her face clearing. 'But if they do, then of course they'll see our number on his collar and ring us so that we can collect him. He is wearing his collar, isn't he?'

'Yes,' said Derek, taking the receiver from her and replacing it. Exactly the same possibility had occurred to him, which was why he'd removed Sam's tartan collar before abandoning the dog. It was now in his car, hidden under some road maps in the pocket beside the driver's seat. 'Yes, of course he's wearing his collar. He'll be found, my love, don't worry.'

He held out both hands, and Christine went to him. He wanted to take her in his arms, but now that she was more relaxed he was afraid of communicating his own increasing tension to her. Bending forward to kiss her forehead he asked, 'Did you have a good day at Southwold?'

Christine glanced up the stairs. Although her mother didn't appear to be loitering at the top, she took the precaution of drawing Derek into the living-room and closing the door.

'It didn't go as well as I'd hoped,' she said despairingly. 'Mum was obviously glad to see her friends, and I began to think she might be prepared to go back to Southwold to live. But after she'd had two large gins at lunch-time she refused even to look at her own flat. I drove her there but she got quite stroppy with me when I tried to persuade her to go in. She wouldn't speak to me on the way home. I'm so sorry, Dee – I did my best to get rid of her, but she's not going to leave us voluntarily and I'm too frightened of the consequences to force the issue. I'm afraid we're stuck with her.'

'Does she intend to come downstairs this evening?' Derek heard himself ask. He prayed that she wouldn't. If he had to see and make conversation with Enid – particularly if she was as civil to him as usual – he doubted that he would be able to go through with the operation.

'No, she's taken her supper up to bed, thank goodness. I don't think we could have stood much more of each other's company. Oh well – ' Christine visibly pulled herself together. 'Talking of supper, you must be hungry. I'll make something for you.'

'No!' Derek had begun to breathe quickly; his mind on what was to come, he jerked out the word. 'No thanks. I'll forage for myself later on. All I want now is to get out of these damp clothes.'

For the first time that evening, his wife looked him over. 'You must have been soaked,' she observed.

'Are you surprised? I've spent hours searching for Sam in the rain.'

Christine's eyes darkened again. Her anguish renewed, she shook her head in bewilderment. 'But that's another thing I don't understand. All right, you wanted to take Sam back to our old picnic place. I'll accept that, even though I can't imagine why you did it in the rain. But why didn't you change before you took him out? Why in heaven's name did you take Sam for a walk in the forest on a wet day in your *office* clothes?'

Derek looked down at himself, and saw that he was still wearing his grey suit with the chalk stripe. The cloth was dark with moisture; there was green-stained mud on both knees, on his thin black shoes and on the cuffs of his pale blue shirt.

Wet, weary, guilty, ashamed, afraid, he was incapable of offering a credible excuse.

'I forgot,' he said.

As he passed the door of his mother-in-law's bedroom, on his way to the bath, he could hear maniacal bursts of television-comedy laughter. He looked at his watch:

eight-fifteen. Packer wanted him and Christine to be out of the house between ten forty-five and eleven-thirty, but what Derek had planned was likely to take them away for a good deal longer than that.

He couldn't be sure, though, for just how long. He was afraid of what he was going to have to do, and he was desperate to get it over and done with, but he daren't risk doing it too early. Nine-thirty would probably be about right ... An hour and a quarter to go.

He ran a hot bath in the hope that it would relax him, but he was so tense that he couldn't stay in the water long enough for it to do him any good. He needed a shave, but his shaking hands made it so difficult to fit the blade into the razor that he abandoned the idea. He wanted a drink, but the whisky was in the living-room and he couldn't face Christine again so soon.

She suspected him, didn't she? She knew he was up to something. God, what a fool he'd been not to think through what he was doing! Why, oh why, hadn't he stopped to change before taking the dog out into the forest?

The true answer was simple enough. He hadn't changed because he was in a hurry to put Sam safely out of the way in a boarding kennel; his clothes hadn't mattered because he didn't intend to do any walking. But if only he'd *thought*, he would have realized that he needed to change in order to give conviction to the lie he proposed to tell Christine.

It was a mistake, a bad mistake. He wasn't used to constructive lying, that was the trouble. He wiped a swathe of condensation off the bathroom mirror with a corner of a towel and stared at the unfamiliar, fearful-eyed face that confronted him. As if it wasn't bad enough to have to go through with everything that lay ahead ... The alibi he planned had seemed to him to be watertight but now, too panicky to think it through yet again, he couldn't be sure.

Fifty-three minutes to go.

He pulled on his towelling bathwrap, padded back to his room and sat on the edge of the big double bed. He needed to rest, but anxiety tightened its grip on his stomach. He felt sick; no longer on Enid's account, but on his own.

But that was the idea, wasn't it? Not to give himself an easy alibi, but to offer expiation for the crime that was to come by putting himself through some form of punishment.

Fifty one and a half minutes to go.

At nine-fifteen Derek stood up, straightened the bedcovers, and put on clothes suitable for an evening at home: an old pair of trousers, a favourite soft shirt with a fraying collar, a light sweater. The casual shoes he chose, though, were substantial enough to go out in.

He felt detached again, as he had done in the Abbey gardens when he had discussed Operation Brickyard with Packer. He observed himself walking downstairs, crossing the hall, opening the living-room door. He noticed that Christine, some sewing material on her lap, hurriedly tucked away a handkerchief and picked up her needle when he looked into the room, but he was too intent on his purpose to allow her unhappiness to distract him.

'I'm going to make a sandwich.' His voice was strangely abrupt in his ears. 'Anything you want?'

'I'd love a cup of tea.' She spoke brightly, though her nose was congested. 'There's some cold lamb in the fridge, if you'd like that. Or you could have – '

'I'll find something,' he said. He closed the door on her, leaned back against it, took two long deep breaths, and then walked steadily to the kitchen, switching on the lights as he went.

It was a large, comfortable room, dominated by an Aga stove and a family-sized pinewood table. A door led from it into a narrow pantry, which housed the freezer on one side and a refrigerator and wine rack on the other. Cans and jars of food were lined on shelves on the walls. At the far end of the pantry, above a built-in slab of marble which would have served to keep food cool in the days before refrigeration, was the north-facing window he had described to Packer.

It was the ideal place for a break-in. *Except that the sodding window was too small!*

The original inner window, of perforated zinc designed to keep out flies in summer, was hooked back against the edge of a shelf. The narrow sash window was fastened with the usual catch, and secured by a screw-type bolt. Derek hunted for the key, found it at the back of the same shelf, fitted it with shaking fingers, unscrewed and withdrew the bolt. Placing bolt and key on the marble slab, he slipped the window catch and tried to lift the sash.

It wouldn't budge. He swore and sweated, got it moving, then jammed it again in his haste. Wiping his damp hands on his trousers, he tried again.

This time the sash opened to its fullest extent. The gap looked no more than eighteen inches by two feet, nowhere near big enough for a man to get through. Oh God ... Derek thrust a handful of fingernails between his teeth in his anxiety.

And then he remembered. Packer, who had gradually assumed gigantic proportions inside his head, was in fact the size of a boy. Packer could do it.

Grunting with momentary relief Derek closed the window and fastened the catch, deliberately omitting to replace the bolt. Then he began to set up his alibi.

Hurriedly, he assembled on the kitchen table the bread board and half a wholemeal loaf, the butter dish, and the foil-wrapped remains of the knuckle end of a leg of lamb. As an afterthought, he filled and switched on the kettle.

His breath was coming more quickly. He snatched an earthenware dinner plate from the dresser, pulled the foil off the cold lamb, and placed the joint on the plate. The shank of bone, left exposed by the meat that had already been eaten, looked like the handle of some primitive tool.

Derek opened a drawer and took out the carving knife.

It was a knife that had been in his family for at least three generations, an old country knife with a yellow horn handle and an eight-inch Sheffield steel blade. The cutting edge had become concave through years of use, and he had sharpened it against the matching-handled steel, as his father and grandfather used to do, only last Sunday. Derek touched the edge gingerly, and drew his finger away with a hissing intake of breath. Yes, it was sharp.

He pushed aside the bread board. Cutting bread had been in his original scenario, but carving a joint would be better because the knife might so unarguably be deflected from the bone. Rejecting the use of the carving fork with its safety guard, he grasped the greasy shank in his left hand and the knife in his right, and gave conviction to his alibi by partially carving a slice of pinkish, fat-rimmed meat.

If the knife were to slip as he used it, the most likely place for the cut would be on his knuckles. But that wouldn't do, wouldn't be serious enough. Letting go of the joint, Derek turned his hand over so that he could see his outspread palm. There were traces on it of grease, and dark fragments of cooked blood. He would have liked to wash, but he was wary now of making mistakes; he wanted no one to doubt that he had been cutting meat at the time of the accident.

Willing his left hand not to tremble, he pressed the point of the knife tentatively against the bridge between his first and second fingers. The skin was tougher than he had thought. He pressed again, a little harder, and shamed himself by gasping and instinctively withdrawing his hand at the first prick of the blade.

He put down the knife and wiped his sweatered arm across his damp forehead. Somewhere on the edge of his consciousness, the kettle was coming up to the boil. He longed to postpone this ordeal: make a pot of tea, go and comfort Christine, try again another time.

But the decision wasn't his to make. Packer was in charge of Operation Brickyard, and Packer would by now be on his way to Wyveling. Derek looked at his watch. Nine thirty-six: if he didn't act right away, he'd cock up the whole thing.

The kettle switched itself off. Derek steadied his left hand by placing the back of it on the kitchen table. He planted his feet well apart, and took a tight grip on the carving knife. Then he drew a shuddering breath, pointed the knife, and slashed his palm from the base of his fingers to within an inch of his wrist.

He gasped with shock, but felt nothing on his hand except a light stinging blow. Staring stupidly at the white line scored across his palm, he realised that all he had done was to break the skin. He'd hardly drawn blood, for God's sake.

Disgusted by his cowardice, he watched as the line of the cut reddened and blood began to seep out from under the overlap of skin. He could feel the sharpness of it now, but he knew that the injury wasn't serious enough for his purpose.

He gripped the knife again. He had begun to shiver, but the

adrenaline was running strongly enough for him to do what was necessary: retrace the line of the cut sufficiently deeply to ensure that Christine would have to take him to the nearest hospital casualty department, twenty miles away in Yarchester, to have it stitched.

It hurt, of course. He could hear his moaning intake of breath, his recurrent ah-h-hs of pain as the blade moved along the line of welling blood and bit into his raw flesh. But then he had meant it to hurt, hadn't he?

Think why you're doing this. Think of poor old Enid, upstairs, whose death tonight this is all about, and punish yourself for being her murderer's accomplice. Don't merely endure the pain, welcome it.

14

'There's no need to shout, Derek. What's the matter?'

He had intended to take his injury to Christine, but the distance from the kitchen table to the living-room had defeated him. Reeling from shock, supporting his left wrist with his right hand, he stood holding out to her a cupped handful of blood that dripped from between his fingers on to the cork tiles of the kitchen floor.

'C-carving meat. Knife slipped.'

'Heavens above – '

Christine flew to his aid, steering him to the sink and thrusting his hand under a running tap. Derek yelped as the cold water hit the lacerated flesh like a blow from a metal bar. He clung to the edge of the sink with his right hand, watching with distant interest as the diluted blood washed pinkly down the plug hole, leaving a jagged V-shaped cut on his palm.

'My poor love! However – ? Well, however it happened, it looks as though it'll have to be stitched. Sit down and hold your hand up.' Christine pushed him on to a stool, snatched some kitchen paper from the roll, and pressed it into his raised hand as the blood began to flow again. 'Clutch this while I make some kind of pad.'

Derek was shivering. He felt white round the gills as he watched his blood trickle from under the quickly-saturated paper, down his wrist and over his watch-strap on to the sleeve of his sweater. But at the same time he was secretly exultant that his part in Operation Brickyard had now been accomplished. He was thankful to be able to submit to Christine's loving care, absolved from guilt by the thought that whatever happened from now on was out of his hands.

There was, though, something he had to establish before he could relax. Christine, having folded a clean towel, had instructed him to hold it pressed against the cut while she telephoned the doctor. But they were patients of a group practice in Breckham Market, and the surgery was too close to home; if a doctor were able to attend to him immediately, he would be back at the Brickyard before Packer arrived. And having gone through all this pain, he wasn't prepared to let the operation be ruined.

'Don't let's waste time with local doctors,' he said, wincing as he pressed hard against the injury. 'Whoever's on call could be out already, and it might be ages before they fix me up. Remember when Les Harding cut himself with his hedge-trimmer last year? I drove him straight to Casualty at Yarchester Hospital, and his doctor said afterwards that it was the best thing I could have done.'

Christine hesitated for a moment, and despite his pain Derek realized how tired she was. Poor darling – after the long drive to Southwold and back, the quarrel with her mother and then the upset over the lost dog, she was in no fit state to take him to Yarchester. His plan had been based on the assumption that she would do the driving, but now he couldn't bring himself to inflict it on her. He'd have to get her out of the house some other way.

'Call the Hardings, love,' he urged. 'One or other of them will be glad to do the driving for you. Only – you will come with me to the hospital, won't you, Chrissie? Please? Sorry to be such a fool, but I do feel groggy – '

His wife was already dialling their neighbours' number. Evidently glad that she wasn't required to drive, she gave him an affectionate glance as she waited for her call to be answered. 'Of course I'll come, if you want me to. Ah, Vera – sorry to bother you but we've got a bit of an emergency ...'

Derek exhaled with relief. His hand was hurting like hell; but he'd cleared the way for Operation Brickyard, and at the same time provided himself with an alibi that no one would ever question.

The Hardings, a tall thin couple a decade older than the Cartwrights, arrived at the Brickyard within minutes. Under

112

the lights that illuminated the outside of the front door, their teeth and glasses shone with friendly concern.

'Tough luck, Derek,' said Les, holding open the passenger door of his Nissan. 'Glad to have a chance of repaying your kindness, though. In you get, old man – oops, mind your hand. You coming too, Christine? Then you can take him straight in to Casualty while I find somewhere to park.'

'That's what I did when Leslie had his accident,' said Vera. 'It simplifies things no end. But we don't want you to go unless you really feel well enough, Christine. You know what hospitals are like, you're bound to be hanging about there for hours. That's why I've come round, to see if you'd like me to go in your place.'

Derek, gingerly holding his towel-swathed hand out of the way as Les fastened the seat belt for him, caught his breath. His wife was not particularly fond of Vera who, over-eager for friendship, invariably touched or patted her arm as they talked; but for all he knew Christine might be thankful to accept the offer and stay at home. And if she did, his plan would be ruined.

'That's very kind of you, Vera,' he heard his wife say, 'but no thanks. I feel fine.'

Good for Christine! Derek breathed again.

'Well, as long as you're sure,' said Vera. 'Anyway, don't worry about your mother – that's the other reason I've come. I'll stay here and keep her company until you get back.'

Appalled, helplessly strapped down, Derek shouted out in protest: 'No!'

Aware that everyone was staring at him, he sought for milder words to deter their well-meaning neighbour. 'We'd hate to put you to that trouble, Vera – wouldn't we, Chrissie? I mean, there's no need for it. Enid's not ill, she'll be perfectly all right on her own.'

'Of course she will,' said Christine, sliding into the car. 'It's very good of you to offer, Vera, but Mum's already in bed, happily watching television. I've told her where we're going, and I've locked the front door, so there's nothing for any of us to worry about.'

'And anyway,' said Les, clipping his own seat belt, 'the old lady's got your beagle for company, hasn't she?'

Derek wished he hadn't said that. But luckily, Christine was calling good-bye to Vera at the time and didn't hear.

It was nearly ten o'clock when they drove out of the Brickyard, and well after midnight before they left the hospital. And in all that time Derek's hand had hurt so much – eight stitches, without benefit of a local anaesthetic – that he had had no difficulty in putting everything else out of his mind. Hadn't even tried to look at his watch until they were half-way back to Wyveling, when he remembered that it had been so sticky with blood that at some stage Christine had unstrapped it.

The two of them were sitting side by side on the back seat while Les Harding drove them home through the moonlit countryside. Derek was holding his bandaged, aching left hand up against his chest. His right hand was resting on his thigh, and Christine had tucked her fingers into his.

'Wha's the time?' he asked blearily.

She took away her hand and looked at her watch by the light of the tiny torch on her key ring. 'Quarter to one.'

Then presumably it was all over. Enid was dead.

The thought left him strangely unmoved. He seemed to be emotionally numbed. He closed his eyes and calmly tried to anticipate what he would see when he went up to his mother-in-law's bedroom – as he must, of course, immediately they got home, to protect Christine from the discovery.

At least Enid's face would be covered by the pillow. Derek was thankful, for all their sakes, that Packer had accepted his suggestion of smothering the old lady. And Christine had said that her mother was already in bed before they left, so with any luck no part of her would be visible. All he would see would be the frilly-edged, flowery pillow, and a mound under the matching quilt. He would have to lift the pillow, of course, just to make sure ... and then he and Christine would be free at last.

He had expected to be, if not overjoyed, then at least filled with relief by the prospect of freedom. But now he found that he was strangely indifferent to it.

Having dreamed for so long of ridding himself of his mother-in-law, his indifference disturbed him. No, not indifference; distaste for something that had suddenly gone sour. He had wanted the freedom for his wife's sake, but now for the first time he looked beyond his own part in her mother's death and realized that while his ordeal was almost over, Christine's was about to begin.

However gently he tried to break the news to her, it was bound to come as a terrible shock. She'd get over it, of course; she'd realize that it hadn't been a bad way for her mother to go. But all the same, during the next few days it was Christine who was going to have to pay for the release he had thought he was giving her.

Poor girl, what had he done to her? As if she hadn't already had more than enough suffering! He felt himself begin to shiver uncontrollably.

'Cold, Dee?' Lovingly, his wife slid her arm through his and held his good hand in both of hers. 'Snuggle up, darling, soon be home.'

Sickened by guilt, Derek was incapable of returning the strong clasp of her hand, or welcoming the pressure of her breast against his arm, let alone of snuggling. Christine loved and trusted him; what he had done to her was unforgivable.

But then he recalled something Packer had said to him: *As a matter of fact, I've never killed anyone before. P'raps I shan't have the guts. P'raps when you get home you'll find the old woman still alive and kicking.*

Please God, Derek found himself praying frantically, as the car's headlights lit up a signpost saying *Wyveling 1½ miles*: please God, don't let it have happened. Don't let me find Enid dead!

'That's odd,' said Les Harding as he turned the car into the Cartwrights' long front yard. 'Your outside lights aren't on.'

'They were when we left,' said Christine.

'Must've fused,' said Derek. He cleared his throat. 'Give me your keys, love,' he added, glad of an excuse to enter the house first, 'and you stay here while I find out.'

'I'll bring my torch,' said Les.

Derek walked apprehensively towards the front door. One-handed, he turned the key, stepped inside and felt for the switches. They all worked. Packer must have switched off the outside lights before he left.

Blinking in the sudden brightness, he saw that Packer had carried out at least the first part of his undertaking. The door of the living-room was open and all the audio and video equipment had been piled in the hall, as if ready to be shifted out. The door of the hall cupboard was also open, and its contents were scattered on the floor.

'Hell's bells,' said Les Harding at his shoulder. 'You've been burgled, old man!'

Derek's mouth was dry, his throat constricted. Unable to think of anything appropriate to say, he let out some kind of croak. He knew that he must go up to Enid's room, but he seemed to be incapable of movement.

It was Christine who got him going. Pushing past him into the lighted hall she took one look at the mess, drew a gasping breath, and went straight to the point.

'Mother! What's happened to Mother?'

Derek caught her up at the foot of the stairs, seizing her in both arms regardless of his injury. 'No, Chrissie, no! Let me go first. You stay with Les – '

Thrusting her into their neighbour's care he took the stairs two at a time, switching on lights as he went. The door of Enid's room was closed. He paused for a moment, trying to quieten his panicky breathing, then turned the handle and pushed the door ajar.

He wanted to hope for the best; but he knew immediately, from the profundity of the silence that issued from the dark room, that Packer had done the job. His mother-in-law was dead.

Pushing the door wider, he took two steps inside. Enid's bed was behind the door, out of the line of light from the corridor, but he could see a tumble of bedclothes and the shape of her body – not neatly covered, as he had hoped, but apparently lying on rather than in the bed.

He reached out for the light switch. Before putting it on he took a steadying breath, and it was then that he noticed the intrusive smell. Enid's room invariably smelled sweetly dusty, of face powder and violet-scented talc. But this smell was rank, alien, as though a visiting animal had left its spraints.

116

He switched on the light. Enid was lying sprawled on her back across the bed, a fluffy slipper dangling from the toes of one bare projecting foot.

Packer had not merely done the job, he had done it with what looked like an obscene enthusiasm. From the lividity of her face, her swollen tongue and the bruises on her neck, it was apparent that Enid had not been suffocated but strangled. And from the way her nightdress had been bundled up to expose her aged flesh, it seemed that murder alone had not been enough to satisfy him.

15

If his mother-in-law were ever to be found dead in suspicious circumstances, thought Detective Chief Inspector Quantrill darkly as he left his Breckham Market home the following morning to start the Wyveling investigation, his colleagues wouldn't need to go far to find the murderer.

Douglas Quantrill and his wife's mother cordially detested each other; had done so ever since they first met. Instead of giving him credit for admitting responsibility for her daughter's pregnancy and doing the decent thing by agreeing to get married, Phyllis Barratt had never forgiven him for seducing Molly.

To be fair (and with a father's hindsight) Quantrill acknowledged that the news that their nicely-brought-up girl had been impregnated by a twenty-one-year-old National Serviceman they had never even heard of must have come as a great shock to Phyllis and her husband. But their shock had been nothing in comparison with his own.

Molly, at nineteen, had been very attractive; but he wasn't in love with her and it wasn't marriage that he'd pursued her for. The loss of his freedom had blighted his young manhood, and it had always rankled with him that Molly's mother, while insisting on a rapid wedding, should have made it so abundantly clear that he was not and never would be good enough for her elder daughter.

The fact that he had buckled down to family life and had eventually made progress in a respectable career had failed to change Molly's mother's attitude. Her husband Jim had been cordial enough as soon as their daughter was safely married, but Phyllis had made it her life's work to be critical of her son-in-law.

Luckily for the young Quantrills, Jim Barratt's job had taken him and his wife and their second daughter Mavis to the north of England. Mavis had married an approved suitor and settled in Harrogate, and visits from any of them to Breckham Market had been mercifully infrequent.

But now Phyllis was widowed. She was old, she had heart trouble, she was unsteady on her pins, her sight was failing. Although she kept insisting that she wanted to remain in her own house in Northallerton, it was clear to her daughters that she could no longer live alone. Something, they agreed, would have to be done about her.

To Quantrill, the solution seemed simple enough. If his mother-in-law couldn't look after herself, she would have to go into a home. But the two sisters, after long telephone consultations, declined to consider any such thing. Their mother had looked after them throughout their childhood, Molly told her husband, and now it was their duty to look after her. They had devised a plan for having her to live with them turn and turn about, for six months at a time, and as Molly was the elder she proposed to take the first turn.

Quantrill had objected vigorously, but his wife refused to budge. After all, she pointed out, he wouldn't see much of her mother because he spent most of his time at work. And now that they had moved to Bramley Road, he couldn't claim that they hadn't enough room.

Looking after one's old parents wasn't just a duty, either, Molly had continued. It was a matter of conscience. *She* didn't want to have anything to feel guilty about for the rest of her life, or to go on reproaching herself for after her mother was dead. And Quantrill, who had made the pressures of his job an excuse for neglecting his own mother during her last ailing years and had been (privately, he'd thought) deeply remorseful ever since her death, had been shamed into acquiescence.

But the reality of having Molly's mother in residence was worse than either of them had anticipated. Phyllis Barratt was as censorious as ever, and now cantankerous with it. Far from being grateful to her daughters for conspiring to take care of her, she had made it plain on her first evening with the

Quantrills that she would never cease resenting being uprooted from her own home. And in the middle of that night, when her son-in-law was called out to the murder, she had stood in his way, dressing-gowned and propped up on her walking-frame, berating him for lack of consideration because the telephone had woken her.

'We shall just have to make allowances,' Molly had said defensively next morning. Quantrill was snatching a quick breakfast before returning to Wyveling, and his wife and teenage son had joined him in the kitchen for a low-voiced discussion before Phyllis put in an appearance. 'She's bound to be upset by the move. After all, she's eighty-four ... '

'Eighty-four's nothing,' said Peter, a note of malicious glee in his voice. He was still hobbling painfully on crutches, five months after an accident on a forbidden motor cycle had nearly killed him, and he had already signalled his intention of milking sympathy and supplementary pocket money from his grandmother. 'She'll probably live to be a hundred.'

'Not if I have anything to do with it, she won't,' Quantrill had pronounced. In reality, of course, he had seen too much of the devastating domestic repercussions of murder ever to contemplate committing it himself. But even so, he couldn't help indulging in a moment's fantasy before setting off to investigate the death of Enid Long.

As a matter of policy, and with the approval of his Superintendent, Chief Inspector Quantrill had postponed the start of the investigation until the morning after the murder. Certain routines – calling in the police surgeon, the photographer, the pathologist, cursorily checking all the rooms, ascertaining the point of entry – had to be gone through as soon as possible, but Quantrill saw no point in having the entire murder squad fumbling about the house and grounds by artificial light. Much better to put the place under guard during the hours of darkness and postpone the detailed investigation until they could see what they were doing.

There was of course no question of the murdered woman's daughter and son-in-law returning to the house, even had they wanted to do so, until the police had finished with it.

Temporary accommodation had been offered them by the neighbour who had witnessed the evidence of burglary, but Mrs Cartwright had begged to go to a particular local friend instead: a fellow cancer-sufferer, her husband had explained, Mrs Sylvia Collins of Church Hill. Having caught a glimpse of her mother's body Mrs Cartwright was understandably distraught, and the police surgeon had given her a sedative.

Quantrill had assigned a policewoman, Val Thornton, to the Cartwrights, to remain with them night and day for as long as was necessary. It always helped a murder victim's family to have one particular officer with them, not only to provide practical support and keep away unwelcome visitors but to encourage them to talk through their shock. This also helped the detectives, because very often some vital scrap of information would emerge from one of these rambling, unpressured conversations.

In this case, though, when it was the victim's son-in-law who had discovered her body, a formal witness statement from him was going to be necessary. Quantrill had already spoken to Derek Cartwright during his initial visit to the scene; now he wanted a longer informal discussion before the witness made his statement.

'We'll go and talk to Cartwright first, then do the major briefing,' Quantrill told Sergeant Lloyd as they drove out to Wyveling. Then he added, in a lamentable lapse of professionalism, 'Pity that man's got an alibi, or I'd have had him down as the natural suspect.'

Hilary Lloyd glanced at her chief inspector with half-mocking affection. 'Oh dear ... Trouble with your mother-in-law already?'

'I told you, it's inevitable. I could cheerfully have wrung the woman's neck when she bawled me out at one o'clock this morning. I wish to heaven we'd stayed in Benidorm Avenue – she couldn't have lived with us there because of the stairs.'

'Come off it, Douglas, you know you don't really wish you were still there. Think how much pleasure you get out of having your own half-acre of land in Bramley Road.'

It was perfectly true. Although Quantrill had bought the established, individual bungalow – on an alarmingly large mortgage – principally to atone for an accumulation of guilt, he regretted nothing about it except its suitability for his mother-in-law.

He had instigated the move, after Peter's accident, to demonstrate to Molly his willingness to make a fresh start: to think in future of his family instead of hankering after his unattainable sergeant. The move had certainly made Molly happy because Bramley Road was one of Breckham Market's most sought-after areas, secluded and yet within walking distance of the town centre. And the bungalow was easier than a house for Peter to hop about in, not just because he was temporarily on crutches, but because his legs had been so badly splintered that despite a restructuring with metal plates and bolts, one of them would always be shorter than the other.

Quantrill had assumed that, in looking for a property to suit Molly and Peter, he would necessarily have to sacrifice his own interests. But he had always been uncomfortable in the cramped modern semi-detached house in Benidorm Avenue, and the generously proportioned bungalow was much more to his liking.

For the first time in his married life he found it a real pleasure to be at home. He liked the privacy of the large garden, with its old apple trees and the vegetable patch he intended to restore to productivity as soon as he could get round to it. He liked the various sheds where – once he got started – he could leave half-finished projects without being accused of making a mess. He liked the sizeable living-room with its open fire on which, next winter, he could throw logs he had sawn himself. It was almost, he felt, like the country life he had been brought up to, though thankfully without the ancient inconveniences of genuine rural living.

He still felt guilty, of course. True, he had put things right both with Molly and with Hilary, in the sense that he was no longer trying to be unfaithful to the one, nor persistently embarrassing the other. His working relationship with his sergeant was now stabilized – enhanced, in fact, by their acknowledged friendship and the support she had given him after Peter's accident.

Quantrill had never been able to admit to Molly that he held himself responsible for the boy's crash. If only he hadn't been so furious when he saw Peter, on a borrowed machine, out with his mates; if only he hadn't distracted the boy by shouting and trying to stop him. Time and again, when he closed his eyes, it was to see his son being flung from the skidding machine, and sliding across the muddy road under a sugar-beet trailer that bumped as it ran over his legs.

Hilary had seen it too. That was why she understood his feelings of guilt. It was also why he couldn't confess them to Molly, because he would never have seen Peter's trial run and attempted to stop it if he hadn't parked his car at the roadside, while on duty, specifically for the purpose of propositioning his sergeant.

If only he hadn't.

But he had. And however deeply he regretted his part in causing the accident, he had at last come to the conclusion that there was no point in wallowing in self-reproach. As far as he could see, circumstantial guilt was an inescapable part of the human condition. If it wasn't about one thing, it was about another. He could understand Molly's attempt to insure herself against it by taking charge of her mother, but he wondered how long it would be before she felt even more guilty because she'd uprooted the old lady, or else because she'd lost patience and treated her unkindly.

As he drove through the gateway of the Brickyard at Wyveling he thought of that other old lady, Enid Long. Someone was guilty of her murder, and that guilt was of a very different kind. Recalling the scene in Mrs Long's bedroom in the early hours of the morning, Quantrill felt properly ashamed of his fantasy about doing away with his mother-in-law. Ordinary everyday guilt was bad enough, God knew. But how anyone who wasn't a psychopath could live with himself after committing murder, Quantrill really couldn't imagine.

16

Derek Cartwright was outraged. If he had known where to find that evil bastard Packer, he would have slaughtered him.

The man was a pervert. Who else would sexually assault an old woman? It was appalling, obscene. No wonder poor Christine was nearly out of her mind with the horror of it.

If only Packer had stuck to the plan and used a pillow, Christine would have been able to cope. In those last few moments in the car Derek had hurriedly thought of a way to minimize the shock for her. He had imagined himself, once he'd established that Enid was dead, leading Christine compassionately into the room; he had assumed that her mother would be lying so peacefully under the covers that it would look almost as though she had died of natural causes.

He could then have gently explained to his wife that Enid had in fact been suffocated. Christine would still have found it distressing, of course, but the atmosphere of dignity would have made the ordeal bearable for her. Instead, while he had stood staring, stunned, she had burst into the room behind him and seen, poor girl, exactly what he saw.

What had happened after that was now a confusion in his mind. Les Harding had been very helpful, though; thank God he was there to do the telephoning, because Derek himself – what with his injured hand, and the shock – had been temporarily incapable of doing anything other than supporting his wife.

And then the police had arrived.

The police were potentially a problem, of course. In prospect, he had been apprehensive about coming into contact with them. He had expected to feel nervous in their presence. He was convinced that they would sense his guilt. But in the event he was so disgusted by what Packer had done that he felt completely distanced from it: what had happened wasn't *his* fault.

Besides, there was no reason why the police should imagine that he had any knowledge of his mother-in-law's murder. They would expect him to be upset, after what he had witnessed. And his alibi was unarguable.

Even so, he had braced himself for some intensive contact with the police. He had assumed that he would be required to make a detailed list of the items that had been stolen from the Brickyard. He had imagined that he would have to spend most of the night taking the detectives on a tour of the property, explaining in full how his mother-in-law had come to be left alone and where, in his opinion, the burglar must have broken in.

But the police seemed not to need him. They had their own way of doing things, and tactfully removing the bereaved from the scene was apparently a priority. Christine was immediately taken care of by a chunky, sympathetic policewoman, who told them to call her Val. Derek was asked a few straightforward questions by the detectives, and advised to make a list of missing items as soon as possible the following morning; that was all. Within a very short time he and Christine were being escorted by Val to the thatched house on Church Hill, where his wife's new friend was apparently expecting all three of them.

Sylvia Collins was in her late middle age, grey-haired but lively and full of chat even at two o'clock in the morning, and quite unabashed to be on view in a mangy old dressing-gown. Its limpness on one side gave away the fact that she, like Christine, had had a mastectomy.

'You poor dear,' she said, giving her stricken friend a hug. 'Hello, Derek, nice to meet you – though not on such a terrible occasion, of course. No, don't even think of apologizing, I'm only too glad to be of whatever help I can. Now, where would you like to sleep? The spare room has twin beds, but I've stripped my double bed – I can make it up for you in a couple of shakes, if you'd prefer that?'

'Thank you,' said Derek, grateful for her considerateness. He knew that on this particular night Christine would more than ever need the comfort of his arms.

But his wife, calmer now, spoke for herself. Her face, numbed by shock, was a pale shiny mask. She seemed to have some difficulty in forcing words through her set lips, and he thought for a moment that he must have misheard her. Then she repeated it: 'No, thank you. It's very kind of you to offer us your bed, Sylvia, but I'd prefer the spare room.'

Long after Christine had been knocked out by a sedative, Derek thrashed about in his narrow bed on the other side of the room. He couldn't rest, in body or in mind. The low, heavily raftered ceiling oppressed him.

He would have liked to get up and go downstairs – wander about for a bit, find the kitchen, make yet another pot of tea. But Val, who had come equipped with a sleeping-bag, had bedded down in the sitting-room and left the door open, and he was afraid of waking her. The last thing he wanted was a private chat over the teacups with a policewoman, however sympathetic.

His hand hurt like hell. 'You all right?' the police surgeon had said after attending to Christine, and Derek had been too proud to ask for a painkiller. He contemplated getting up and raiding Mrs Collins's bathroom cabinet for aspirin or something, but the bathroom was downstairs and he would have to pass the sitting-room to get to it.

He turned over and thumped his pillow with his good hand. God, what a hideous thing Packer had done. So much for all his talk of being a professional! Derek hated him for abusing poor old Enid, and for causing Christine such extraneous grief. He'd give anything to see him locked away for life. Anything except his own freedom, of course.

Though he dissociated himself completely from Packer's actions, he knew that he could do nothing to dissociate himself from the man. The two of them were interdependent. The only way he could conceal his own foreknowledge of Enid's death was by taking good care to shield Packer from the police.

He would have minded less about doing this if only everything had been right between himself and Christine. After all, the whole purpose of the operation had been to regain the privacy they valued as a happily married couple. But their former loving relationship seemed to be going wrong already.

Despite their earlier quarrel over his loss of the dog (and that fretted him, now he remembered it: was Sam all right, out there alone in the forest?), Christine had been entirely sympathetic about his cut hand. But almost from the moment when she saw her mother's body, her affection for him had seemed to cool.

He had immediately taken her in his arms, of course. He'd held her close for most of the time from then until she was sedated. But come to think of it, Christine hadn't once turned voluntarily to him. Far from responding to his loving care she had on occasion fought impotently against it, shouting at him to leave her alone.

Derek had put it down to shock. She needed him, he knew that; she would be only too glad to cling to him when they were at last alone. But he'd been wrong, and the fact that she had rejected the offer of a double bed, when they had never before not slept in one, had hurt him deeply.

Perhaps the sight of the terrible things that a man had done to her mother had temporarily alienated her from men. That could make sense ... except that he wasn't just any man, he was the considerate husband she'd known and loved for over twenty years. Why in God's name should she turn against him now?

Did she suspect him? Did she hold him in any way responsible for her mother's death?

There wasn't any reason for her to do so; or was there? Well, he'd made it clear enough that he wanted to get rid of Enid ... and Christine had certainly been suspicious about the way he had taken the dog to the forest in the rain.

Even in the middle of her distress over her mother, Christine hadn't forgotten Sam. 'He would have kept away any burglar,' she had sobbed to Sylvia. 'Oh, why did Derek have to go and lose him, today of all days – '

Naturally he had lamented with her, reproaching himself aloud for his carelessness. Not that Christine had been in a fit state to take in what he was saying, but he wanted to make the point for the benefit of Sylvia Collins and Val. They had both been quick to tell him that he mustn't blame himself. It was just one of those terrible coincidences, they'd said, speaking with such sincerity that he's almost believed them.

But Christine, with her wifely intuition, was less likely to dismiss the episode. That was why her withdrawal filled him with such anxiety. He didn't for one minute think that she would give him away, whatever her suspicions; but that was not the point. Derek didn't want a bitter loyalty from his wife, he wanted – needed – her love and trust. Without that he had nothing.

Sick with worry, he looked longingly across the room towards the dark shape of the other bed. What with his guilt, and his fears, and the hurt of his hand, he wanted to lie close to Christine as much for his own sake as for hers.

Eventually Derek slept. And dreamed. And what he dreamed was the old nightmare of strangling his mother-in-law.

But now the details were different, more specific. The throat that his fingers grasped was not inert, but warm and trembling. The flesh was flabby, but there was an underlying resistance to his pressing thumbs, a resistance that he knew he could crush if only he squeezed hard enough.

The throat was Enid's, indubitably. As he began to work on it he could see her familiar, admirably cared-for features; at first smiling, then looking at him with perplexed enquiry, then starting to bulge under the pressure he was applying to her windpipe. He was horrified, appalled by what he was doing. But try as he might he couldn't stop until, on an instant, he woke.

He shot up in bed, dry-mouthed yet covered in cold sweat. It was all so vivid, and he was afraid. When he realized that he had only been dreaming again and that he hadn't really murdered Enid, he could have wept with relief.

He turned to Christine for comfort, expecting to find her beside him in their double bed. And then he remembered.

17

At least the police didn't suspect him.

It had been unnerving, when he returned to the Brickyard on the morning after the murder, to see the police in possession. Worse, he was admitted to his house only under escort. But all of them were friendly and considerate, and as he went round deciding what items were missing he kept reminding himself that the very young constable was with him merely to ensure he didn't get in the way of the men with the lights and the cameras and the tweezers and the plastic bags, the dusting-powder and the tapes.

And what did it matter if any of them noticed his edginess? They would expect him to be shaken after finding his mother-in-law murdered, and his bandaged hand would draw attention to the fact that he was in some pain.

He was most reluctant to go into Enid's bedroom, and the police understood that too. When he told them that he really wouldn't know whether anything of hers was missing or not, they said they were satisfied that the intruder hadn't disturbed her room and that he needn't go in.

But he couldn't prevent himself from glancing through the hinge of the open door as he passed. Her body had been removed, of course. Her bed had been completely stripped. It was ridiculous to imagine that a stripped bed looked defenceless, and yet that was Derek's impression: without its buoyant duvet and pillows it seemed pathetically small for the large room. Its irrevocable emptiness was exactly what he had striven for, but now that he saw it he turned away, choked.

'I daresay you could do with some coffee,' said the very young constable, contriving to seem avuncular in spite of his downy cheeks. 'If you'll start writing up your list – you can use the big room that looks over the garden – I'll bring you a cup. Then the DCI and Sergeant Lloyd would like to hear whatever you can tell them about last night.'

The list of stolen property wasn't long. Packer had at least stuck to that part of their agreement. Although a few small items were missing from the living-room, most of the things that had been taken were Derek's own valuables that he had purposely planted in the hall cupboard.

But the saving of her treasures would be of precious little comfort to Christine now. As he sat at the dining-room table trying to steady his hand sufficiently to make a fair copy of the list, Derek thought of the last time he had been in that room – just two days ago, when he had helped his wife put up the striking blue and green and lilac curtains. That was when he'd finally realized that the only way he could rid her of her mother was with Packer's help. But what a mistake it had been to forbid the man to ransack the house! If the bastard had expended his energies on that, he might have been less violent with poor Enid.

The detectives arrived at the same time as the coffee. Derek's stomach dipped as they walked in and introduced themselves. The big, tweedy, Suffolk-voiced chief inspector had spoken to him sympathetically in the middle of the night, but the woman detective was new to him. She was in her early thirties: tall and thin and dark, wearing stylishly casual clothes, and with a frowning scar on her forehead; more sophisticated than the chief inspector, a different proposition altogether.

'We're making use of your kitchen, I'm afraid, Mr Cartwright,' she said as the constable set down a tray with three steaming mugs. 'But we do bring our own coffee – catering size.'

She had an unexpectedly attractive smile, and she made a point of moving her chair so that she wasn't facing him inquisitorially across the table. By the time she had asked after his injured hand, and after his wife (Christine had been sitting motionless in her lop-sided dressing-gown in Sylvia Collins's kitchen when he left, too withdrawn from him to take any notice when he said where he was going) Derek felt more relaxed.

The chief inspector apologized for taking over his house and promised to let him have it back as soon as possible within the next few days. Derek asked when he would be able to make arrangements for his mother-in-law's funeral. It had been part of his plan to get that under way as soon as possible, thinking that it would help Christine to have something practical to discuss, and that the sooner her mother was buried, the sooner she would be able to come to terms with what had happened. He was dismayed to hear that the body was now within the jurisdiction of the coroner, who would release it for burial at his own discretion; possibly not for some time.

The detectives explained that Derek would be required later to make a formal witness statement about the finding of the body. Meanwhile, they wanted to be clear about the sequence of events at the Brickyard during the course of the previous evening.

Derek was ready with his story. He told them the truth in so far as he wanted them to know it, beginning with his arrival home after his mother-in-law had gone up to her room, tired after her visit to Southwold, and his decision to make himself a sandwich.

He had originally intended to mention the loss of the dog, thinking that it would explain both his late return and his clumsiness with the carving knife, but Christine's questioning last night had decided him against it. After all, he wasn't being accused of anything. If he started offering explanations, the detectives might wonder why. Keep it simple, that was the safest plan.

Besides, he would get quite enough cross-questioning from the rest of the family when they arrived later in the day. Derek was very glad that Tim and Richard and Lyn were coming so promptly, for Christine's sake. For himself, he felt apprehensive. He'd softened the detail as much as possible when he telephoned them with the news, but they weren't children, they would have to be told exactly what had happened to their grandmother, and when they heard it they would be horrified. Angry, too.

They were certain to want to talk it over and over with him, questioning him about all the circumstances – and that would include his loss of the dog. Derek realized, now, how that incident cast a shadow over his otherwise perfect alibi. He looked covertly at his watch, which he was wearing on his right wrist because of the bandages on his left. He couldn't do any driving himself, but Les Harding had kindly agreed to take him to the forest in search of the dog as soon as the detectives had done with him.

Derek was reasonably confident of finding Sam. With any luck the beagle would still be somewhere near where he'd parked him. The forest was a favourite dumping-ground for unwanted dogs, and Derek had more than once reported to the police that he'd seen some wretched animal wandering by the roadside, dashing anxiously towards every approaching car in the forlorn hope that its owners had returned for it. If he and Les could pick up Sam this morning, Christine would be comforted, and the rest of the family need know nothing about it.

'So you went to your mother-in-law's room,' the chief inspector was saying, 'as soon as you saw the hi-fi equipment piled in the hall?'

'Yes. I was a bit stupefied, because of the pain from my hand, but Les Harding said, "You've had a burglary," and my wife said, "What about Mum?" so I went straight up to her. It was so quiet that I was afraid she might be dead, but I never imagined anything quite so horrific. Do you think she disturbed the burglar? Was that why he killed her?'

'That's what it looks like. It's a unique tragedy for your family, Mr Cartwright, but I'm afraid it does sometimes happen these days.' The chief inspector, a heavily handsome man a few years older than Derek, shook his head with middle-aged gloom. 'Time was when burglars were professionals, and we could rely on 'em not to use violence. But now there are more and more opportunists about, and some of them – like this one – don't hesitate to kill if they're disturbed. It's a very sad business.'

'An opportunist?'

'Looks like it. This is the first domestic burglary we've had in Wyveling, or any of the villages round about, for some years. Professionals don't work rural districts unless they're after church antiques or big country houses. This chap must have seen your place, thought you were all out, and decided to try his luck.'

'Will you catch him?'

The chief inspector shed his gloom. 'That's what we're here for,' he said.

For the first time since the start of their talk, Derek felt uneasy. Until now the detective had seemed no more alarming than any other stolid countryman, but the quiet confidence of his words was disconcerting.

'I mean – ' Derek hoped he didn't sound anxious ' – did he leave any clues, or anything?'

'Oh yes,' said the sergeant, equally confident. 'To begin with, we know he's a small man. He climbed through the pantry window, you see.'

Derek tried to look surprised. 'I wondered how he got in.'

'He smashed the glass and unfastened the catch. Luckily for him, the window wasn't locked. Mrs Cartwright seems to be puzzled about that – she told Val she was sure she hadn't unlocked it.'

'Ah no, I unlocked it myself yesterday evening when I went to the pantry for some food. There was a large spider scuttling about. Christine hates spiders, so I opened the window and put it outside. I know I closed the window again, but I must have forgotten to lock it. Would a man really have to be small to get through it, though? Mightn't this one have been tall and thin?'

'Not according to the footprints he left,' said the sergeant. 'We're definitely looking for a small man, probably somewhere about five foot six. And we know that he has very dark hair.'

Derek gaped at the description of Hugh Packer. For a moment he felt close to panic. How could they know so much already? And as for Packer being a professional – it had been criminally careless of him to leave so many traces. With all that information the police couldn't fail to catch him. God what a fool he'd been to trust the man –

Wait, though. Think.

He retrieved his dropped jaw, swallowed hard, and began to feel steadier. All right, so the police knew what physical type they were looking for. But the advantage of this operation, based on the strangers-in-a-traffic-jam encounter between himself and Packer, was that no one knew of any connection between them. And even if the police were to round up every small dark man in the east of England, they still needed good evidence before they could pin the crime on anyone.

'Did he leave any fingerprints?' Derek asked casually.

'He took great care not to,' said the chief inspector. 'No doubt he thought he was doing a clever job. But then he made the mistake of leaving us something even more significant – his genetic fingerprints.'

Derek blinked uneasily, trying to remember where he'd come across the expression. Something he'd read in the *Daily Telegraph*, or one of the Sunday colour supplements, probably. Or perhaps he'd seen it on the *Crimewatch* programme. Yes: DNA, genetic fingerprinting – didn't it give positive proof of identification if the police tested the suspect's blood? Hadn't it been used already to catch more than one murderer?'

'Did he leave bloodstains?'

'No, his semen. The pathologist has sent a sample of it to the forensic science lab.'

Derek pushed back his chair in disgust and strode to the window, so angry that he could see nothing through the glass but Packer's wolfish image. God, what an idiot the man had been, to put them both in such danger of discovery. And what a sadist, to have used poor Enid like that.

He turned back towards the room, his fists clenched. 'What he did to her was wicked,' he burst out. 'Raping an old lady – it was *wicked*.'

The detectives, who had been going through his list of missing items, looked up at him with surprise.

'Certainly,' said Chief Inspector Quantrill. 'But less wicked than murdering her, wouldn't you say?'

'Oh – yes of course!' Sensing that he'd aroused their interest, Derek tried to amend his words. 'I mean – '

Sympathetic again, the detectives agreed that they knew what he meant: bad enough that the poor old lady had been murdered, without being raped as well. 'If it's any comfort,' the chief inspector added, 'the pathologist says she would have lost consciousness by the time the rape took place.'

Derek slumped back into his chair, shaking his head in disbelief. 'I know this sort of thing happens, I've read about it in the newspapers. But I've never understood it. How can any normal man *want* sex with an old woman?'

'He isn't normal,' pointed out the sergeant, 'or he wouldn't have done it. And rape isn't about sex, it's about the exercise of power. Not, I'm afraid,' she added apologetically, 'that that will be of any comfort to your wife. It's all going to be very hard for her to live with.'

Derek was grateful for Sergeant Lloyd's understanding. 'Well, at least Christine and her mother weren't very close,' he said. 'That'll make it easier for my wife. It wasn't exactly a loving relationship – it's just the fact that her mother died in this terrible way that has shattered her.'

The sergeant gave a thoughtful nod, and said nothing.

'And of course you've already had more than your share of family problems,' said the chief inspector kindly, 'what with your daughter's death, and Mrs Cartwright's cancer. I understand that she's worried about your dog, too. Didn't it go missing yesterday? She seems to think – rightly or wrongly – that the man wouldn't have broken in if the dog had been there.'

Derek had ceased to be surprised that the detectives knew so much. He was tempted to try to laugh off the beagle's usefulness as a guard dog, but he guessed that belittling Christine's worries might not go down too well with the detectives. Better to show them that he treated the loss of the dog seriously, and give them the story he had given his wife.

'Christine's quite right,' he concluded. 'Sam might well have deterred the intruder and I blame myself, entirely, for losing him.'

'No need to be too hard on yourself, Mr Cartwright. You couldn't have lost the dog at a worse time, as it happens, but you weren't to know that. Tell you what – as you can't drive, I'll get the patrol man in that area to keep a look out for your beagle.'

The chief inspector opened his briefcase, produced a large-scale map and spread it on the table. 'Now – whereabouts were you at the time?'

Derek breathed more easily. Obviously they had seen nothing suspicious in his story, thank God. He would have preferred to do without police assistance, but in his anxiety to comfort Christine and – hopefully – get the dog back before the family assembled, he pointed out the road where he had last seen Sam. The two detectives eyed the distance from there to Wyveling, and then looked up at him.

'That's a long way to go to take your dog for a walk,' suggested the chief inspector mildly.

'Well, I – I had to visit a client in that area.'

'Of course,' said the sergeant, 'you're in life assurance, aren't you? Right, then, I'll get a message through to the patrol car: one fully grown beagle dog, black, white and tan, yes?'

'Yes. And thank you very much.'

The detectives made ready to go. There had been nothing at all alarming about the interview, but as they stood side by side they gave the impression of being a potentially formidable team.

The sergeant smiled at Derek. 'Can't promise anything, Mr Cartwright, but we'll do our best.'

'To find the murderer,' said the chief inspector, 'as well as the dog.'

With Les Harding's assistance Derek spent the rest of the morning in the forest. He found the right area without much difficulty, but on a sunny Sunday, with parked cars and people about, everywhere looked different. He couldn't identify exactly where he had left the car, or which of the many forest rides he had walked the dog in. While Les continued to drive slowly along the narrow roads, looking about and stopping to ask anyone he saw, Derek plunged in and out of the pine trees, holding his aching hand up against his chest and calling, calling.

But Sam was nowhere to be found.

18

'We need to talk to you, Dad.'

Lyn had inherited her attractive face and figure, and her colour sense, from her mother's side of the family; her lack of sentimentality came direct from Enid. Derek had seen his daughter shed tears for her grandmother during the course of the afternoon, but primarily she seemed to be angry. When she eventually cornered him outside Mrs Collins's back door, Lyn's eyes were fierce and her voice had an edge to it.

Tim and Richard stood behind her, less fierce but equally determined. Crowded round by his progeny, Derek tried to offer excuses: there was nothing he would like more than a good long family chat, but with him staying there and them at the Hardings' it wasn't really possible to hold a private conversation, was it? Better to wait until they could get back home, to the Brickyard.

'No, we're going to talk tonight,' said Richard. 'Mum doesn't want the Hardings to feel obliged to feed us, so I've arranged a meal at the Five Bells, at seven o'clock. All right?'

Derek did his best to get out of going. He didn't want to leave their mother, he said; but he knew that after the emotion of her children's homecoming she had fallen into an exhausted sleep. He couldn't face the stares and sympathy of the villagers, he said; but his efficient younger son had arranged for them to eat in a back room. The food at the Five Bells was notoriously poor, he protested finally, and all three of them looked at him with something like contempt. 'For God's sake, Dad,' Tim growled through his massive beard, 'at a time like this, what does it matter?'

None of them had been close to their grandmother, and

Derek had been surprised by the strength of their grief. The first hours after their arrival had been filled with sorrow and outrage, and with compassion for their mother. Now, though, they were showing signs of restlessness.

Had Enid died of natural causes, the need to make arrangements for the funeral would at least have kept them all occupied. Had they been in their own home, there would have been meals to prepare and routines to follow. As it was, there was nothing for any of them to do; the murder enquiry had pushed them to the side of their own lives. Derek supposed that Christine would want her mother's funeral to be at Southwold, where her father was buried, but there was obviously no need to discuss it with her yet. And anyway she was still reluctant, for whatever reason, to talk to him.

His children escorted him to the Five Bells by way of the field path, with the sun setting behind Doddenham church on the other side of the valley. It was only a matter of days since he had last used the path, but during that time the cow parsley and docks had grown by inches, narrowing the way so that they had to walk in single file.

'If we meet anyone, I'll do the talking,' Richard said as he strode ahead. But as Derek followed, with the other two close behind, he felt considerably more apprehensive about the coming conversation with them than about any chance encounter with a neighbour.

They rounded the churchyard wall unseen, skidded down through the spinney behind the Five Bells, and sneaked into the pub through the back door. The landlord, mumbling with suppressed curiosity, showed them into a little-used room that smelled of rising damp. While he fetched their drinks his wife, tiptoeing reverentially, served them with platters of gnarled rump steak and oven-ready chips, garnished with peas from the freezer and squishy tomatoes.

Derek couldn't eat; couldn't have eaten, even had the meal been appetizing. Richard sawed up his steak for him, unasked, but all Derek did was sip whisky, push the food about with his fork, and watch his children refuel themselves.

He was fond of them, as he hoped they were of him, but he found it difficult to relate to any of them. He privately deplored the casual expletives and the taste for beer that Lyn had brought home from medical school; he resented being organized by Richard; and he simply couldn't come to terms with being addressed as 'Dad' by such a whiskery man as Tim, who looked exactly like the sepia family photographs of his own great-grandfather.

Derek and Christine had done their best to give the three of them – as well as Laurie – a happy childhood. But in comparison with some unharmonious couples they knew, who had centred their emotions on their children, he and his wife had always and unequivocally given their devotion to each other.

Christine mattered to him far more than Tim or Richard or Lyn. If, as he suspected, they were ganging up on him because he'd lost the dog, he could comfort himself with the knowledge that what he'd done had been entirely for his wife's ultimate benefit. With any luck, Sam would be found. And Derek was still convinced that when she'd had a chance to get over the horror of what that bastard Packer had done, Christine would be thankful for the freedom he had won for her.

What his children had to say, initially, was mild enough. They were frustrated because they could do nothing useful, and embarrassed by the Hardings' hospitality. Richard and Lyn both had exams to face, Tim was in the middle of erecting barriers round part of a Suffolk beach that was a breeding sanctuary for the little tern, and now that they had all done what they could to comfort their mother they were anxious to get away as soon as possible.

'We thought we'd push off tomorrow,' said Richard. 'But we'll be back next weekend to see Mum – if you're still here, that is. And of course we'll be at the funeral, whenever and wherever.'

Tim growled agreement. 'But before we go, Dad,' he said, wiping beer from his whiskers, 'we want to know what your plans are.'

They were all looking at him.

'Plans?' said Derek.

'You must have been making some, for Mum's sake,' said Lyn impatiently. 'What are the two of you going to do now?'

In fact, his plans had never extended beyond getting rid of Enid. He had supposed that, once the funeral was over, he and

Christine would be able to return to normal almost immediately. That had been the whole idea, to regain their home for themselves for as much – or as little – as remained of Christine's life. But now that Packer had fouled things up, Derek could see that his wife was going to take longer than he'd imagined to get over her mother's death.

'It's difficult to plan anything,' he explained, 'until the police let us have the Brickyard back. But I think I'll take your mother for a holiday as soon as possible, somewhere in Devon or Cornwall, just to give her a chance to recuperate. Then perhaps I could leave her with her Long cousins in Swindon while I come back to work. I'll have the house redecorated while she's away – the hall and our bedroom, anyway, and of course your grandmother's room. That'll have to be completely refurbished.'

Lyn drew a sharp, audible breath. All three of them were staring at him as though they couldn't believe their ears.

'*Refurbished*?' she exploded. 'Christ – have you gone completely out of your mind?'

He stared back, affronted. 'What d'you mean?'

'You can hardly go on living at the Brickyard after Gran has been murdered there,' said Tim gruffly.

'And even if *you* could,' said Richard, 'Mum certainly can't.' His shoulders sagged; he suddenly looked very young. 'We've lost poor Gran, and we've lost our home as well. It's good-bye to the Brickyard for all of us.'

Derek was speechless.

It had never occurred to him that there would be any problem about continuing to live at the Brickyard. But it wasn't his fault that he hadn't thought of it. If only that bastard Packer had carried out the plan and quietly smothered Enid, Derek was sure that Christine would have had no qualms about going on living there.

The family were right, though. After what she'd seen last night, Christine would find the house unbearable. The village too; probably the whole area. So now, in her state of health, she was going to have to go through all the harassment of trailing about the countryside viewing other properties, and then the upheaval of moving. Poor, poor Christine – what she was being put through . . . and all on account of that devil

Packer! God, what he wouldn't do to him if ever he saw him again –

Derek pushed aside his plate. 'You're right, of course,' he admitted. 'I'm sorry – I just didn't think.'

'You never do think, do you?' To his astonishment, Lyn began blazing at him from across the table. 'At least, not as far as Mum's concerned. You never bother to take her feelings into account. You're simply planning to do what suits you, and assuming that it's in her best interests as well as your own.'

'That's not true!'

'Oh yes, it is, I've seen it happening before. You think of her only in relation to yourself, never as a person in her own right.'

Derek was hot with indignation. 'You don't know what you're talking about. I'm devoted to your mother.'

'Oh yes – you've always made a big thing about that, haven't you? All right, I know you care about her, Dad. But you don't even begin to understand her. F'r instance, you've obviously no idea how shattered she's been by that mastectomy. Don't you realize what a devastating thing it is for a woman?'

'Of course I realize it. God knows I've done everything to reassure her that it doesn't make her any less attractive – '

'Attractive? To you, you mean?' Lyn slammed back her chair in disgust.

'There you go again! That's absolutely typical. Can't you see that it's not the way you feel about her that matters, it's the way she feels about herself? She's been a deeply unhappy woman – and I'm furious with you for not letting me know as soon as she found the lump in her breast. There was probably no need for her to have a radical mastectomy. That hospital's notorious for doing it as a matter of routine on every breast cancer patient. If only you'd told me I'd have come home right away and discussed the alternatives with her – and kicked up a fuss at the hospital if necessary. *Why* didn't you let me know, Dad? Why didn't you give me a chance to help her?'

'Because it was nothing to do with you, Lyn,' said Derek sharply. 'It was a matter for your mother and myself.'

'"And yourself"! It's her body, not yours – and not some out-of-date consultant's either. Well, all I can say is, thank God for Sylvia Collins – at least Mum's now got someone sympathetic to talk to.'

'Except that you can't go on staying with Mrs Collins indefinitely,' pointed out Richard. 'And Mum won't want to go back to the Brickyard even for one night. You could always use Gran's flat in Southwold, I suppose – only it's too far from your office. So where will you go?'

Derek propped his elbows on the table and rested his aching head on his one good hand. Lyn's attack had been so unexpected, so bloody unjust. She'd got it all wrong about him and her mother, but he was too weary to argue with her. And how the hell could they expect him to make any decisions, when he was still in shock after the horror of last night?

'I don't know,' he mumbled. They could see the bandages on his left hand – didn't they understand that it hurt? Couldn't they leave him alone?

'And the other thing we need to sort out, while we're here,' growled Tim, 'is what happened yesterday afternoon. How did you come to lose poor old Sam? Why on earth did you take the dog for a walk in the forest in the pouring rain – and in your office suit? What exactly were you *doing* yesterday, Dad?'

Derek was saved by a loud knock on the door. He hurried to answer it, and found the two detectives there.

'Sorry to intrude, Mr Cartwright,' said the chief inspector, ducking his head as he came through the low doorway. 'We're on our way back to Breckham Market, and we just wanted a final word with you.'

'Final for tonight, that is,' said Sergeant Lloyd. She smiled at the younger Cartwrights, and Derek reluctantly introduced his family. Hands were shaken, but the detectives refused the offer of a drink.

'We're giving a press and television conference later this evening,' explained the chief inspector, 'and appealing for possible witnesses to come forward. Better steer clear of alcohol until that's over.'

'Do you suspect anyone?' asked Lyn.

'No, it's early days yet. But at least we've got a possible lead. Someone noticed a man with binoculars hanging about beside a parked car by the bridge on the Doddenham road, on the day before Mrs Long's death.'

Derek's mouth went dry.

'Couldn't it have been a bird-watcher?' he said.

The sergeant turned her head. 'Did you see him, too, Mr Cartwright?'

'No, no. It's just that you said he had binoculars – and that's quite a well-known spot for bird-watching.'

'First I've heard of it,' muttered Tim.

'As it happens,' said Sergeant Lloyd, 'the person who saw him thought he was a bird-watcher. Apparently he was wearing all the gear. But he's described as a small man, and he was looking towards the field path from which we think the murderer approached your house, so we'd very much like to talk to him.'

'Or to anyone else who might have seen him, or who noticed his car,' said the chief inspector. 'If he had no connection with the murder, we'd like to eliminate him from our enquiries.'

Derek took several deep breaths in an attempt to steady his heartbeat. The standard police phrase had an ominous ring to it, but there was no need to panic. Even if anyone could remember any details of the car, Packer had said that he had since changed the number plates. No one could possibly trace the man that way. Relax.

'What we came to see you about, though, Mr Cartwright,' said the chief inspector, 'is your dog.'

'My dog?'

'Yes, I'm afraid we've had no sightings from our patrol car. What I thought, though, since Mrs Cartwright is so concerned about him, is that we might give him a mention to the press. We do our best to keep reporters away from the family, as you know, but they've got a job to do and no doubt they'll be glad enough to use the lost dog story. If you'd like us to release it, that is?'

Derek swallowed, trying to moisten his mouth. 'Er – yes. Yes, of course – please do.'

'Thank you very much, Chief Inspector,' said Tim, standing squarely opposite his father. 'We'll all be grateful if Sam can be found. What we don't understand – we were just saying this to Dad when you arrived – is how he ever came to be lost.'

'I couldn't help it,' said Derek. 'I didn't *want* to lose him.'

'Nobody said you did,' argued his first-born, looking more

patriarchal than ever. 'But what bothers Mum – and us – is why on earth you took him all the way to the forest in the pouring rain.'

'I told her: it wasn't raining when I set out.'

'And you were wearing your office suit, so she said.'

'I was going to visit a client.'

'You don't have personal clients,' said Richard.

'Not exactly a personal client – a bank manager, a useful contact.'

'On a Saturday afternoon?' said Lyn.

'Yes – just a social call, really. He'd invited me to visit him at his home, near Fodderstone.'

'Fodderstone?' said Tim. 'That's on the other side of the forest from Two Mile Bottom.'

'Who said anything about Two Mile Bottom?'

'You did,' said Lyn. 'You told Mum that was where you lost Sam, at our old picnic place.'

Derek had forgotten. He glanced at the detectives, and saw that they were listening with undisguised interest. Sweat sprang out on his hairline, and he had to will himself not to wipe it away.

'No, I didn't,' he said. 'She must be confused. I told her I took Sam for a run there, before the rain started. It was later, on the way back from Fodderstone, that I let him out of the car and he went chasing off after a rabbit. It wasn't my fault – '

'Could happen to anyone,' intervened the chief inspector, curtailing the family argument. He reached for the latch of the door. 'Let's hope we can get the beagle back for you, with the help of a bit of publicity.'

'Ah yes – ' said the sergeant. 'There's just one detail I forgot to ask you, Mr Cartwright. Was your dog wearing his collar when he ran off?'

'Er – '

'You told Mum he was wearing it,' said Tim sternly. 'A tartan collar,' he explained to the sergeant.

She raised one eyebrow at Derek, seeking confirmation.

'Yes,' he said, by now slightly desperate. 'I'd forgotten.' Then he turned on his children, his patience snapping: 'Good grief, d'you think I'm a computer? Do you imagine I've got total recall? If you'd been through what I went through last night – '

144

From the corner of his eye he saw the detectives leave the room. God, what a fright that had been! But they didn't suspect anything, surely? No, of course they didn't. There was no reason why they should.

It was just that *interested* look of theirs that he couldn't get out of his mind. Had they noticed the give-away sweat on his forehead? What were they saying about him? Had it occurred to them that there might be something significant about the dog's disappearance on the very day of Enid's murder? Because once they made that connection –

'Derek Cartwright', said Sergeant Lloyd as she sat in the Chief Inspector's car and fastened her seat belt, 'is a very worried man. What do you make of this dog incident, Douglas? What's he covering up?'

Quantrill snorted, half-disapproving, half-amused.

'What I think,' he said, 'is that Cartwright took the chance of making a Saturday afternoon visit to a secret girlfriend, with dog-walking as an excuse. Now the animal's lost, what's putting him in a muck sweat is that his family is just about to find him out.'

19

Derek would have preferred to avoid his children the following morning, but they insisted on making a search for Sam before they left and they needed him as a guide. They also needed to use his car, because Tim's pick-up truck wasn't big enough for the four of them.

The Sierra was in its usual place at the front of the Brickyard, under the old cart shed where Derek had left it on Saturday evening when he returned from the forest. Now, though, it was blocked in by police vehicles. The very young constable who had escorted him round the house the previous day hurried out with an apology, and began to clear their way.

Derek stood alone in the yard, blinking dazedly in the sunshine after another dream-disturbed night. His damaged hand felt easier, but Tim had commandeered his car keys. The constable moved a police Rover, judged that there was now enough room for Tim to reverse and turn the Sierra, and beckoned him out of the shed.

What was happening, there on Derek's own property, seemed to him totally unreal. He felt choked with worry; less – at the moment – on account of Packer's crime than on account of the unexpected and wholly unfounded charges his children had levelled at him last night.

Since he had no way of disproving what they thought, except by telling the truth about what he had done on Saturday, he had said nothing. As a result, his children despised him for being unfaithful to their sick mother. And if Christine had come to the same conclusion – which would account for her withdrawal from him – then the basis of their marriage had already been destroyed. God, what a mess everything had turned out to be . . . And all he'd ever intended was to make life easier for Christine because he loved her.

'You've got some nasty scratches on your bodywork, Mr Cartwright,' observed the very young constable as he signalled Tim to stop reversing the car. 'Recent, too.'

He bent to examine the driver's door and Derek joined him, not really caring about the scratches but feeling that he ought to show an interest. Tim lowered the window, and stuck out his bearded head for an alternative view; Lyn and Richard walked up from the gateway to see what was happening.

The slate-blue car was badly in need of a wash. Its Saturday journey through the wet countryside had left it sprayed with mud. And there, on the driver's door, in paw-prints and scrabbles and long raking scratches, some of which went right through to the metal, was clear evidence that Sam had frantically objected to being abandoned.

Derek heard himself gulp.

The constable, thank God, seemed not to think the marks suspicious. He took a good look at them, and agreed with Derek's gabbled improvisation: yes, the dog might well have returned to the car while his master was searching for him, tried to get in, and then rushed away again when he heard himself being called from elsewhere.

Tim and Richard and Lyn glanced their disbelief at each other, and then stared at their father with hostility. But at least they said nothing in front of the policeman.

They told Derek exactly what they thought of him as they drove to the forest but he stuck to his story, hoping fervently that the beagle would be found and that some at least of the family pressure would be taken off him. But when all four of them had called and searched for an hour or more, hurrying up and down grassy rides and blundering through thickets in vain, it became clear that Sam was irretrievably lost.

'For God's sake look after Mum,' said Lyn, by way of farewell. Every bit as beautiful as Christine had been at the same age, she was spitting hostility at him: 'Stop being so bloody selfish, Dad. Try to think about her needs, for a change.'

Derek flinched, but said nothing. What was the point? Too

many angry things had been said already, and no one now believed the truths he told. He stood outside Mrs Collins's house, watching as Tim drove off in the Sierra, taking Lyn and Richard to catch their respective trains. Christine went with them, venturing out for the first time since her mother's death. He would have liked to wave to her, but she didn't look back.

Hungry at last, he went to the village shop and bought bread rolls, cheese and fruit. The owner and the other customers stopped talking immediately he went in, but Derek was indifferent to the embarrassed silence, the lowered eyes and the covert glances. Enid's murder was in the past; it was his future with his wife that he was concerned about.

As he ate his food in Sylvia Collins's garden, Val the policewoman joined him to report that her colleagues had just finished their work at the Brickyard. They would be moving out that afternoon, and she herself would be leaving too; no doubt, she said, to the Cartwrights' – not to mention Mrs Collins's – relief. There was just the formality of Derek's statement about finding the body to be gone through, if he wouldn't mind accompanying her to Breckham Market police station. When he'd finished his lunch, of course.

There was nothing difficult or alarming about making the statement. The police were so very much easier to deal with than his children. He didn't see either of the detectives but all the uniformed officers were considerate, even about his loss of the dog; having checked that Sam had not yet been found, they discussed with him their press release for the next day's local paper.

By the time Val drove him back to Wyveling, Christine had returned. Thankfully, though, Tim had taken his truck and gone. Val collected her toothbrush and sleeping-bag, said her thanks to Mrs Collins, shook him and Christine by the hand and told them that she'd stay in touch. She handed Christine a card with the telephone number of the police station: 'If there's anything you want to know, or if you just want to talk, don't hesitate to give me a ring.'

Then Derek and his wife were alone together.

They sat on a wooden bench beside Sylvia Collins's goldfish pond, Derek at one end, Christine at the other. She stared straight ahead, her face so pale and the skin round her eyes so bruised-looking that he was afraid she was ill.

'Are you in pain, my love?' he asked, stretching his good hand tentatively towards her. She shook her head. He left his outstretched hand resting hopefully on the bench for a few moments, then cleared his throat and shifted himself to a less suppliant position.

'The police are moving out of the Brickyard this afternoon,' he said. 'It'll be good to have our own home back. Not to move into, I mean,' he added hastily, observing Christine's shudder, 'but it'll give us a chance to sort ourselves out, won't it? Change our clothes, sit in our own garden.'

'I can't go back there,' she said in a remote voice. 'Not to live, ever.'

'Of course you can't, Chrissie, I know that. I never expected you to. We'll decide what to do when we've had a chance to draw breath, but what you need first is to get away for a bit. We'll have a holiday, shall we?'

'No thank you, Derek.' She still wouldn't look at him, let alone call him by his affectionate name, or touch him.

'Would you like to go to Southwold, then? To your mo- To the flat?'

'No.'

Derek didn't know what to say next. After a few moments Christine said, 'I shall go away on my own, as soon as I feel able to drive. I'm still too shaky for that at the moment. I'll go and stay with Trish.'

'Who?'

'Trish Wilson. We were at school together, we write every Christmas. She and her husband have a farm in Derbyshire, and I can rent one of the barns they've turned into holiday cottages.'

'Derbyshire? But that's much too far away! Why don't we rent a cottage nearer Cambridge, so that we can share it – or at least so that I can be with you for as long as possible at weekends.'

'No. I'd rather be alone.'

A silence fell between them; lengthened, deepened. It seemed particularly cruel that the natural world should be burgeoning into new life all around them – birds bustling in the greening hedges, toads croaking and splashing in the pond – just at the time when their married life was juddering to a stop.

Derek felt numbed. How could this be happening, when they'd always been such a secure couple? When they'd been through so many trials together? When he loved Christine so much that he was prepared to do anything for her, even to the extent of –

Well, he wouldn't think about that. The death of Enid had nothing to do with what was happening between him and Christine. Understandably, she was rejecting him because she thought he had been unfaithful to her. But since he hadn't (hadn't ever been, wouldn't ever be), surely he ought to be able to convince her?

'It isn't true, Chrissie,' he said urgently. 'The family's got it all wrong. I love you, you know that. I've always been faithful to you. I've never so much as looked at another woman, and I never will.'

'The children didn't say anything about it,' said Christine distantly, 'though I'm sure they guessed. They didn't need to say anything. I worked it out for myself on Saturday evening.'

'But I've just told you – it's not true! I swear to you I've done nothing wrong. Good God,' he burst out, 'do you take me for a liar as well as a lecher!'

She gave a shrug of indifference. 'It hardly seems to matter, now.'

'Not *matter*? What do you mean? Don't you care whether or not I've been faithful to you?'

'I would have cared very much', she said in a level voice, 'if it had occurred to me earlier that you hadn't been. I cared for a time on Saturday evening. But now, quite frankly, it seems to be of very small importance.'

She stood up. 'I need some space, Derek. It's not you that's the problem, it's me. I need to think things out on my own. Sylvia has kindly said that I can stay here until I'm fit to drive to Derbyshire – but no doubt you'll want to go elsewhere straight away.'

'But how long are you going for?'

'I don't know. I really don't know.'

Anguished, he stumbled to his feet. 'I don't understand what's happening to us, Chrissie. We're not going to part company, not after everything we've been through together! We're a couple, we have been since we were teenagers. We're *us*, and I won't let you go.'

She began to walk away. 'I'll send Trish's address to you at your office before I go,' she said. Then she paused and glanced back at him: 'Don't forget that you're due at the doctor's surgery on Friday to have your stitches out.'

Derek looked dumbly down at his bandaged hand. It seemed to be of no importance at all.

At the Brickyard, the very young constable was taking a second look at Derek Cartwright's Sierra before the police moved out.

'What do you make of this, Sergeant Lloyd?' he called to the detective as she crossed the yard to her own car.

Hilary joined him under the cart shed. As they examined the marks in the dried mud on the driver's door of the Sierra, PC Mills told her how Cartwright had explained the scratches away.

'But I've been thinking about it,' he said, 'and I'm not satisfied that he was telling the truth. Yes, all right, some of the paw prints are clear enough. No doubt they were made when the car was stationary. But look at the angle of these scratches – '

'You're right, Shaun,' said the sergeant. 'Some of them are more horizontal than vertical. And some of them trail away on the back door. It looks as though the car was moving when the dog tried to get in.'

Shaun Mills stood up, frowning. 'I wouldn't have thought it of Mr Cartwright. He seems such a decent man, not at all the sort to get rid of a poor old dog by dumping it.'

'I wouldn't have thought it of him either – but you can never tell, can you? If this was what he went to the forest for, then we were probably wrong about the secret love affair. But all I can say is,' concluded Hilary Lloyd crossly, 'that if his family has been giving him a hard time over a non-existent affair, then it serves the wretched man right.'

20

Derek was so dazed by what had happened between Christine
and himself that it was only when he emerged with a suitcase
from the now-deserted Brickyard that he realized he had gone
upstairs and done his packing without giving Enid's murder a
thought. And now that it crossed his mind, he felt completely
disassociated from it.

He sat in the Sierra and tried using the gear lever and
handbrake with his bandaged hand. Driving to Cambridge was
going to be difficult, but not impossible. What did it matter that
his hand would hurt? His emotions had already taken a far
worse battering.

He booked in at the same Cambridge hotel he had used on
Friday night, then drove round the corner to his office. His
colleagues were surprised to see him, because he had
telephoned first thing that morning to say that his
mother-in-law had suddenly died and he wouldn't be at work
for the next few days. But they were sympathetic and
incurious, accepting his explanation that there was nothing he
could do at home and he was glad to get away for a bit from the
old lady's friends and relations.

Fortunately the *East Anglian Daily Press*, which that morning
carried a front-page account of the murder, didn't circulate as
far as Cambridge. Derek expected that the news would reach
his colleagues eventually, but he had no intention of telling
them. Nor did he say anything about his move to the hotel,
partly out of hurt pride and partly because he didn't want to
become the subject of office gossip.

He had hoped that work would take his mind off his
personal problems, but it didn't. Or, rather, it did every so

often; but then the recollection that Christine had rejected him would come springing back, more painful than ever.

There was no point in continuing to sit in his office staring at his monitor after the rest of the staff had gone home. The trouble was that he didn't know what else to do. He thought about going to the health club, but he was in no fit state either to swim or to exercise.

For a time, oblivious of his surroundings, he walked the streets of Cambridge. He stopped at a pub for a drink and something to eat, but the bar was a noisy student haunt and he didn't feel inclined to linger. Abandoning a sinewy chicken drumstick, he bought a half bottle of Bell's and retreated to his hotel room.

The first whisky went straight down, almost unnoticed except for the shudder effect. Clutching the second, he sat on his bed and contemplated the telephone. He always rang Christine when he was away for a night, and he longed to talk to her now. He couldn't believe that everything wasn't all right between them, just as it always had been.

And perhaps it was. Perhaps he'd allowed a mere tiff to balloon to monstrous proportions in his mind. Christine was probably sitting in Sylvia Collins's house now, waiting anxiously for his call. After all, she'd thought to remind him about having the stitches out of his hand, so there was no doubt that she cared. Perhaps if he opened the conversation as though nothing had happened, the problem would go away.

He swallowed the second whisky, dialled Mrs Collins's number, and asked to speak to his wife.

It seemed to him that several minutes elapsed before Christine came to the telephone. There was a crackle on the line which made it difficult to judge her mood, but her formal 'Hallo Derek' was not encouraging.

'Hallo Chrissie! How are you, darling?'

'I'm all right, thank you.'

'Good!' He would never normally pronounce the word so heartily, but anxiety falsified his tone. 'I had a lot of work to catch up with, or I'd have rung you earlier. I'm staying at the usual hotel near the office. Would you like to make a note of the telephone number, dearest?' He read it off to her. 'Got that?'

'Yes, thank you,' she said. The line had cleared, and he could tell from her voice that she hadn't bothered to write the number down.

'Chrissie!'

Abandoning his casual act he gripped the receiver tightly, with his bandaged as well as his good hand, as though by doing so he could hold on to her. 'You know I love you. You only, ever and always. Let me drive over now, tonight, and bring you back here. Or anywhere, as long as we're together. *Please.*'

'Oh, Derek ... Can't you understand?' There was a weary sadness in her voice. 'I'm distressed and confused, and I need to be on my own to try to sort things out. Don't hassle me, please. Just – good-night.'

She cut him off. He sat quite still for a few minutes, staring at the receiver he was holding. Then he slammed it down, and grimly set about finishing the remainder of the bottle.

His secretary had already cancelled his appointments for the rest of the week; just as well, as far as the following day was concerned. Derek woke with a foul taste in his mouth, a sore hand and a pounding hangover. But those were the least of his troubles.

He made a cup of coffee in his room and stood with it at the window looking out at the Chesterton road and the willows beside the Cam. It was raining again, just as it had been last Saturday morning, before everything started to go wrong. Oh God, if only ...

If only.

Chrissie. Christine.

Without her his life was meaningless. He didn't know what to do with the day that lay ahead, let alone with the week. And as for months and years ... the bleakness was terrible to contemplate.

Wretchedly, he pulled on his clothes and drove out to the health club; somewhere to go on a wet Tuesday morning, that was all. He sweated some of the alcohol out of his system in the sauna, took a shower, and then wandered over to the jacuzzi.

A young couple were just emerging from the bubbling grey

water. Glad to be able to have the whirlpool to himself, Derek sat on the underwater seat, leaned back with his arms stretched out along the edge, closed his eyes and hoped that the power jets would pummel his body into temporary oblivion.

Almost immediately he heard someone else approach. As he moved his long legs, with reluctance, to accommodate the newcomer, he saw through half-open eyes that the masculine body lowering itself into the water opposite him was startlingly simian in appearance: smallish but strongly muscular, and coated with hairs that curled blackly round the edges of the white trunks.

He widened his eyes. The body was now submerged; only a familiar swarthy head and handsome face showed above the water.

'Well, if it isn't you, Derek!' said Hugh Packer. 'Small world, eh?'

'What the hell are you doing here?'

'Don't be like that! This seemed a good place for us to talk, but it's cost me a packet to get in. I had to book a room in the hotel before they'd let me use the facilities, and buy the swimming gear as well. Still, it'll be worth it in the end. You're pleased with the job I did for you, I hope?'

'*Pleased.*' Gaping with rage, Derek shipped a mouthful of frothy water. It was the need to cough that initially prevented him from launching himself bodily at the man. After that, it was only the fear of drawing the attention of the club staff that restrained him.

'You bastard, Packer!' he hissed. 'You've ruined my life because of what you did. I've lost my wife. I've lost everything else I love and value – my children, my home. And now you have the nerve to ask me if I'm pleased! My God, if we weren't in public view I'd – '

Packer was making tutting noises. 'How very careless of you to lose all that, Derek. But don't blame *me*. You should have thought about the consequences before you agreed to the plan, shouldn't you?'

Under cover of the bubbles Derek lashed out with one leg, trying to slam his heel against the smaller man's groin. But the water absorbed the force of the blow, and all he managed to do was thump Packer's thigh. For the first time that morning the man revealed his sharp wolfish grin. It reminded Derek of exactly what Packer had done to Christine's mother.

'You bloody pervert,' he said through his teeth. 'How could you rape a poor defenceless old woman?'

'Interesting you should ask that,' said Packer in a tone of cheerful detachment. 'It wasn't anything I'd *intended* to do, believe me! It – well, it sort of came over me. Nothing to do with sex, you understand. God, no. That's what I've got a wife for.'

He paused, with the tip of his tongue protruding slyly from between his red lips. Derek, remembering the big, unhappy, strikingly attractive young woman who was married to the man, spared her a moment's sympathy.

'As far as I was concerned,' Packer went on, 'it was just a spontaneous reaction. Nothing personal at all. I'd never actually despatched anyone before, you see, so there was a great sense of power in knowing that I'd got her life in my hands and I could do whatever I wanted with her. Mind you, she put up a resistance – but that only added a bit of spice to the proceedings.'

Derek was nauseated. 'Bastard,' he spat; 'you bastard! You promised me you'd do it gently, with a pillow.'

'No I didn't. That was your idea. I decided it would be in your best interests if I used my hands, because then you wouldn't have to pretend to be surprised when you found her.' Packer chuckled. 'And I was right, wasn't I? I bet you were so shocked that you fooled everybody. Oh, it really was a brilliant operation, wasn't it?'

'You're insane!' said Derek. 'Get out of my sight or – '

Packer was already standing up, though not at Derek's insistence. Instead, with charming courtesy, he was handing an elderly woman – limping arthritically, but game in her swimsuit and floral bathing cap, and dripping after coming out of the pool – down into the jacuzzi.

'One more step,' he was saying to her, while she murmured delightedly in response to his concern. 'Steady! There you are, have my seat, I'm just going anyway. All right? Comfy? Perhaps this gentleman wouldn't mind moving his feet ...'

Derek shifted them, mumbling an apology to her. He stared with hatred at Packer's extraordinarily hairy back as the man swaggered off. At that moment, Derek felt that he would give anything to see him locked away for what he had done. It would mean confessing his own part in the planning of Packer's crime, of course; but it was such a very small part, and now that he had lost Christine the prospect of being tried for it hardly seemed to matter.

Except that he still couldn't believe that he had lost her, not for good. And as long as there was some hope of their getting together again, he'd be a fool to do anything to discredit himself in her eyes. No: let the evil little bastard go, and good riddance to him.

Derek stayed in the jacuzzi, enduring the conversation of the arthritic woman and a retired couple who had joined them, until he felt sure that Packer would have gone. Then he showered, dressed, and went cautiously into the foyer-bar of the hotel. There was no sign of the man, thank God. With luck, he would never see him again.

He decided to leave the Post House immediately; for anywhere, it didn't matter. Running through a drizzle of rain to his car, he unlocked the door.

He was in the act of getting in – his head bent, his left knee raised – when he heard a slap of footsteps from behind and felt a violent shove on his right shoulder. Caught off balance, he pitched sideways across the driving seat. At the same time his keys were snatched from his right hand.

He was in no doubt who had done it. Beyond protest, he watched Hugh Packer letting himself into the front passenger seat.

'What do you want?' he said dully, staring straight ahead.

'What do you think I want?' said Packer, surprised. 'You must know what I'm here for. I've carried out my part of our bargain, and now it's your turn. I've come to tell you what arrangements I've made for you to kill my father-in-law.'

Derek was so shocked that for a few moments he said nothing at all.

He'd forgotten. In all his anxiety and trouble, he had

completely forgotten that a bargain had ever been made. And now that his life had been ruined by Packer, he had absolutely no intention of carrying out the part that had been allotted to him.

'Go to hell,' he said.

Packer shrugged. 'Say what you like, but you're going to do it.'

'I am not! I couldn't, for one thing. I couldn't bring myself to kill anyone, let alone a helpless old man.'

'But this'll be easy. No violence, no physical contact of any kind.' Packer unfolded a large-scale map and pointed out an isolated rural property near Newmarket. 'This is where we live, Winter Paddocks. There'll be a Pony Club meeting going on just up the road, here, next Sunday afternoon, so that'll be an ideal time for the job. You'll be able to park your car with the others without being noticed. The field they're going to use as a car-park adjoins our wooded grounds, and you can slip in through a back gate in the wall, here.

'Belinda and I will be out, spending the day with a cousin of hers in Ely. Normally she'd hire a trained nurse to sit with her father, but I've fixed it so that the woman who's coming on Sunday is an untrained nursing assistant. They'll be together in the sun-room from about one-thirty onwards – the old man always has a sleep there after lunch. You can approach it on this side, from a shrubbery at the foot of the terrace, without being seen.

'At two-fifteen I'll make a telephone call to draw the woman out of the sun-room. I'll pretend I'm someone else, and persuade her to write down a complicated message for me. While she's away, you'll nip into the sun-room and open an old croquet box that you'll find just behind the garden door. Inside it there'll be a lidded plastic cup, identical to the one my wife will have left beside Sidney – but the orange juice in this one will be laced with insulin.'

Derek had been listening with an unwilling fascination as the man went through the details. Packer had planned it well – just as he'd planned Enid's murder. But Derek wasn't going to do it.

'No!' he said.

'What could be simpler?' protested Packer, sounding almost

158

injured. 'All you have to do is swap the cups, and then clear off. The woman will give Sidney the drink during the course of the afternoon, and he'll rapidly go into a diabetic coma. Belinda's been trained to recognize it, just as a nurse would, but this woman will think he's having a good sleep. By the time we get home, Sidney will have died of natural causes. A nice peaceful end for him, no suspicion devolving on me, no trouble for you. All right?'

'Wrong!' said Derek angrily. 'I won't have any part in this, or anything more to do with you.'

'That'll suit me perfectly,' said Packer, folding up his map. 'We shan't see each other after this morning, anyway. I'm driving a Jag up to Scotland for a customer tomorrow, and I'll be away until Saturday night – that's why I'm giving you your instructions now. Do you understand them? Any questions?'

'Didn't you hear me?' Derek exploded. 'I tell you, *I am not going to do it*. You can't make me.'

'No?' said Packer. His brown eyes hardened and his mouth took an ugly line. Seizing Derek's bandaged hand, he slammed the palm against the knob of the gear lever. Derek gasped as the pain stabbed up his wrist and through his forearm.

'Just you remember this,' Packer said, thrusting his face so close that Derek caught the tainted heat of his breath. 'I've already killed once, and I found it very stimulating. I wouldn't at all mind having another go. If you don't get rid of the old man for me – this coming Sunday, exactly as I said – then I'll get rid of you.'

21

At Breckham Market police headquarters, Detective Chief Inspector Quantrill and Detective Sergeant Lloyd were assessing house-to-house reports and witness statements.

The reports revealed that no one had seen or heard anything untoward at or near the Brickyard on the night of the murder. The only significant statements were those of four local drivers, who had all noticed what they thought was a bird-watcher using binoculars to survey the village from the back road between Wyveling and Doddenham on the morning of the day before the murder. Their descriptions differed in detail, but they were agreed that the man's car was old and light-coloured, and that he was short and swarthy. He had not come forward in response to the chief inspector's television appeal, and identifying him had now become a matter of urgency.

'If he's our man,' said Quantrill, 'we've got to revise our thinking, haven't we? We've been assuming that the murder was done by an opportunist burglar, and that the Brickyard was a random target. But this man was sussing out the territory a day in advance. No doubt he could see that the field path would make an ideal way of approach to the properties that back to it, but why should he pick out the Cartwrights' place? Even if he decided in advance that it was the most likely target, when it came to Saturday night he'd have had to pass the back gardens of a dozen other houses, one of which would have been in complete darkness because the occupants were away, in order to reach the Brickyard. No opportunist would do that.'

'It certainly suggests that he knew what he was after,' agreed Hilary. 'He doesn't seem to have found it, though, does he?'

She picked up the list of missing items, and read through it with a deepening frown. 'There's nothing here that's of any serious value or interest – a camera, a couple of very small silver trophies, a chequebook, credit cards, £200 in cash . . . He must have expected to find something more substantial than this. Come to think of it, though, I don't remember having seen anything in the house that looked as though it would be of particular value, apart from the audio and video equipment that most households have.'

'Perhaps the Cartwrights were known – or suspected – to have something valuable hidden away, and the old lady disturbed him before he found it,' said Quantrill.

'Yes . . . But if he murdered the poor old soul because she interrupted his search, why did he bother to take away with him the bits and pieces on this list? You wouldn't think he'd lumber himself with inscribed trophies, and potentially incriminating items like the chequebook and credit cards.'

'At least if he tries to use them we'll have a good chance of catching him. *If* he actually took them, that is,' said Quantrill. 'What I'm beginning to wonder is whether Derek Cartwright's list of missing items isn't a cover-up.'

'For what?'

'For whatever it was the man set out to burgle the Brickyard for. Perhaps he found what he wanted, and Cartwright isn't prepared to own up to having had it in his possession.'

'Then it would have to be something serious,' said Hilary. 'Seriously criminal, I mean, if Cartwright isn't prepared to confess it in order to help us find his mother-in-law's murderer. What do you think? Drugs?'

'No,' said Quantrill decisively. 'He's a family man, and no one who's gone through the anxiety of bringing up children could contemplate dealing in drugs.'

'His children didn't seem all that fond of him, when we met them in the Five Bells,' said Hilary. 'In fact they were ganging up on him, weren't they? It was obvious that they didn't believe a word of his story about what he'd been doing on Saturday afternoon, and I don't blame them. Derek Cartwright isn't at all the pleasant, ordinary, decent man I took him for.'

'Why do you say that? Because he dumped his dog in the forest?'

Hilary shook her head. 'That simply reinforces my opinion of him. No, what bothers me is something we both noticed when we first talked to Cartwright. There seemed to be something disordered about his thinking. Do you remember how enraged he was because his mother-in-law had been raped? His anger was perfectly understandable, up to a point – but his moral priorities seemed to be all wrong. The real horror, for any normal man, would be the fact that she'd been murdered.'

Quantrill had a great respect for his sergeant's opinions on human behaviour. She had qualified as a nurse before changing careers to join the police, and although she often pointed out that she wasn't a psychiatrist he continued to regard her as his expert on the subject. When it came to mothers-in-law, though, he considered himself his own expert.

'There's nothing abnormal', he said sharply, 'if your mother-in-law lives with you, in not being sorry when she dies. But you can certainly regret the *manner* of her death, and that was probably what Cartwright was doing. He couldn't grieve over losing her, but he was angry because of the terrible way it happened. What's odd about that?'

'It would be less odd', argued Hilary, 'if we had any evidence that Derek Cartwright shared your feelings about mothers-in-law. But from what his wife said in our policewoman's hearing, he'd always got on better with her mother than she did. Apparently that's why Christine has been so shattered by her mother's death. Because the two women didn't get on – and in fact quarrelled on their return from Southwold, parting without a kind word – Christine's full of remorse as well as grief.'

'Her husband seems to think she'd have got over her mother's death soon enough, if only it hadn't been so horrifying,' said Quantrill.

'That's exactly what I mean about his thinking being disordered. He told us that Christine would "get over" her mother's death more easily *because* theirs wasn't a loving relationship, but of course the opposite is far more likely to happen. The guilt of having been less than kind to her mother will probably eat away at Chrstine for the rest of her life – and would do even if the old lady had died of natural causes. That's something her husband seems incapable of understanding.'

Douglas Quantrill, who knew all about the persistence of

feelings of guilt, didn't propose to discuss the subject. 'It's not the Cartwrights' relationship I'm interested in,' he said, 'it's what Derek is trying to conceal from us. Once we know why his house was targeted, we may know where to look for the man who broke in. I think we'd better borrow the keys of the Brickyard again and search it thoroughly, including the attics, cellars and outbuildings.'

'And if whatever-it-is has already gone? If the man found what he was after, and Cartwright – as you suggested – made this list as a cover-up?'

'Then we'll probably come across these so-called missing items hidden away somewhere on the property.'

Hilary agreed, and studied the list again. 'The more I look at it, the more suspicious this seems. Cartwright must think we're idiots to believe that a murderer would take these away with him. Or else he's desperately anxious for us not to discover the truth because it would incriminate him in some way.'

'Perhaps he guesses who broke in,' said Quantrill, 'and now that a murder has been committed he's afraid we'll have him as an accessory. Come to think of it, perhaps he *was* an accessory to the break-in. What about that business of dumping the dog? Perhaps his object wasn't to get rid of an unwanted animal, but to make the break-in easier.'

'But why should he want to do that?' said Hilary. 'We can hardly accuse him of planning a fraudulent claim on his insurance, on the strength of this pathetic list of stolen items.'

'Hmm.' Quantrill scratched his jaw. 'It looks as though we're not going to make any headway on this case until we can find out what Derek Cartwright's been up to. We've got no information on him, I suppose?'

'Nothing at all. He's a model citizen, as far as we know.'

'Where is he now?'

'Back at work in Cambridge, and staying in a hotel there. Do you want me to keep an eye on him?'

'Not until we've given his house a thorough going-over. And after that, I'd like you to see what information you can get out of Mrs Cartwright.'

'I rather think that she's a loyal wife,' said Hilary. 'Loyal wives don't usually give much away about their husbands.'

163

'Doesn't that depend', said Quantrill, 'on what the man has actually done?'

22

Derek Cartwright was afraid. He had no doubt that Packer would carry out his threat to get rid of him if he didn't assist in the killing of the man's father-in-law.

He hated the thought of doing so, of course: what decent man wouldn't? And yet, as Packer had reminded him before they parted, Sidney was so handicapped as a result of his stroke that his life had become a burden to him. Remembering the frustration in the old man's eloquent single eye, Derek conceded privately that to give him a massive overdose of insulin might well be an act of mercy.

But he wanted no part of it. True, the role that Packer had allotted him was simple, even inoffensive; but so had been his part in Enid's death, and look what had resulted! He and Christine had already suffered enough from that, and all he wanted now was to be left in peace to sort out his problems with her and restore their former happiness.

Time, though, was not on their side. The possibility that her cancer might recur was Derek's basic fear, more potent than Packer's threat. If Christine were to fall ill, she would need him. He had to stay alive for her sake; and if that meant doing as Packer had said, then he would do it.

Still sitting where Packer had left him, in his car in the Cambridge Post House car-park, Derek looked at his watch. Now that he had made up his mind to do the job, he longed to get the old man out of the way as soon as possible. But Sunday was the appointed day – and here it was only eleven-twenty on Tuesday morning! How was he going to get through such an eternity of time here in Cambridge on his own, without the support of the woman he loved?

There was no way. It couldn't be done. Derek took another decision, started the engine, and turned his car in the direction of home.

Home was where Christine was. He drove along the village street with hardly a glance at the Brickyard, and stopped outside the thatched house on Church Hill. Sylvia Collins, who was taking advantage of a fine April day to repaint her yellow back door with more will than skill, greeted him cheerfully and told him that his wife had just gone out for a walk.

Knowing that Christine was unlikely to have gone through the village, where she would have had to encounter people she knew, Derek set out along the path that ran below the churchyard wall. Although it was no more than two days since he had last walked there with the family, it seemed more like weeks; certainly the vegetation had shot up to knee height, and the lime trees overhanging the wall were in much fuller leaf. There was no sign of Christine there, or on the field path, or in the spinney behind the Five Bells, or on the Doddenham road, but as he returned, walking along the top of the churchyard bank for a better view, he saw from the corner of his eye a movement in the church porch. Christine was there, apparently wandering restlessly from one side to the other.

Derek scrambled over the low wall and hurried towards her, up the gravelled path between the leaning gravestones and the cypresses. It was unfamiliar territory. In all the years they had lived in Wyveling he had been to the flint-built medieval church only once, for the Hardings' daughter's wedding. Christine had been an occasional attender, usually at the major festivals of the Christian year; but religion was one of the things they had never discussed.

As she saw him approach she composed herself and stood still. 'The door's locked,' she greeted him distantly, as though he were a passing stranger who had come to look at the monuments in the church.

Derek entered the porch and tried to turn the iron handle. The massive silver-grey oak door remained firmly closed.

'Ah, there's a notice here that says who holds the key. I'll go and get it for you,' he said.

'Don't bother.'

Christine sat down on the stone bench inside the porch, and stared straight ahead. Her features seemed still numbed by shock; only her hands were mobile, plucking restlessly at the fabric of her skirt.

Derek sat beside her, at a respectful distance but angled so that he could look at her. 'How are you, my love?'

'Physically? All right, thank you.'

They were silent for a few moments. Despite the warmth of the spring day, the interior of the porch was as cold as a stone tomb. Shivering a little, dispirited by Christine's continuing indifference, Derek looked round him at the roof bosses mutilated by ancient vandalism, the damp-stained walls, the faded notices, the worn flagstones, the bird-droppings.

'Let's go somewhere else,' he urged.

'You go if you want to. I didn't ask you to come here.'

'I had to see you. I want to be with you, Chrissie. I can't be happy without you.'

Her shoulders sagged. 'How can you talk of happiness, after what's happened to my mother?'

'Oh my love –'

He stretched his hand towards her. It happened to be his damaged hand, the bandages now disarranged and grimy with use, and the thought crossed his mind that perhaps it was no bad thing to remind her that he had been suffering too. 'I know it's been a terrible shock for you, but the worst is over. We're still us, and now we've got our future to think of.'

Christine shook her head, and said nothing more. She hadn't even noticed his outstretched hand, let alone offered to rebandage it for him. 'Which day am I due to have my stitches out?' he asked presently in a humble voice.

'On Friday. The casualty doctor at the hospital gave me a letter for you to give to the doctor when you go. It's with my things at Sylvia's. I'll drop it in at the health centre for you.'

Derek hoped that this might be an opportunity to prolong their encounter in pleasanter surroundings. 'I'll come back with you to the house for it,' he offered.

'There's no need. I have to go to the health centre anyway, to pick up my prescription before I leave for Derbyshire.'

'You're still set on going there?'

'Yes. I should be fit to drive by the weekend.'

'Oh, Chrissie ... Why can't we go somewhere together?'

She sighed. 'We've been through all that, Derek.'

'Well – if you *must* go away on your own, at least let me drive you there.'

'I'll be perfectly all right, thank you.' She stood up, and for the first time took a look at him. 'Anyway, your hand must make driving painful.'

'It does,' he said, holding it out conspicuously as he got to his feet. 'But I wouldn't mind, if only we were together. I love you, you know that.'

She turned and began to walk away down the churchyard path. He strode after her, and caught at her good arm with his good hand. 'Do you hear me, Christine? *I love you.*'

She pulled away from his grasp and went on walking.

'Sam is still missing,' she said over her shoulder. 'Don't talk to me about love, Derek, until you're prepared to tell me the truth about why you dragged him out to the forest on Saturday afternoon.'

'The dog has nothing to do with this,' he protested, following her out of the churchyard and along Church Hill. 'What I'm concerned about is *us*.'

'I'm concerned about Sam,' she said, 'because he can't look after himself. You can, and so can I.'

She opened the front gate of Mrs Collins's garden, walked through, and shut it against him without another glance.

23

Right, then. *Right*. Derek drained his second glass of whisky. If Christine was more concerned for the wretched dog than she was for him, let her go to Derbyshire on her own. Let her do what she liked. But when she wanted to come back to him, she would have to make the first move, because he was damned if he would plead with her ever again.

It had been a bad afternoon. He had accelerated out of Wyveling in a fury, and spent the next few hours burning up petrol in an attempt to put as great a distance as possible between himself and his wife. At one point, seeing a signpost to Parkeston Quay, he had contemplated driving aboard a ferry bound for Holland. Losing himself on the Continent for a few weeks would not only teach Christine to appreciate him, but would get that bastard Packer off his back as well.

Then he remembered that he hadn't got his passport with him.

Abandoning the idea, he drove back to Cambridge, parked his car at his hotel, and went out for a drink. He needed someone congenial to drink with, though; after the second whisky, it became imperative to find some friends to tell his domestic troubles to. And so he consulted his pocket diary for the phone numbers of two hockey-playing acquaintances who lived in Cambridge, good old Dave and good old Andy, and invited them to join him.

Derek's subsequent recollection of the evening was hazy. The three of them had been in and out of several pubs, back-slapping and drinking and reminiscing. Then his friends had enquired about his bandaged hand, and that had reminded him of what he wanted to tell them: his wife, he heard himself say with a choke of grief, had unaccountably walked out on him.

Good old Dave and good old Andy, as solid a defensive pair as any forward could want behind him, both on and off the pitch, had given him exactly the support he needed. They'd refilled his glass, put fraternal arms across his shoulders, and assured him that if his wife had been misguided enough to leave a first-class husband like him, he was better off without her. Wives were ungrateful, irrational, and nothing but trouble, they said. Think yourself lucky, old mate! Now you're a free man you can spend every evening like this, having a good time with mates who're only too glad of your company.

For as long as it took them to drain their glasses, Derek basked in the glow of alcohol and true friendship. But then good old Dave and good old Andy looked at their watches, said Help, was that the time? and hurried home to their wives and families, leaving him more alone than ever.

He felt emotionally exhausted. Wanting to drown himself in sleep he bought a half bottle of Bell's, for the second evening in succession, to take back to the hotel. But he needn't have bothered. Tanked up already, he passed out on his bed partially clothed before he'd even got the bottle open.

Inevitably, his sleep was bedevilled by bad dreams. When he woke, sweating cold and crying out with anguish, it was because this time the face under his strangling hands was not Enid's, but Christine's.

And there was still the other prospective horror that he had to attend to: getting rid of Packer's poor old father-in-law.

Next morning, as he sat sweating hot in the sauna at the health club, mentally going through Packer's instructions again and again to be sure of getting them right, Derek knew that he couldn't just hang about waiting for Sunday to come.

Today was Wednesday, the day Packer had said he would be driving up to Scotland. Since there would be no fear of meeting him on the old man's property, Derek decided that he might as well go there now, today, to look the place over. It would give him an occupation, as well as easing the way for what he had to do on Sunday.

He showered, dressed, went into Cambridge to buy an

170

Ordnance Survey map from Heffers, and took off for Newmarket. According to the map, the house Packer had pointed out was about four miles south-west of the town, on a minor road that went nowhere in particular.

It wasn't until Derek was within half a mile of the place, on a tree-lined road that led straight to Winter Paddocks, that it occurred to him that he was doing a very risky thing. All he had thought of was the necessity of avoiding Packer; the house was so isolated that he hadn't anticipated being seen by anyone else. Now, with stomach-dipping apprehension, he realized that precisely because the place was isolated, anyone who saw him was likely to notice him.

If he parked his car anywhere near the house while he sneaked round the grounds – as Packer had parked his car by the bridge at Wyveling – he would probably be spotted by a local passer-by who would report the fact to the police as soon as the murder enquiry started. And whereas Packer couldn't be traced through the car he had been driving, Derek could certainly be traced through his.

Alarmed, he decided to turn at the next convenient field entrance and belt back the way he had come. But then he took a deep breath and told himself to calm down. There were no other vehicles on the road at the moment, and the countryside was deserted. What possible risk would be involved in driving slowly past the house and making a mental note of the extent of its grounds, and the whereabouts of the field that the Pony Club would be using as a car-park on Sunday?

He eased his foot off the accelerator. On his right, a tall brick wall joined the road at a right angle and continued for about two hundred yards, its straightness broken by an inward curve towards a pair of ornamental iron gates. The gates were closed. The road was still empty. Derek slowed to a crawl, and prepared to take a good look.

A wide gravelled driveway led to a substantial, square, creeper-covered house set among lawns and flowering shrubs and mature trees. On one side of the drive was a great copper beech, its new leaves a translucent pink in the sunlight. The property was much more attractive than its name suggested, and far more imposing than Derek had imagined. Must be worth a fortune.

171

As he stared, impressed, something moved. The trunk of the copper beech had temporarily obscured his view, and now he saw with alarm that there were people in the gardens less than fifty feet away. A wheelchair with a huddled occupant was coming into sight: the old man in person, being pushed by his daughter, the generously built young woman who was wasted on that bastard Packer. She had evidently heard the car's engine slow, and she was looking questioningly in Derek's direction.

Panicking, he put his foot down and roared away. Fool! What a fool he'd been to take that risk!

How much had she seen? Had she hurried to the gate, identified the make of the car, noticed the colour, taken the number? If she had, then she would be sure to put the police on to him as soon as her father died. God, how could he have been so stupid as to give himself away like that!

He was almost back into Newmarket before he stopped jittering. As his heartbeat steadied, he forced himself to think logically about what had happened. And, logically, he had to admit that it was most unlikely that Belinda Packer would have done any of the things his imagination had suggested.

All right, so she had looked towards the gates when she heard a passing car slow almost to a stop. Well she would, wouldn't she? Quite naturally, she would think that someone had come to call. But the owners of properties as attractive as Winter Paddocks must grow used to having their houses stared at by inquisitive passers-by, and when the car drove off again she would almost certainly have thought nothing more of it. *Of course* she wouldn't have abandoned her father's wheelchair in order to run to the gate to try to identify a passing vehicle!

Panic over.

Or at least, that particular panic was over. Derek's moment of relief evaporated as he remembered that he still had to face Sunday's ordeal. Sneaking up on a defenceless old man in order to swap a mug of orange juice for a deadly overdose of insulin might be a less distasteful way of committing murder than some, but it was still murder, and the thought of it gripped him with fear.

Supposing the old man saw him? Packer had said that his father-in-law always had a sleep after lunch, but what if the telephone were to wake him? True, since the old man couldn't speak intelligibly he wouldn't be able to give the intruder away; but that wasn't the point. Derek was horrified by the thought that, in the act of swapping mugs, he might look up to see Sidney's eloquent single eye fixed accusingly on him.

Would he have the callousness to go through with the swap while his victim watched? Would he have the nerve?

If he didn't, Packer would kill him. But if he did, could he live with what he had done? Or would Sidney Brown's stricken face begin to alternate with Enid's in his already intolerable dreams?

Derek drove on. Too agitated to endure the snarl-up of race-day traffic in Newmarket, he circled back into the countryside. He felt thirsty, dehydrated by last night's intake of alcohol, but although it was after mid-day and the pubs were open they held no attraction for him.

What he really needed was a haven such as he and Christine had once enjoyed at the Brickyard. He longed for peace of mind. He ached for the touch of love.

But the Brickyard days were over, and he had nowhere else to go. With the recent past a nightmare, and nothing in prospect but fear, he hustled through the maze of country roads in a desperate, instinctive search for some way out of his problems.

When he realized that he was back again on the road that led to Winter Paddocks he felt a genuine shock of surprise. He had formed no conscious intention of returning. But now he came to think of it ... Now he came to think of it, this might be where he could find his solution.

He slowed as he approached the entrance, but this time there was no sight of Belinda and her father. His earlier worries about being noticed had gone, and so he pulled in immediately outside the closed gates and switched off his engine.

He knew now, for sure, that he wasn't going to kill Packer's father-in-law. He couldn't possibly bring himself to commit murder; he wasn't that kind of man. And what had just occurred to him was that if Belinda were to see and identify him while he was looking round this afternoon, then the operation would have to be called off. It would be far too risky to go ahead, knowing that Belinda would probably mention his name to the police at the subsequent investigation.

Packer would be furious, of course. Derek would have to ring him on Saturday night to tell him of the 'accidental' encounter, and no doubt the man would give him an earful of invective. But that wouldn't matter. However much Packer might rage about his incompetence, he couldn't accuse him of lack of zeal. As long as Derek hadn't finally refused to take part in the operation, Packer would have no reason to kill him.

Besides, it had begun to seem most unlikely that the man would ever carry out that particular threat.

Having seen Winter Paddocks, Derek felt certain that Packer wasn't trying to get rid of his father-in-law just because the old man was a burden both to himself and to his daughter. What Packer really wanted, without doubt, was access to Sidney's considerable wealth. And in those circumstances, why would he waste his time and ingenuity on killing Derek? Packer's sole concern would surely be to find another way of disposing of his wealthy father-in-law without himself coming under suspicion – and that, reflected Derek with some satisfaction, should take the bastard a long, long time.

The wheelchair had come into view again. Belinda was pushing her father through a distant part of the gardens. With a lightened heart Derek opened the gate and hurried towards them along the sun-warmed gravel paths, past the copper-pink beech, past the blueing racemes of wisteria that covered the side wall of the house, past the sun-room, the tulip-bordered terrace, the lily pond, the lawns. Then, as he drew near the father and daughter, his pace slowed.

He had been seen. The wheelchair was stationary, turned towards him, and the old man was staring at him with a penetrating single eye. But his own gaze was on the tall, fair young woman who stood waiting for him, her heavy-lidded eyes shyly averted but her back straight, her throat splendidly curved, her figure full and strong and whole.

God, she was magnificent –

Now he knew why he had come.

24

At Wyveling, the police were swarming over the Brickyard again. This time they were searching for evidence to support the detectives' theory that Derek Cartwright knew why his house had been targeted for a break-in.

Sergeant Lloyd had of course given Mrs Cartwright a more tactful reason for wanting to borrow the keys of her home. They would like to take a second look round, she had said simply, and Christine had expressed neither surprise nor objection. She herself would need to go back to the Brickyard later in the week, she told the sergeant, to pack what she wanted to take to Derbyshire, but she dreaded going into the house; the police were welcome to borrow the keys again, if that would help them find her mother's murderer.

Christine might have been more concerned had she known exactly what the police intended to do. This time, instead of concentrating on the scene of the crime, they went through the building systematically from the attics to the cellars: investigating every cupboard, moving every article of furniture, emptying bookcases, rolling back carpets, prizing up floorboards, sniffing the contents of containers. When they had finished with the house they turned their attention to the outbuildings, the front yard, the garden and the dustbins.

But nothing came to light that could be regarded in any way as suspicious. In terms of criminality (though not perhaps of housekeeping; Hilary Lloyd, who would have liked her own flat to be immaculate but resented spending her free time on housework, was always heartened to find how much grubbiness lurked in the corners of even the best-kept homes), the Brickyard was clean as a whistle.

There was no evidence that Derek Cartwright had been engaged in any kind of activity that he might want to conceal from the police. Nor was there any sign of the items that Cartwright had listed as having been stolen. Quantrill's theory that he might have hidden them on his property, as a cover for the theft of something incriminating, proved to be completely unfounded.

Sergeant Lloyd was still reluctant to believe that a burglar who had committed murder on the job would have hindered his getaway by taking the goods with him, but she solved her problem by instigating a search of the areas bordering the field path between the back gate of the Brickyard and the car-park of the Five Bells. On Wednesday morning, one of the missing items – an old briefcase in which Derek Cartwright had told them he kept his spare chequebooks and credit cards – was discovered in the spinney at the back of the pub, dumped in a bed of stinging nettles just off the path.

All the other items on Cartwright's list were found inside the briefcase. Presumably, the detectives decided, the villain had filled it and left it ready to take away when he had finished burgling. After being disturbed, and murdering the old lady, he must have snatched up the briefcase as he left the house. Then, on his way back to his car, he must have thought better of taking anything so identifiable with him.

'That answers your query about the missing items,' said Quantrill, 'but it still doesn't explain Cartwright's behaviour. Dumping his dog, and then leaving the pantry window unlocked, just a few hours before the break-in sounds more like collusion than coincidence. But what about his cut hand?'

'Perhaps he staged his own accident, so as to leave the way clear for the break-in,' said Hilary.

'Yes – but in fact he didn't leave the way clear, did he?' Quantrill objected. 'The house wasn't left empty, unfortunately, otherwise we wouldn't be investigating the old lady's murder. But I'm still not convinced that this was an ordinary burglary-gone-wrong. We've been all through the house and we know for sure that there's nothing of special value or interest in it. At the same time, we know that a man answering to the description of the murderer was seen sussing the place out the day before. So what could have brought him here?'

'I suppose it's still possible that he got away with what he wanted,' said Hilary. 'If there'd been any collusion, Cartwright would naturally be reluctant to tell us. Even so, I really would have thought that the murder of his mother-in-law would have shaken him into talking.'

'I'm not so sure about that. P'raps he was only too glad to get rid of her,' suggested the chief inspector with feeling. Life in the Quantrill household was a good deal less harmonious than usual. Bad enough to have had his wife supervising his consumption at every meal; now her mother had commandeered the job, and was doing it with relish. 'P'raps he feels grateful to the man.'

'Do stop being snide about mothers-in-law, Douglas,' protested his sergeant. 'I don't suppose yours likes living with you any more than you like having her there. The least you can do is try to be nice to her – after all, time's on your side.'

'Just as well something is,' muttered Quantrill, rather ashamed of his suggestion. A detective, of all people, understanding the appalling reality of murder and its effect on the bereaved, should know better than to talk about it lightly. But if you didn't, sometimes, the horror of the job would be unbearable.

'What we need,' he went on firmly, 'is some good hard evidence. We both suspect that Cartwright could tell us a lot more, but we're handicapped by not being able to prove that he knew the reason for the break-in. If we can't find some evidence to link him with the man who did it, we'll have to forget about him and start looking for a completely new lead.'

'Do you want me to talk to his wife?'

'No – we'll go to Cambridge and see if we can find out anything about him there. Then we'll pick him up, and start to put on the pressure about what he was *really* doing on Saturday afternoon. You've got the address of his office, Hilary? And the name of the hotel? Right, m'dear, let's get going.'

Derek Cartwright's junior colleagues in the Anchor Life Assurance office had assumed that the regional marketing manager was at home on account of the sudden death of his wife's mother. When the detectives told them that she had in fact been murdered, while her son-in-law was at Yarchester Hospital late on Saturday evening having a cut hand stitched, they were astounded. Derek had come back to the office for an hour or so on Monday afternoon, and had made no mention of the murder!

But then again, they agreed when they'd finished exclaiming, you could understand why: he was probably too shocked to want to talk about it. And now they realized why he'd looked so wretched on Monday – though at the time of course they'd put it down to his injured hand.

Derek Cartwright was well respected. A good boss, said his up-and-coming assistant, demanding maximum effort from the sales force but giving them a hundred per cent encouragement and support. Everyone liked Derek, though he wasn't one for socializing. On the occasions when he spent a day at the office, he wouldn't go to the pub for lunch, but to the Post House health club for a swim. And after work, he always headed straight for home.

His assistant was at a loss to know why Derek should be staying in Cambridge this week. He hadn't mentioned, when he came in on Monday that he intended to do so. Certainly he'd said he was glad to get away from home for a bit, after the upheaval of the old lady's death, and that was understandable. But heaven knew why he was staying on. He hadn't been in touch with the office since Monday, and he'd cancelled all his appointments for the rest of the week.

Talking of cancelled appointments, though, his assistant remembered, Derek had done something very odd on Friday afternoon. He'd kept an appointment with the manager of Lloyd's Bank in Saintsbury in the morning, but he'd failed to keep his afternoon appointment with the personnel director of a brewery, one of the town's major employers. Hadn't cancelled it, though – they'd had a blistering telephone call from the personnel director to say that he just hadn't turned up. 'Str'ordinary. Derek had been trying to sell a new company pension scheme to the brewery for months, and it was unthinkable that he should have forgotten. He'd sack any of the consultants who missed an appointment, no excuses accepted! But then, he'd seemed very edgy for the past couple of weeks. Uptight. Brooding about something. No, his assistant had no idea about what.

Derek Cartwright's pretty secretary agreed about his recent edginess. No, she couldn't imagine what he was doing in Cambridge – she simply couldn't understand why he wasn't at home with his wife at a time like this.

No, she was quite sure that Derek wasn't spending the time with a girlfriend! He was a devoted family man. There were photographs of his wife and the little girl who'd had Downs Syndrome on his desk, and he'd told her all about his family: what the older children were doing, Laurie's sudden death, his wife's fight against cancer. He'd had more than his share of domestic problems. But even so, he wasn't the sort to run after other women. He was a thoroughly *nice* man, who'd never breathed an unkind word against his mother-in-law, which was more than she could say for some of the men in the office. He obviously liked the old lady, so no wonder he was upset over her murder. And as for his earlier edginess, well, she'd put that down to his wife's health.

Yes, she supposed it would be all right if the detectives took a look round Derek's office to see if there was some indication of what he might be doing this week. But she didn't think they'd find anything that would help them; and she was right.

Derek Cartwright wasn't remembered by name at the health club, but both T-shirted supervisors recognized the snapshot that Sergeant Lloyd had appropriated from the family pin-up board in the downstairs cloakroom at the Brickyard. Yes, he came in occasionally on the strength of his company's block membership. In fact he'd been there that morning.

They'd seen much more of him that usual during the course of the past week. On Saturday night they'd been quite worried about him. Saturday? No – p'raps Friday; yes, Friday, that was it.

He'd nearly done himself in on the power-sport equipment. That was something you always had to watch for, middle-aged men trying to prove they were young and giving themselves a heart attack in the process. But this one was very fit for his age.

He'd had a recent assessment, and he'd warmed-up properly, so there was no reason why he shouldn't go through the full routine. But he wasn't merely exercising, he was making himself suffer, and he just wouldn't stop. They'd given him a couple of warnings, and in the end they'd had to haul him off, as much for the club's sake as for his own.

They'd been quite relieved to see him alive and back again on the Saturday morning. He was in again yesterday afternoon, with a heavily bandaged hand – apparently he'd accidentally cut himself. He couldn't swim or exercise because of the hand, but he'd used the sauna and the jacuzzi.

No, he didn't seem to be with anybody on any of his visits. He might well have talked to other people, but they couldn't possibly remember who was there at the same time. Hotel guests were entitled to use the club facilities, so there were always visitors about as well as members. And there was always a lot of chat, especially in the jacuzzi. You can't sit knee-to-knee with a stranger in a hot tub without exchanging the odd word.

Yes, they said, producing the register, everyone using the club has to book in, stating whether they're members or hotel guests. And yes, the hotel does have a photo-copier – no problem.

The shrewdly mature receptionist at the private hotel just round the corner from Derek Cartwright's office was the daughter of the proprietor. She told the detectives that Mr Cartwright had arrived on Monday, asking to take a room for an indefinite period. She had thought it a little odd, because normally he stayed only for the occasional night. He was there last Friday, a most unusual night for him to stay, and he hadn't said a word then about wanting to come back this week.

As a matter of fact, he hadn't looked at all well when he arrived late on Friday evening – both she and her mother had noticed that. He hadn't come down to breakfast on Saturday morning, and he'd seemed very tense and agitated when he paid his bill. For some reason he hadn't used his company credit card, but his own card – most unusual, for a businessman. She'd thought perhaps he had given it to her by mistake, but he said quite forcefully that this was one bill he was paying for himself.

When he came back on Monday night he'd looked even worse, though by that time he had his left hand bandaged so he was probably in pain. And last night he'd come in late, looking dishevelled with drink. Most unusual for any of their guests, and if she hadn't seen it with her own eyes she would never have believed it of Mr Cartwright.

No, she had no idea where he went during the day. Wasn't he at work? She had every reason to suppose that he was coming back tonight, but goodness knows when, or what state he'd be in. Certainly the detectives could take a look at his room – and if they particularly wanted to see Mr Cartwright, she would be only too glad for them to stay until he returned.

Carwright's room revealed nothing of any significance, until the wardrobe was opened. The interior smelled strongly of whisky; clothes had been tossed haphazardly on to the shelves. Stashed away at the back was one half-bottle of whisky, unopened but with the seal roughly broken, and one half-bottle that was empty.

Convinced that Derek Cartwright was a deeply worried man who had been through some on-going crisis ever since Friday afternoon, the detectives decided to accept the owners' daughter's offer. Seated in the hotel's breakfast room, with a pot of tea to keep them going, they worked through the photo-copied pages of the health club register while they waited for Cartwright's return.

25

Derek had never allowed himself, except in the most general way, to acknowledge the attractions of women other than Christine. His reaction to the sight of Belinda Packer took him completely by surprise.

Embarrassed by the fact that she had quickened his pulse, he decided to behave as though they had never met. After all, he had no reason to suppose that their one brief moment of physical contact on that hot afternoon at the roadside had registered with her as it had with him. Perhaps her averted eyes, as she waited in the garden beside her father's wheelchair, indicated nothing more than indifference; perhaps she didn't even remember him.

'Excuse me,' he said courteously, not so much ignoring the old man as too intent to notice him, 'but I was hoping to see Hugh Packer. We have some business to discuss. My name's Derek Cartwright, I'm regional marketing manager for Anchor Life Assurance.'

Belinda lifted her head. As they looked at each other across the wheelchair, almost height-to-height, Derek knew that she did remember. Her blood was rising, suffusing her strong, curved throat and handsome features with a self-conscious red, and she greeted him with artless enthusiasm.

'Oh – it's *you*.'

'Yes,' he said. He was staring at the column of her throat, shocked to see that the skin was marred by a scattering of bruises, some fading, one particularly recent and livid.

'Hugh isn't here.'

'I know.'

'I'm so glad to see you.'

182

The radiance of her greeting temporarily deprived him of his wits. But then a gobble of protest from her father reminded them that they were not alone.

The old man's daughter bent to him immediately. 'You remember Mr Cartwright, Dad? That day when we took you to hospital to have your wrist X-rayed, and then got stuck in a traffic jam on the way back. It was very hot, and Mr. Cartwright – '

'Derek.'

She dazzled him with a glancing smile. ' – Derek kindly helped me move you into the shade. Remember?'

Sidney's single eye indicated recognition. Seeking her further approval, Derek gave him a friendly greeting and asked him about his wrist, even though he knew the answer would be incomprehensible.

'But what about your own hand?' said Belinda with concern.

Derek was so accustomed to its ache, and had so adjusted himself to the inconvenience of driving with bandages on, that he had almost forgotten about the injury. For the past twenty-four hours he had deliberately blocked its cause out of his mind, and he didn't intend to revive the memory now.

'Oh, it's just a bad cut.'

'It needs rebandaging.'

'Yes, I suppose so.' Looking at the bandages, he realized how grubby and loose they had become. He gave an uncertain laugh, wanting to make the most of the opportunity she was so transparently offering, yet half-ashamed of his willingness to be involved. 'It's a bit difficult to do, single-handed.'

'I could do it for you, if you like.'

'Would you?'

'Gladly.'

She was gazing at him with an urgency that went beyond attraction. Her pale eyes under their heavy lids had a beseeching look; they seemed to be signalling distress. And no wonder, poor girl, he thought with compassion, glancing again at her savaged neck. That evil bastard Packer –

With a growing sense of elation, he realized that there was no reason for him to feel ashamed of wanting to linger. Belinda was in trouble; she needed help, and needed it more than she

183

knew. He hadn't angled for her attention for his own sake, but for hers. What decent, honourable man could do less?

Belinda left him in the sun-room with a cup of coffee while she took her father elsewhere to give him his lunch. Then she wheeled in the old man for his afternoon nap, and led Derek through the opulent house to a bathroom where she could attend to his hand. Her first touch made him catch his breath, but although the colour rose again under her skin she kept her eyes on what she was doing. Her hands were large but well-shaped, her fingers deft.

'You're obviously an expert,' he said with admiration as she began to roll off the soiled bandage.

'I always wanted to be a nurse. I started to train, but then I had to give it up to look after Dad.'

There was regret in her voice, and Derek wondered with alarm if he had misinterpreted her unhappiness. Was it her father who was her real problem? Had her husband planned to get rid of the old man as much for Belinda's sake as for the money? With a new lurch of anxiety, he prayed that Belinda wasn't about to encourage him to go ahead with the killing.

'Do you very much resent having to look after your father?' he asked apprehensively.

'I did at first. I missed the company of other girls. And then, I'd grown up to hate Dad's boozy lifestyle. But he was a most affectionate father when I was small, and now that he's dependent on me I see this as my chance to repay him. Oh, I get tired and depressed, and sometimes angry – who doesn't in these circumstances? But I'm not resentful. This is my choice, and I really wouldn't have it any other way.'

Derek breathed again, and Belinda eased the final stained layer of gauze from his hand. 'Good heavens!' she said, counting: 'Eight stitches – how on earth did you get such a bad cut?'

'I was making myself a sandwich. The knife slipped.'

'Ouch, that must have hurt!'

She covered his scored palm with a fresh dressing, and produced a new bandage. 'Er – talking of sandwiches,' she elaborated, 'I usually have one for lunch, after I've fed Dad.

Would you like to – ? I mean, do stay, if you have the time.'
She looked straight at him, blushing again: 'As long as you're
not expected at home, or anything?'

She was trying to discover whether he was married. Elated
by the significance of her question, Derek answered without a
blink. 'I'm not expected anywhere. I'm living in a Cambridge
hotel at the moment – and I'd love to stay, thank you.'

Well, he'd told her the truth, hadn't he? He wouldn't lie to
her, he wasn't that kind of man. All the same, as she
rebandaged his left hand he couldn't help thinking it a piece of
luck that he didn't wear a wedding ring.

'Belinda –

Sharing sandwiches in the sun-room, and keeping down
their voices so as not to disturb her sleeping father, had given
their inconsequential conversation a kind of intimacy. Derek
was reluctant to break it, until she made some reference to her
father's diabetic condition and the need to keep his blood-sugar
in balance with insulin injections.

With jolting dismay he realized that by coming to Winter
Paddocks and making himself known to Belinda he had not,
after all, extricated himself from Packer's plan to kill his
father-in-law. Derek had thought of it as committing murder.
Well, it would be committing murder. But Packer had
cunningly arranged it to seem like a straightforward imbalance
of insulin: death from natural causes. There would be no
suspicious circumstances, and therefore no police investigation.

And if there wasn't going to be a police investigation, it
wouldn't matter that Belinda had met him, would it? She
couldn't possibly connect him with her father's death, and
therefore he wouldn't be able to use this 'accidental' meeting as
an excuse for not committing the murder ... Oh God,
conplication after complication –

But now, as they walked out into the garden, Derek rapidly
devised another stratagem. He had, anyway, intended to warn
Belinda against her husband. With luck – for her sake, and for
his – he might be able to persuade her to take her father away
from Winter Paddocks. Then, on Sunday evening, he could
telephone Packer and say that he had tried to do the job, but
that the old man had gone. The perfect let-out.

He drew a long breath, and embarked. 'Forgive me for asking you this, but are you in love with that husband of yours?'

Startled, she turned to him with wide, nervous eyes. Her hand went instinctively to her throat. 'No! Oh no.'

'Then for God's sake – Look, I'm sorry, but I've met him several times on business and I think he's a very unpredictable, dangerous man. Why do you stay with him?'

'Because we're married,' she said.

'Oh, Belinda!' He could hardly believe that a woman so beautiful could have so little self-esteem.

'I know what you're thinking,' she said, 'and it's true. Hugh married me for money, I knew that all along. But I was lonely in this great house, and I needed someone to help me with Dad – and Hugh can be very charming, you know. At least, he often was, to begin with, until he found out that I haven't any money of my own.'

'And now he's violent with you?'

'He always has been, I suppose ... But more so, lately. He can't bear the thought of having to wait for the money until Dad dies.'

Derek stopped walking. They had reached some stone steps leading down from the terrace to the lawn, and beside the steps was a thicket of lilac bushes, already in full leaf and hinting of colour to come. Presumably this was the shrubbery that Packer had told him to lurk in before swapping the old man's drinking cups.

'Listen, – ' he said, taking her arm to prepare her for the shock. 'You're absolutely right about your husband. He can't bear to wait, and what's more he doesn't intend to. He's already trying to get rid of your father.'

Her eyes grew even wider. 'Get rid – ?'

'Yes. He's planning to give Sidney a massive overdose of insulin. Not to administer it himself, he's too clever for that, but to get someone else to do the job for him.'

'Oh, God – ' Belinda sat down abruptly on the low wall of the terrace. Derek, sitting close beside her, took her hand; she seemed hardly to notice, let alone respond. 'I might have known,' she said dully. 'But, Derek – how do you know?'

'Because he asked me to do it for him.'

186

'What?'

'Don't worry, I'm not going to! Apparently he tried me because no one knows we're acquainted, so he thought I could get away with it. And he seems to be convinced that anyone will do anything for money.'

His carefully thought-out explanation failed to interest her; she was high-coloured, breathing quickly, near to panic. 'Have you told the police?'

'Not yet.' He tried to calm her gasp of protest: 'How can I go to the police? I've got no proof, it would only be my word against your husband's. He'd probably tell them that he meant it as a joke.'

'But you *must* go to them. If Hugh means it – and I'm quite sure he does – then he'll find someone else to do it for him. If you won't tell the police, Derek, I will!'

He hadn't bargained for that response, or for such a display of anger. 'Of course I'm going to tell them,' he said quickly. 'But not while you and your father are still living here, it's too dangerous for you. That's why I came today, while your husband's away, to warn you. He's in Scotland until the end of the week, isn't he?'

'He said he'd be back on Saturday.'

'Right, we'll get you and your father away to safety before then. Where can you go? Relatives?'

'I've some cousins in Ely who sometimes look after Dad so that I can have a break ... Yes, I suppose we could go there. But that'll probably be the first place Hugh will look – he knows they're expecting the two of us to lunch this coming Sunday.'

'So he told me. That's the day he wanted me to dispose of your father. Oh, don't worry, Belinda, everything will be all right. If you'll arrange to go to your cousins' tomorrow, I'll put the police on to your husband just as soon as he returns.'

Derek held her hand in what he hoped was a reassuring grip. In reality, though, he was filled with misgivings. For all her lack of sophistication and self-esteem, Belinda was an intelligent woman. She would expect him to go to the police, and she would know that if he did so they would want to interview her. Derek had no doubt that, when nothing happened, she would go straight to the police herself.

And fool that he was, he had told her his real name and the company he worked for!

It would mean nothing to the Cambridgeshire police. But they would find out that he lived in Suffolk, and as soon as the Suffolk police were told Packer's name, that would be it. Oh God, what a mess . . . Wherever he tried to turn, there was no way out.

Belinda had begun to shiver with delayed shock. Derek put his good arm round her shoulders and gave her a hug. Emotionally, he felt nothing but compassion for her. But the splendid firmness of her body, its youth and warmth, had the immediate effect of reviving his long-suppressed sexual drive.

It also blocked his ability to think. Hounded as he was by guilt and worry and fear, he sought urgently for refuge, a place where he could forget.

'Belinda, dearest – don't cry. Everything will be all right. I'll look after you, I promise.'

'Don't say that,' she objected, pulling away from his encircling arm. 'Don't *say* that.'

'Why not?'

'Because you can't look after me. You're married.'

'I don't see how you can tell.'

She gave a sad, wobbly laugh. 'The nice men always are,' she said, standing up and walking away from him down the garden steps.

Desperate not to lose her, Derek strode after her. 'I'm not lying to you,' he protested. He caught her by the upper arm, forcing her to stop and turn towards him, and as she did so felt her breast brush against his hand. Desire rose, making him reckless. 'Yes, legally I'm married, but not in any other sense. We haven't had sex for a year or more, and now my wife has left me.'

'For someone else?'

'No – she just says she doesn't want to live with me any more. What I told you earlier is the absolute truth. I'm living on my own in a wretched little Cambridge hotel, and I'm every bit as lonely as you are.'

Her eyes were misting over with sympathy, and he took advantage of it,

188

'I hate living in that hotel. I hate being alone, I'm lost. Can I stay here with you tonight, Belinda? Tonight, and tomorrow night?'

'You said I'm to take Dad to Ely tomorrow.'

'No, Friday. Friday will be soon enough.'

'But what will happen after that?'

'We'll work something out.' He drew her to him and began to stroke her hair and kiss her. 'Oh my dearest, it'll be all right. Everything will be all right, I'll look after you, I promise – '

He tightened his arms as though to crush her, and she went rigid with fear. Loosening his hold, he silently cursed that animal Packer for what he had done to her.

But then her fears seemed to dissolve. 'Oh, Derek,' she said, putting her arms round his neck, melting. He could feel all the length and amplitude of her body, magnificent and richly whole, and he knew then that the months of frustration were over, he had found his refuge.

26

In Cambridge, Detective Chief Inspector Quantrill and Detective Sergeant Lloyd were still waiting for their major witness to return to his hotel. During the evening they had made use of Cambridgeshire police facilities to fax the relevant pages of the health club register to the CRO, in the hope of discovering that Derek Cartwright had been using the club as a rendezvous with a known criminal, but the reply had taken them no further forward. None of the names entered during the same period as Derek Cartwright's related to anyone with a criminal record.

At five p.m. the detectives had accepted the hotel proprietor's offer of another pot of tea. At seven p.m. they had gratefully accepted her offer of an extremely late late breakfast. At nine p.m. they recognized that they had outstayed their welcome, and went outside to wait in the chief inspector's Rover.

A number of guests, most of them reps, stiff from a long day's driving, entered the hotel during the course of the evening. Derek Cartwright was not among them.

At ten p.m. Sergeant Lloyd telephoned the Brickyard, on the off-chance that he might have returned to Wyveling, but there was no reply. She then rang Christine's friend, Mrs Collins, putting her enquiry casually so as not to cause alarm, and learned that Derek wasn't there either. He was staying in Cambridge, said Mrs Collins helpfully; Christine knew the name of his hotel, should she ask her?

At eleven p.m. the lights in the hall of the hotel went out. The doors had been locked for the night.

'Blast!' said Quantrill, starting his engine and heading out of the city. 'After all that, the man's done a bunk.'

'His things are still there,' said Hilary.

'Yes, but what do they amount to? A pair of casual trousers, spare shirts and socks, a razor, a toothbrush. Enough to make us waste five hours waiting for him, but nothing to bring him back for if he's scared.'

'We can't be sure that he's scared. Perhaps he's simply staying with his girlfriend.'

'What girlfriend?'

'The one you first thought of. The one you said he might have gone to visit on Saturday afternoon, while his wife and her mother were out.'

'Oh, her. I thought we'd abandoned that theory. Aren't we assuming now that Cartwright went to the forest to get rid of the dog?'

'Yes, and we're also assuming that he did it in preparation for the break-in. But the only evidence of collusion we can find is circumstantial, and I'm beginning to wonder whether there isn't another explanation for that. We know he had a row with his wife when he came home on Saturday evening without the dog. If he was also feeling guilty about a secret girlfriend, then he must have had a lot on his mind. Perhaps it's not surprising that he forgot to lock the pantry window, and was clumsy enough to cut his hand.'

'But that doesn't account for his peculiar behaviour on Friday – forgetting an important business appointment, half-killing himself on the power equipment at the health club ... '

'Oh, but it does account for it,' said Sergeant Lloyd. 'If you were right about his girlfriend, and his secretary is right about his being a good family man, then he must be going through a terrible emotional conflict.'

She sighed impatiently. 'It's probably the usual story: the girlfriend's putting pressure on him to leave his wife, but he won't; and on the other hand, he can't bring himself to give up the girl. I haven't any time for men who try to have it both ways – it's so juvenile. Though I will say this for Derek Cartwright,' she added more fairly, 'at least he seems to have the decency to know he's behaving badly, and to be putting himself through hell on account of it.'

Quantrill thought it prudent, on behalf of the misunderstood male sex, to concentrate on his night driving and maintain a dignified silence. At home, his mother-in-law – between bouts of dietary instruction – was driving him mad with men-are-so-selfish earfuls, and he could do without any contributions from Hilary; even if she happened to be right, as well as relevant.

'Sorry, Douglas,' said his sergeant, leaving him to decide whether she was apologizing for what she had said, or for her abandonment of the collusion theory.

'So what you're suggesting now,' he said, 'is that Derek Cartwright really does know nothing about the break-in. Well, you may be right – but that still doesn't explain why the Brickyard should have been targeted, does it?'

Hilary gave another sigh, this time perplexed. 'The only reason I can think of is that it's a substantial house, set well back from the road. The man with the binoculars must have thought that he could slip in by way of the field path, pile up the loot, and then bring in a vehicle and load it up without being noticed.'

'But *what* loot? Who'd go to all that trouble, just to steal a video recorder and a hi-fi, and some unremarkable bits and pieces?'

'I know, it simply doesn't make sense ... Just what did the man go there hoping to gain? As far as we've been able to discover, nothing in particular.'

Quantrill's headlights picked up the sign for the Breckham Market turn-off. As he left the busy A45, and thought for a moment of the pleasures and turn-offs of home, it occurred to him that there was in fact one person who had made a clear gain out of what had happened at the Brickyard: Derek Cartwright, who had been relieved of the company of his wife's mother.

But Hilary would never forgive him if he made another tasteless gibe about mothers-in-law. And because he too wanted to have it both ways – Hilary's friendship, at least, as well as the better parts of marriage – he kept his thoughts to himself.

27

On Thursday morning, Christine Cartwright drove her car for the first time since her mother's murder.

She still felt weak-kneed and shaken, but she was determined to do it. Sylvia Collins had been wonderfully kind, and had urged her not to think of leaving the thatched house before she was really fit, but Christine knew that if she didn't make the effort now she would find it even more difficult later. Besides, much as she liked Sylvia, she was anxious to get away to Derbyshire. She needed to be alone.

She hoped to be ready to travel on Sunday, a day she had chosen so as to avoid the worst of the heavy traffic in the industrial Midlands. If she used the car every day between now and then, gradually rebuilding her confidence, she thought she would be able to manage the distance. Her first trip, she decided, would be very short: to Breckham Market, eight miles away, where she had made an appointment to visit her doctor.

She had been so groggy during the past few days that she was beyond knowing whether the cause was physical or emotional. As a recent cancer sufferer, she had inevitably become more aware of her body's signals. Although she tried to be calm and practical about it, she couldn't help fearing that any persistent ache or minor pain, any feeling of nausea or weakness, might herald the onset of the dreaded secondaries. Her present discomforts were, she told herself, almost certainly emotional in origin, but it seemed wise to have a check-up before she went away.

Like most families in Wyveling, the Cartwrights were registered with the nearest group medical practice. This had advantages, in that the practice was housed in a purpose-built health centre with excellent community-care facilities, but a disadvantage was that the patients never knew which of the five doctors they would see. Christine acknowledged the efficiency of the system, but she found it impersonal, and she was disappointed that there was no woman doctor in the practice.

The one permanent figure at the health centre seemed to be the receptionist, who sat at a desk in the busy waiting-room with her name displayed on a badge: Mrs Molly Quantrill. She was a plumply pretty woman in her late forties, carefully coiffured and fussily dressed. She looked up as Christine entered and gave her a big smile of recognition.

'Good morning, Mrs Cartwright! I do hope you're keeping well. Lovely weather for April, isn't it?' Then her face crumpled in dismay; clearly, she had just remembered that Christine's mother had been murdered only a few days previously.

Pink with embarrassment, she jumped up and patted Christine on the arm. 'Oh – I am most terribly sorry, my dear! Such a dreadful thing to have happened, and after all you've gone through, too – '

Christine nodded, finding it difficult to speak. But Mrs Quantrill couldn't stop: 'Of course, I only know what I read in the local paper,' she said hastily, guiding Christine to a chair. 'I don't hear any of the details – my husband doesn't talk about his work at home, I can assure you of that. You'll have met him, I suppose? Detective Chief Inspector Quantrill.'

She said it with some pride, and Christine nodded again. The events of the weekend had conjoined into one hideous blur, but she could vaguely associate the name with a large man who had spoken to her at one point. 'Yes, I remember him. He was very kind – '

But then, everyone had been very kind. She had been swamped with kindness ever since her mother's death, and she found that this was one of the hardest things to bear.

Christine knew that she didn't deserve such kindness. She felt an impostor. How could people – not only friends and neighbours, but the police as well – freely bestow so much kindness on her when she, Enid Long's only child, had been so unkind to her own mother? Unkind even on the day of Enid's death, when she'd been so angry with her mother for refusing

194

even to look at her Southwold flat that they had travelled back to Wyveling in furious silence. So unkind that she had allowed her mother to go off to bed without attempting to make amends, or even wishing her good-night.

It was a terrible thing, to have parted for ever in such petty anger. Christine didn't know how she was going to live with it. She had already been racked by guilt on two occasions, but each time she had been able to take some positive action: first by devoting herself to Laurie's upbringing, then by taking her mother into her home. But what could she do now? Her life had suddenly been emptied of all purpose.

She had her husband, of course, but Derek wasn't dependent on her. He was perfectly capable of looking after himself. Dear Derek – he was such a good husband and he'd done his best to help her through this crisis, but he simply couldn't understand her relationship with her mother. He seemed to think she didn't care – though to be fair to him, it was only now her mother was dead that Christine herself had come to realize just how much she cared. And now it was too late to say so.

That was why she'd had to part company with Derek, temporarily: because he couldn't begin to understand her shock and grief and remorse. She knew she had hurt him, and she was sorry; she'd tried to explain that this was nothing to do with him, but he didn't seem able to take it in, and she couldn't go on explaining. At least he'd got his work to keep him busy, just for two or three weeks while she went to Derbyshire to sort herself out away from all this terrible local kindness. She had told her friend Trish that her mother had recently died, but she certainly didn't intend to reveal to her how it had happened.

'Mrs Cartwright, dear!'

Molly Quantrill, her soft brown eyes brimming with sympathy, was calling her for her appointment. 'Dr Rogers will see you now.'

Christine was sorry that it was Dr Rogers, her least favourite among the partners. It was he who had first examined her after Derek had felt the lump in her breast. Dr Rogers had always been most reassuring, but he was what her medical-student daughter Lyn spoke of scathingly as a paternalistic male doctor. He didn't encourage his patients to express their views, and

Christine had never felt able to talk to him. Besides, she disliked his bristling eyebrows and unhygienic moustache.

He too greeted her with kindness, and offered his sympathy on her bereavement. He enquired after her general health, took her temperature and pulse, listened to her lop-sided chest, asked her a number of specific questions, and told her that she seemed to be in satisfactory physical health after her treatment. But when Christine said that she proposed to drive to Derbyshire on Sunday for a holiday, he vetoed it sternly.

A holiday, certainly, he agreed; but it was much too soon after her mother's tragic death for her to go careering off on her own. She had been badly shocked, and shocks like that took a long time to get over. Couldn't her husband take her? Well, if he was too busy at the moment, why not wait until he could spare the time? Much the best thing for her to stay quietly at home and give herself a chance to recover.

Christine said nothing. What was the point? As long as her health was satisfactory, she intended to go to Derbyshire as planned. She would be sensible about it, taking the drive slowly and making frequent breaks; all she really needed from Dr Rogers was a repeat prescription for the tablets she had had to take since her treatment ended.

As he wrote out the prescription, Christine remembered that she still had in her handbag a letter addressed to the practice.

'My husband will be coming in tomorrow to have some stitches taken out,' she said. 'He cut his hand rather badly on Saturday night, and some friends took him to the hospital casualty department. The doctor who stitched him up gave me this letter for you.'

Dr Rogers opened the envelope and glanced at the scrawled note it contained. Christine, standing and buttoning her coat, saw that he was frowning. 'Er – sit down, please, Mrs Cartwright,' he said abstractedly, reading the note again and gnawing at his moustache.

Christine sat down, puzzled, while the doctor read it a third time.

'I don't believe I've met your husband,' he said.

'Probably not. He's one of those lucky people who're never ill.'

'Is he a worrier? Any business problems, would you say?'

Well, of course Derek was a worrier. Why else would he have those bad dreams that woke him, twitching and sweating and whimpering, night after night? But she wasn't going to tell Dr Rogers that.

'My husband has a responsible job, and I've no doubt he does have the occasional worry. Why do you ask?'

'And what about your personal relationship?'

Their personal relationship was most certainly not a subject that Christine wanted to discuss with Dr Rogers. 'What about it?' she replied civilly.

'Mrs Cartwright – ' said the doctor slowly, swivelling in his chair. He was so clearly searching for words that Christine began to feel alarmed. 'There are some people who find it almost impossible to talk about their problems. But when they reach a point of desperation, they sometimes put out what we call a cry for help.'

Christine stared at him, the surface of her mind irritated by the condescension of the doctor's 'what we call' phrase, the rest of it swamped by anxiety.

'Do you mean – ? Are you trying to tell me that Derek's cut was a suicide attempt?'

'No, no. Please don't imagine that. There was nothing potentially life-threatening about the injury. But I'm afraid – according to the doctor who stitched them – that the cuts were self-inflicted.'

Christine could have laughed with relief. 'But we know that! Derek went out to the kitchen to make himself a sandwich. He was carving a joint of cold meat, and the knife slipped, so of course it was self – ' She paused. 'Did you say *cuts*? Plural?'

'I'm afraid so. One cut can be accidental, but a second cut almost – but not exactly – in the same place can only be deliberate. That's the reason for this note. We don't want your husband to do anything quite so drastic again, do we? And now we know about it, perhaps we can try to relieve some of his problems.'

Christine nodded dumbly. *Poor Derek* was all she could think, gulping at the glass of water the doctor offered her; *my poor Dee*.

'When your husband comes to have his stitches out,' continued Dr Rogers, 'whichever partner sees him will try to find out what's wrong. But if, as I rather suspect, it's a personal matter – ' he quirked his eyebrows at Christine' – then you are the only one who can help him,'

'What makes you think it's personal?' she said dazedly.

'Oh, come, Mrs Cartwright – here you are, badly shocked less than a week after a tragic bereavement, and your husband is too busy at work to take you away? So busy that he can't even spare the time next Sunday to do the driving for you?'

He put a kindly hand under her elbow and led her to the door. 'Try some bridge-building,' he advised. 'And if you can't do it on your own, ask Mrs Quantrill for the address of the Marriage Guidance Council.'

The doctor had handed her over to his receptionist, saying that Mrs Cartwright needed a quiet rest before she drove home. Mrs Quantrill had taken her to a small side room, and had trotted in a few moments later with a cup of tea.

Resting on an examination couch, Christine drank her tea and wept. After a time, having decided what she must do, she wiped her eyes and combed her hair and went to the pay-phone in the foyer.

First she rang Derek's office, and discovered that they had heard nothing from him since Monday.

Then she rang directory enquiries, and asked for the number of his hotel. She was greatly relieved when the hotel receptionist confirmed that he was staying there, but her relief turned to anxiety when she learned that although Derek's things were still in his room, he had not slept there the previous night.

She began to panic. Oh God, what had happened to him? Was he so desperate because she had ignored his appeals that he was now seriously contemplating killing himself? Oh no, not that –

Her hands were shaking so much that it was difficult to search through her bag, but eventually she found what she was looking for. 'If there's anything you want to know, or if you need to talk,' Val the policewoman had said as she gave her the printed card, 'just ring me.'

Without a moment's hesitation, Christine dialled the number of Breckham Market divisional police headquarters.

198

28

Chief Inspector Quantrill was not best pleased to have been excluded by Sergeant Lloyd and WPC Thornton from their long conversation with Christine Cartwright. Christine would probably talk more freely without him there, Hilary had said, adding that the three of them were going to do it over morning coffee in the comfort of Breckham Market's best hotel.

'Well?' he demanded impatiently, when she returned to the office. 'Does Mrs Cartwright know where her husband is?'

'No, she has no more idea than we have,' said Hilary. 'Quite genuinely, I mean. She's not doing a cover-up for him, Val and I are both confident of that.'

'Why does she think he deliberately cut himself?'

'Like us, she assumes that he must be having an affair. It's very difficult for her to admit it, after umpteen years of what she thought of as an ideally happy marriage, but that's what she realized on Saturday, when he was so obviously lying about why he took the dog out in the rain. She sees the business of cutting his hand as a cry for help after the row they'd had.'

'Humph,' said Quantrill, who regarded such goings-on as wimpish. 'Still,' he admitted, 'it must have taken a hell of a lot of courage for the man to make an initial cut, and then enlarge it – '

'Yes. But I can believe that he might have put himself through the ordeal because of a deep emotional conflict. I can't believe he'd do it just to facilitate a break-in.'

Quantrill agreed, but pensively. 'And what about Cartwright's disappearance last night? How does his wife account for that?'

'Emotional conflict, again,' said Hilary. 'Apparently she went right off her husband after her mother's murder. It was nothing to do with him, it was her relationship with her mother that was the problem, but in effect she brushed him off when he was seeking a reconciliation. When she heard that the cuts were deliberate, she thought immediately that he must have taken her withdrawal to heart. Val and I have tried to persuade her that he wouldn't have done anything suicidal, but that leaves her convinced of the other possibility – that he's gone back to the girlfriend.'

'And that's what you think?'

'Yes. But I'd feel easier if we put out an alert for him, just in case he's contemplating anything stupid.'

'I agree about the alert,' said Quantrill, 'but for a different reason. This case smells to me of collusion. I don't want his wife to be alarmed, but we need to find Derek Cartwright as soon as possible and sort him out. I want him to be either completely eliminated, or charged.'

'Charged with what?'

'You're not going to like this, Hilary. I know you've told me to stop going on about mothers-in-law, but this case doesn't begin to make sense unless we reverse our previous assumptions. Perhaps Derek Cartwright wasn't colluding with a burglar who just happened to kill the old lady. Perhaps he arranged the burglary as a cover for his mother-in-law's murder.'

An alert went out on local radio and television on Thursday evening, saying that the police were anxious to know the whereabouts of Derek James Cartwright of Wyveling, last seen in the Cambridge area and known to be driving a slate-blue Ford Sierra, registration number F 285 KAH.

But in the rural isolation of Winter Paddocks, the car was securely garaged, and Derek and Belinda were neither listening to the radio nor watching television.

29

Douglas Quantrill had devised a master plan to enable him to keep both his sanity and his temper while his mother-in-law was in occupation of his home. Quite simply, it involved staying right out of her way.

So far, it had worked. The bungalow was large enough for him to dodge her, and his irregular hours meant that he could make a point of avoiding her regular meal-times. But Thursday evening was going to be different: Alison, his favourite daughter, who lived and worked in Yarchester, was coming home to see her grandmother. Molly had arranged a family supper for the occasion, and Quantrill was much too fond of Alison to attempt to duck out of it.

At first it went reasonably well. Quantrill let the others do all the talking and embarked on his meal in peace, proudly aware of what a lovely girl Alison was, and observing how affectionately and patiently she dealt with her grandmother. But then he made the mistake of asking Peter to pass the salt.

His mother-in-law immediately upbraided him for eating too much salt. It was very bad for a man of his age, she informed him. He was simply asking to be carried off by a heart attack – and who would provide for his wife and family then, she would like to know?

Molly looked embarrassed. Peter snickered. Intolerably provoked, Quantrill slapped down his knife and fork.

'It may surprise you, Phyllis, but I've made ample provision for my family in the event of my premature death. And now if you'll excuse me I've got some work to do. I'm trying to find a man who's killed his mother-in-law – and frankly, there are times when I feel considerable sympathy for him.'

Fuming, he stalked out to the kitchen. Alison followed him almost immediately, and slipped her arm fondly through his. 'Oh, Dad – '

'I can't stand it,' he declared. 'I cannot stand it. Dammit, Alison, why should I have to put up with it, in my own house?'

'I know . . . it's very hard on you. But she's an old lady, you must try to be patient with her.'

'Hah! Being old's got nothing to do with it, she's been like it ever since I've known her.'

'Well, I'm afraid you'll just have to try to bear it, for Mum's sake. It's part of family life, isn't it? One of the good parts, with the generations taking it in turns to look after each other. Even you'll be old one day, Dad.'

'Thanks for reminding me. That's all I need to cheer me up.'

Alison gave his arm a sympathetic squeeze. 'Is the murder case going badly?'

'Oh, I dunno. It's frustrating, as much as anything.'

'Did the man really kill his mother-in-law?'

'Not directly, but we suspect he put someone else up to it. He certainly cleared the way, if nothing else. It was very cleverly done. I doubt we'll ever catch the actual murderer, except through the victim's son-in-law. And we still haven't enough evidence to charge him when we find him, we'll have to rely on getting a confession.'

'Why did he want to murder his mother-in-law? For money?'

'No, or we'd have suspected him sooner. But then, I should have realized that you don't need any specific motive for wanting to get rid of your mother-in-law. The fact that she's *there* is motive enough.'

Alison snatched away her arm. 'That's not funny.'

'It's not meant to be. It's just an observation.'

'Well, it's a very mean one. And you really ought to apologize to Grandma for what you said.'

'No, I'm damned if I will! She started it.'

'I know, and I'm going to have a quiet word with her about that before I go. But only if you promise never to let fly at her like that again.'

'Oh – all right, if you insist. Anyway, I suppose I should be grateful to her for pointing me in the right direction on this case.'

'That's my nice Dad. For that, you can rely on me to look after you when you're a cantankerous old man.'

'That'll be a comfort. But don't forget that it'll be rough on your husband, whoever he's going to be. He's not likely to take kindly to having a father-in-law in residence, is he?'

'He'll just have to put up with it,' she said firmly. Then she chuckled. 'Tell you what, Dad. Supposing I marry Martin – '

'You won't!' said her father, appalled. Martin Tait was the least favourite of his colleagues, a vaultingly ambitious university graduate who, in the space of five years, had soared from sergeant to detective chief inspector without ever having got his feet wet.

'I might,' said Alison. 'And if I do, and he becomes a chief constable – just think what a marvellous time you'll have when you're old, driving him mad by giving him the benefit of your experience!'

Undeniably tickled by the idea, Quantrill went to answer the telephone. The caller was Hilary Lloyd.

'Douglas – I'm at the office. Thought you'd like to know that the Cartwrights' dog has been found.'

'Has it?' He was only mildly interested. 'Well, I'm glad for Mrs Cartwright's sake. That should cheer her up a bit.'

'Yes, but that's not all. Things are looking up for us, too. There's some useful information with it.'

'I'm on my way,' said Quantrill.

Hilary navigated him through forest darkness towards the boarding kennels from where the information had come.

'A Mrs Rachel Dean rang the station this afternoon,' she said, 'saying that a young couple had just arrived at her kennels with a beagle they'd found wandering in the forest on Sunday. A PC went to collect it, and she told him what the couple had told her: the beagle wasn't wearing a collar, and they thought it had probably been dumped. They were sorry for it, and decided to give it a good home.

'Two days later, they saw the press release about the Cartwrights' missing beagle. By that time, though, they'd fallen in love with it. And because the press release said that the missing dog was wearing a tartan collar, and the one they'd found was collarless, they kidded themselves that it wasn't the same dog.

'But then their consciences smote them – particularly as the press release said that Mrs Cartwright's mother had been murdered. So they decided, today, to turn the dog in. But they were afraid of getting into trouble for not doing so earlier, and instead of ringing us they took it anonymously to the nearest boarding kennels.'

'If Cartwright removed the dog's collar,' said Quantrill, 'it certainly sounds as though he abandoned it intentionally.'

'Yes – but our information's even more interesting than that. The PC says that Mrs Dean told him that a man called there on Saturday afternoon wanting to leave a dog for just one night. He gave his name as David Carter, and his address as Flint Cottage, Fodderstone.'

'Did he? And does anyone of that name live at that address?'

'No, it's a false one. There's no one by the name of Carter in Fodderstone, and what's more there isn't even a place called Flint Cottage.'

'But was the dog a beagle?'

'Mrs Dean can't recall. For some reason she refused to take it. But I'm sure the man must have been Cartwright, and that he dumped the beagle as an alternative way of geting rid of it while the murder was taking place. If Mrs Dean can identify him, we'll really have him in a corner.'

Barn Farm Boarding Kennels was not easy to find in the dark, but Hilary was a good navigator. Quantrill eased his Rover up the pot-holed track and stopped at the farm gate, leaving his headlights on to enable them to read the assorted notices. Hilary got out, approached the hut labelled *Reception*, and rang the bell.

A light came on in the porch of the farmhouse on the other side of the yard, and from somewhere among the dark outbuildings a couple of dogs began to bark. Presently a small muffled figure came towards them, flashing a torch. 'We're from the county police,' called out Hilary reassuringly. 'Is that you, Mrs Dean?'

The detectives followed her into the hut, blinking in the sudden light, and apologized for disturbing her. 'Thad's all ri',' she gasped heroically, through a cold and a chesty cough. It was obvious that she had a temperature; she was radiating heat like a mobile gas stove. When Hilary commiserated with her she explained that she'd had her cold since before the weekend, and that her husband was even worse, but they were taking it in turns to keep going because of the animals.

Quantrill began to question her about the man who had brought in the dog on Saturday, but it soon became clear that she was in no fit state to identify him. She peered with bleary-eyed willingness at the photograph Hilary showed her, but couldn't recall having seen the man before. 'I didn't take in his appearance,' she explained. 'Except that he was wearing a suit. I remember thinking that it was ridiculous for him to have come out to a place like this on a wet afternoon in a light grey suit.'

'Did he say what breed his dog was?' asked Hilary.

'No – I started to fill in the register, as you see, but we didn't get as far as the breed. When he said he hadn't brought the vaccination certificate, I had to refuse to take the dog in.'

Rachel Dean turned aside to smother a cough. The detectives glanced at each other, reluctant to go on bothering her but tantalized by her reference to the man's clothes. One of Cartwright's family had mentioned, when they were grilling their father at the pub, that he had gone to the forest in his business suit.

'Did he say why he hadn't brought the vaccination certificate?' asked Quantrill

'Only that they'd never boarded the dog before. He was so persistent – aggressive, even. I nearly gave in when he explained why, because I felt sorry for him. But then he tried to bribe me, offering a week's money if I'd keep the dog for just one night, and what with my cold and everything I felt I'd had enough.'

'Why did you feel sorry for him?' said Hilary.

'Because he told me it was a family emergency. He was desperate to get somewhere-or-other as quickly as possible, because of his wife's mother. He said that she wasn't expected to live through the night.'

30

Belinda Packer was mortified.

The afternoon and evening of Wednesday, when Derek had
come to Winter Paddocks for the specific purpose of rescuing
her from Hugh and then had swept her into his arms, had been
the happiest hours of her whole life. Derek was everything she
admired in a man — tall (taller even than she was),
good-looking, ardent, but also gentle and considerate;
romantic, but at the same time thoughtful and honourable. The
nicest possible kind of man, the potential husband she had
always longed for.

Their first embrace had been so passionate that if Derek had
wanted to take her there and then, in the garden just below the
terrace, Belinda would have yielded to him. But, considerate of
her reputation, he had asked if any domestic staff were about.
There weren't, because she had help only in the mornings, but
that had reminded her that her father might need her. Mutely,
they had agreed to contain themselves, and she had drifted
through the rest of the day's duties in a haze of happiness,
knowing that the night was going to be theirs.

And when the night came, and they shared her bed, she was
so entranced that she didn't mind that Derek's initial ardour
had abated. (After all, she'd had more than enough of that kind
of thing from Hugh.) It didn't matter a bit, she assured Derek
truthfully; really, she would much rather just relax in his arms,
and touch and smile and talk.

What demolished her romantic dreams was the discovery
that the only person Derek wanted to talk about was his wife.

On Friday morning Christine decided to return to the Brickyard for a complete change of clothes. What gave her the courage to go back to the house, for the first time since her mother's murder, was the fact that Sam was with her.

Val, the policewoman, had come to the thatched house the night before, saying that a collarless beagle had been found in the forest. Could she identify it, Val had asked? But Sam himself had provided instant identification, hurling himself at his mistress with flailing rudder and barks of joy. Christine had hardly known whether to laugh or to weep, so she had done both, and now she felt revived.

She was still extremely worried by her husband's disappearance, but at least that gave her something to think about other than her mother's murder. She was thankful that the police were trying to find Derek, and reassured by Val's promise to let her know as soon as there was any news.

As she entered the house, uneasily alert to its alien atmosphere but heartened by Sam's company, she concentrated her mind on her husband. Which alternative did she prefer: that Derek was so distressed by her apparent rejection of him that this time he had made a much more serious cry for help? Or that he was perfectly well, and staying with another woman?

Either way, it seemed to her, the once-secure foundation of her marriage had been badly shaken. Derek had always been so strong, such a rock in times of trouble – and heaven knew there'd been more than enough of those. If he'd finally cracked, she couldn't be surprised. If he was so frustrated that he'd found another lover, she couldn't entirely blame him. But whichever it was, she knew that she could never rely on him again.

She was still fond of him, of course; but things would never be the same. How could they be, after all that had happened? As she went through the house collecting soiled linen, staying upstairs for as little time as possible and averting her eyes from the door of her mother's room, she found that she was already mentally sorting and packing her possessions, preparing to move out.

She was in the kitchen, having fed Sam and now feeding the washing machine, when the front-door bell rang. A large young woman stood outside in the gravelled yard, not on the doorstep but several feet away, as though she did not expect to be welcomed.

'Mrs Cartwright?' the caller said nervously.

'Yes?'

'My name's Belinda Packer. I – er – '

She seemed incapable of continuing; but Christine knew instantly who she was, and why Derek had gone missing.

The girl was young enough to be their daughter, but that was only to be expected. Her thin skin and wispy hair and pale, beseechingly blue eyes detracted from what might have been a stunning beauty, but Christine knew that it wasn't only the girl's face that would have attracted Derek. She had never before had cause to be jealous, but now she found herself bitterly resenting this full-bosomed stranger for being in possession of what she had lost.

'I suppose you're Derek's girlfriend?' she said harshly.

Belinda Packer seemed taken aback. 'Oh, well – I wouldn't exactly put it like that,' she said apprehensively. 'I mean, we only met – met properly, that is, apart from in a traffic jam – on Wednesday. And we're not – we haven't – I mean, he loves you far too much to be unfaithful to you.'

'Where is he?' said Christine, still annoyed but rather less so with the girl than with Derek.

'I'm not quite sure, at the moment. He's been staying with my father and me, near Newmarket, but we parted this morning. He thinks I'm going straight to Ely, where we took Dad yesterday, but I felt I had to come to you first.'

'Is he all right?'

'Yes, apart from his hand. Well, physically all right. But he's in a dreadfully mixed-up state, not just about really loving you, but about other problems. He's been having terrible nightmares, and I don't know how to help him – except to beg you to let him come back home.'

Christine sighed. Then she gave the girl a wry smile. 'I think you'd better come in and tell me about it.'

31

Derek could find no way out of his problems. Every stratagem he tried resulted in different worries, fresh complications.

Persuading Belinda to remove her father from Winter Paddocks had seemed to free him from carrying out Packer's plan to murder the old man. But then he'd realized that Belinda would insist on telling the police of her husband's intentions, innocently informing them that Hugh had tried to involve Derek Cartwright of Anchor Life.

He had done his best to get out of that one by helping her take her father, on Thursday, to stay with their Ely relatives. While Belinda settled her father in, Derek pretended that he was going to the police station to tell them what he knew about Hugh.

Afterwards, when they met at the Lamb for a drink before returning to Newmarket, Belinda had wanted to know exactly what he had said to the police, and what they had said to him. Fortunately he was getting better at constructive lying. He told her that he had given the police a full statement, and convinced her that everything was now under control and there was nothing she needed to do.

At least he hoped he'd convinced her. But how could he be sure? He knew that he'd been over-elaborating, and that Belinda had looked at him several times with concern. Did she guess that he was lying? And if so, would she get in touch with the police herself as soon as he'd left her?

It was this fear that had made him suggest that they should still spend Thursday night together at Winter Paddocks. It would give Belinda a break from her father, he said, and it would be very much nicer for him than going back to his

Cambridge hotel. No complications this time, he promised; just friendship.

And that had worked, on one level, staving off at least some of his worries for a few hours. Belinda had been very sweet to him. But when she announced that she would of course tell her solicitor about Hugh, Derek knew that his chances of going unmentioned were lessening.

He'd begged her not to involve him – for fear, he said, of disrupting his chances of a reconciliation with his wife. But although Belinda sympathized and agreed, he felt that it was unrealistic to expect her to be more concerned about him than about her husband's threats. It could only be a matter of time before the police were alerted, and began to connect his name with Hugh Packer's.

Even if Belinda did her best to shield him, there was still Packer himself to be feared. What would the man do when he returned to Winter Paddocks and found his father-in-law gone? He couldn't blame Derek for it, or for the fact that the original plan for murdering the old man on Sunday was now off. But Hugh Packer wouldn't just give up. He wouldn't abandon his plan because his father-in-law wasn't at home on one particular day, he'd simply switch it to a later date.

Packer wouldn't consider using any other accomplice, either. Why should he, when he'd already got Derek Cartwright stitched up? No, it would be a repeat of the same old situation, with the evil bastard following him wherever he went and hounding him until he did the job. There would be no release from Packer, Derek knew that now, until he had committed the murder.

On Friday morning, after the inevitably dream-tormented night – spent this time in Belinda's spare room – Derek parted from her with some relief. She was a splendid, generous girl, and he knew he'd done the honourable thing by warning her against her husband; but he wished to God he hadn't jeopardized his own security in the process.

Now, though, all the thoughts and emotions he could detach from his private problems centred on Christine. He loved her. He needed her. He wanted to go home.

But did she love and need him? And anyway, where was

home? For him, it would always be with her, wherever she was. But supposing she wouldn't allow that? Suppposing she still rejected him – what was he to do?

All that he knew for sure was that he had to go to Christine, as soon as possible, and attempt a reconciliation.

He gave Belinda a hasty, absent-minded farewell hug. Then he opened the double gates, watched her drive Sidney's Rolls through (with a moment's regret that yesterday, when he'd driven the powerful car for her and her father, he'd been too fraught to enjoy the experience) and waved her away to Ely. He had already moved his Sierra out of the garage block, locked the doors and given Belinda the keys. Now, returning to his car, he discovered that he had a flat tyre.

Cursing, and hampered by his still-aching hand, he pulled off his jacket and got down to the job of changing the tyre. It would have been just his luck to have had to do it in the rain, but in fact it was a very warm morning for mid-April. The sun on his back as he worked, jacking up the car and prizing off the hub cap, gave promise of as much heat as there had been on the day when he'd met Hugh Packer in the traffic jam, and by an idle comment started the process that was inexorably ruining his life.

But none of it was his fault, it was Packer's. No decent man would take a stranger up on a casual remark and twist it into a conspiracy to murder. Hugh Packer was evil. For a moment, imagining that he saw the man's wolfish face reflected in the hub cap, Derek remembered the satisfaction he had once gained from lashing out at him and knocking him down.

He picked up the wrench, and rested for a moment on his haunches before tackling the wheel nuts. How much more satisfactory it would be, it occurred to him, as he hefted the wrench in his good hand, to clobber Packer with a weapon like that! To kill him, even –

Well, yes. And perhaps he could do it, as long as he struck the man in hot blood. But he couldn't do it with premeditation. As he applied the wrench to its proper purpose, grunting with the effort of loosening the wheel nuts, Derek knew that he could never bring himself to use premeditated violence against anyone. He simply wasn't that kind of man. Besides, his dreams were terrible enough already.

Finishing the job, he packed away his tools and wiped the dirt from his good hand with the rag he kept for the purpose. There was nothing he could do about his soiled bandages – but come to think of it, if today was Friday, and he thought it was, then he was due to go to the health centre to have the stitches out.

He would have to go through Breckham Market on the way to Wyveling, so he might as well have his hand done before seeing Christine. No – on second thoughts, he couldn't bear to waste time. He wanted to talk to her as soon as possible. And anyway, if she saw how neglected he looked, she might be more favourably disposed towards him.

He drove out through the gates, stopped the car, and went back to close them. He was just driving off when he saw that another car was approaching down the narrow tree-lined road, and so he pulled back in front of the gates to give it room to pass. But as the car neared, it slowed.

He didn't recognize the vehicle, and when it rolled to a stop beside him he knew why. The man behind the wheel was Hugh Packer, his darkly handsome face distorted by a scowl. As Packer got out of the car and slammed the door, Derek felt his stomach dip.

'What the hell are you doing here?' Packer demanded.

Derek wound down his window. With anxious inspiration rather than presence of mind, he heard himself reply, 'I came to look the place over, so that I'd know my way round on Sunday.'

'You bloody fool! Now you've ruined my plan – Belinda's probably seen you.'

'No, she hasn't. And the plan's off. I saw her take her father away in the Rolls about twenty minutes ago.'

'How do you know the plan's off? They may be back by lunch-time.'

'I don't think so. When I first drove past, I saw her loading suitcases into the car.'

Packer swore, and strutted rapidly up and down in thought. Derek had forgotten – he always forgot, because in his mind the man assumed the proportions of a monster – how small he was in reality.

'Belinda will have left a note for me in the house,' decided

212

Packer, returning to the window. 'I expect she's taken Sidney to Ely – I was supposed to be going there with her on Sunday, so she'll want me to join them. All right, then: this Sunday's off. But I know she won't stay away for more than a few days, because the old man's difficult to cope with away from home.'

He took a pocket diary from his blazer and riffled it through. 'The following Sunday will suit me almost as well. I'll book a table for lunch somewhere for Belinda and myself, and arrange for the untrained help to sit with the old man.' He bent towards Derek, displaying his canine tooth in a narrow smile. 'Right, so we'll make it Sunday week.'

Derek swallowed. Here they were, arranging the date of an old man's death, and Packer was treating it with no more emotion than he would a game of golf. 'I'm not sure – ' he began, trying to invent a previous engagement; but Packer shot out his hand and grabbed him by the knot of his tie, threatening to choke him.

'Then you'd bloody better *make* sure, Derek,' he said. A bead of spittle gleamed on his tooth. 'I want this over and done with, understand?'

Derek nodded, with difficulty. Packer released his hold. 'The only snag', he said as if to himself, 'is that there'll be no Pony Club event that Sunday, and no car-park. I'll have to find somewhere for you to pull in off the road.' He stabbed a finger at Derek: 'Wait there!'

Speechless with anger, but impotent to do anything else, Derek sat waiting. He watched Packer check that there was no traffic in sight, and then swagger briskly along the road beside the garden wall. Where the wall turned in at a right angle among the trees, Packer disappeared behind it.

Within a few seconds Derek saw him emerge, apparently satisfied that he had found a suitably hidden parking-place. Standing on the narrow grass verge, Packer beckoned imperiously. Obedient still, Derek put the car in gear and began to roll.

There was nothing premeditated about what he did then. His mind seemed to have closed down. But the mounting fear and loathing he felt for Hugh Packer released a surge of adrenaline that impelled him to attack, with whatever weapon he had available. On instinct, he shifted the engine into second gear, slammed his foot on the accelerator, turned the wheel and went straight at his tormentor.

Packer saw him coming, but didn't seem to believe what he saw. Quite clearly, from the initial look of annoyance on his face, it simply hadn't occurred to him that Derek would ever fight. Then the man's expression changed, from annoyance through perplexity to unease, and then to abject fear.

Packer turned to run. Colliding with a tree trunk, he almost bounced back into the path of the car. Still trying to run, he twisted his body round, opened his mouth in frantic appeal and flung up his hands, as if to ward off the mass of metal and glass and rubber that Derek was propelling towards him.

Outwardly calm, Derek felt a thump against the bumper and saw Packer shoot up into the air, growing a foot taller in front of his eyes. He braked, swinging the wheel to avoid the tree. Packer fell towards him, hands monstrously outstretched, momentarily filling Derek's view before he landed with a crunch, face down on the bonnet. Then, slowly, as if he were shrinking, he began to slide backwards off the nearside of the car.

Derek sat and watched as the man's hands scrabbled for a grip on the smooth metal. Then one hand caught hold of the nearside windscreen wiper, pulling the blade away from the glass but clinging to it to arrest the body's slide.

Packer lifted his black curly head to reveal a bloodied face. His eyes were staring, his nose was awry, his mouth was closing and then gaping wide. He tightened his grip on the windscreen wiper. Veins stood out on his forehead as he struggled to pull himself higher. But as he did so, the wiper bent towards him under the strain, and his head fell with a thump. Leaving a smeared trail of blood on the paintwork, he slid sideways off the bonnet and almost disappeared. Only the forearm and the hand that clutched the tip of the wiper blade remained in Derek's view.

Everything was suddenly very quiet. The engine had stalled with the impact, and the reverberations of it had died away. Derek sat rigid, still without thought, watching that hand.

Gradually, almost imperceptibly, the grip was loosening. The fingers, each with its crest of stiff black hairs, seemed to be losing their strength. But Derek kept on watching, fearing that any moment the hand would tighten and Packer's menacing face would reappear.

Instead, the hand went. One second it was there on the bonnet, weak but still flexed; the next, it had collapsed like a puppet's and gone.

Derek blinked and shook his head. He hardly dared believe it. He looked again, but there was nothing to see except the smears of blood on the bonnet of the car; and they convinced him.

Packer was dead. He didn't matter any more.

But it was too soon to feel relief. Derek looked anxiously up and down the road. Was anyone coming? Would he be seen, and his car remembered?

For once, though, luck seemed to be with him. The road was empty; his engine started sweetly. Backing away from what lay crumpled on the verge, he drove off without giving it a glance.

Three minutes later, having encountered no other vehicle, he was able to mingle his car with the traffic on a busy road. Within ten minutes he was at a service station on the Newmarket by-pass, putting the Sierra through an automatic car wash. And no sooner had he watched the bloodstains on the bonnet being sudsed away, than relief came rinsing over him.

He was free. All his Packer-related problems had disappeared. He had finally found a way out.

32

Derek went straight to the Brickyard. It didn't occur to him that Christine would be anywhere else.

He walked in through the back door and along the kitchen corridor, and found her sitting on her tall stool at the ironing board, folding one of his shirts. 'Dee!' she said, looking across the board at him with surprise and concern; but he knew she wouldn't have called him that if she hadn't been pleased to see him.

'Hallo, darling.'

He wanted to give her a great hug and tell her how much he loved her; he wanted to tell her that everything was going to be all right from now on, as long as she still loved him. But it was difficult, with the ironing board in the way. Compromising, he leaned hopefully towards her. With affection, but briefly, she met his mouth with hers.

They enquired after each other's health. Christine said she was feeling much better, and Derek was thankful to see that she looked it. He was telling her that he intended to go and have his stitches out that afternoon when, with a clatter of nails and a *woof*, their beagle came pushing through the door behind him.

'Sam!' cried Derek. In truth, for the past two or three days he'd forgotten about the dog completely. But that didn't mean he wasn't overjoyed to see it. No wonder Christine was looking better! With the beagle's return, Derek felt – however obscurely – that they were a family again.

'Oh, Sam, you're back!' He crouched down, holding out his good hand. 'Come to Dad, then, you great old silly – '

The little tri-coloured dog was already half way towards him, stern wagging. Now it checked, its domed forehead wrinkling with perplexity. 'Come on,' coaxed Derek. 'Good boy, good old boy.'

The beagle skirted cautiously round him and stood at Christine's feet, whining softly, watching him. Its tail still wagged, but without much enthusiasm. Fancying that he saw reproach in its eyes, Derek stood up abruptly. The dog was found, and he wasn't going to think about the way it had been lost.

'Have the police spoken to you yet?' asked Christine. There was no alarm in her voice but his spirits plummeted. Oh God – had someone seen him on the Winter Paddocks road after all?

'What about?' he asked nervously.

She continued with her ironing. 'Chief Inspector Quantrill's been trying to get in touch with you. He thinks you may be able to help him – something to do with Sam getting lost, I believe. He wanted you to ring him as soon as you got back.'

Derek breathed again. 'What's the point, now Sam's found?' he said lightly. Then, 'Oh, Chrissie – its wonderful to be at home with you. We've been through such a terrible patch, but it's over now. Let's forget all about it and make a fresh start, shall we?'

Christine put down her iron. She was looking at him as though he were a stranger.

'Derek,' she said, with an emotional break in her voice. 'Haven't you forgotten something? My poor mother was brutally murdered, upstairs in this house, less than a week ago. How can I "forget all about it"? I doubt if I'd have been brave enough to come here this morning, if Sam hadn't been with me. I certainly can't come back here to live. If you and I ever make a fresh start together, it will have to be somewhere else.'

He was shattered by disappointment. '"If we ever"? But we must – I can't live without you. I'll go anywhere, anywhere you like, as long as we're together. I love you, Chrissie!'

She sighed. 'And I love you, Dee. But it's no use pretending that things are the same, because they're not. We've grown apart. We need a break from each other, for a time at least. You stay here, if what's happened doesn't worry you, and I'll go to Cambridgeshire.'

'Don't you mean Derbyshire?'

'No, I've changed my mind. I couldn't be happy there, doing nothing and being of no use to anyone. Sam and I have been invited to Winter Paddocks, to stay with Belinda Packer and her father.'

Derek sat down abruptly, and stammered out his astonishment. Christine looked critically at the garment she was ironing.

'You'll want some new office shirts – Marks and Spencer, size 16½. Yes, I've met Belinda. She came to see me this morning, and we got on extremely well. I'm going to help her look after her father.'

'But you've no idea how handicapped he is!' Derek protested. 'For heaven's sake, Chrissie – you've been tied down for so much of your life, first by Laurie, then by your mother. I thought you'd be thankful to be free!'

'Yes,' she said soberly, 'I suppose that's what everyone must think. But in practice it's different. I need to be *needed*, you see. I've felt adrift ever since Laurie died, as though I'd left some important business unfinished. And now Mum's dead, too, I think that helping Belinda will give me a sense of purpose. Besides, the poor girl's afraid of her husband. He's a brute, and she intends to get a legal separation from him as soon as possible, and then a divorce. If I'm staying with her, it'll help to keep him away.'

Derek didn't stop to analyse his emotions, or to think. His need for Christine was paramount, and he spoke from frustration and jealousy. 'Well, you've no need to go to Winter Paddocks on that account! Belinda won't have any more problems with her husband, because he's dead.'

'Dead? He can't be . . . She was here talking about him, half an hour ago. What's happened, Derek? How do you know?'

He shouldn't have told her, he realized that immediately. With anyone other than Christine, the mistake would have finished him. But as long as she was the only person who knew, he was sure he could make her understand. She had said that she still loved him, that was the all-important thing. As long as she loved him, he knew he could count on her loyalty.

'Hugh Packer was one of my clients,' he began, careful with his explanation. 'That was why I went to Winter Paddocks, to see him, but he was away. Then Belinda told me what a violent man he was – how he'd married her for her father's money, and was trying to get rid of the old man with an overdose of insulin.

'Well of course, knowing that, I wouldn't have him as a client any longer. I was driving away from the house this morning, after Belinda had gone, when he arrived unexpectedly. We met just outside the gates. He tried to stop me, to talk, but I didn't want anything to do with him. I accelerated, and suddenly there he was, right in front of me. There was absolutely nothing I could do – '

Christine, iron in hand, was staring at him with horror. Derek watched apprehensively as the blood, which had made such a welcome return to her cheeks, drained away, leaving her white and ill. 'And you ran over him? *You* killed him? Oh, how dreadful – what a terrible experience for you!'

'Yes – yes, it was.'

'What about the police? What do they say?'

Derek swallowed. This was going to be the difficult part. 'I haven't told them. No – listen to me, Chrissie, you must understand. There was no one else there. No witnesses at all. When I saw that Packer was dead, naturally I drove straight off to find a telephone.

'But then I realized that the police would start asking questions. They'd find out that Packer had been cruel to his wife, and that I'd spent a couple of nights at Winter Paddocks – though not making love to Belinda, I swear – and they'd assume that I did it deliberately. If I told them, I could never convince them that it was an accident.'

Christine abandoned the iron. Her pallor had been replaced by a flush of anger. 'What do you mean, Derek? "If you told them"? Of course you must tell them! Accidents happen, the police know that. They'll be able to judge how it occurred from your tyre marks. You've got to tell them – you can't leave a man lying dead on the road.'

'But Chrissie, darling, you must think this through. The police may get it wrong. They may misinterpret my tyre marks, and then I'll run the risk of being tried and imprisoned, just for an accident. Surely you don't want that to happen?'

Christine looked at him with incomprehension. 'Well of

course I don't. But that isn't a valid reason for not owning up. It's a criminal offence to cause a road accident and not report it. Besides, hit-and-run drivers are despicable. I couldn't possibly live with you ever again if I knew you'd been responsible for someone's death and were too cowardly to admit it. I don't see how you could live with yourself. What's happened to you, Derek? You always used to be such a good, honest man.'

'But it's not as if I'd knocked down an innocent person,' he argued desperately. 'Hugh Packer is evil. Chrissie – more evil than you know. Surely you don't expect me to give myself up for the sake of someone like that?'

'You can't start playing God, Derek. It isn't for you to judge whether a person deserves to live or to die.'

Her moral certainty embittered him. All very well for Christine to take that stand, when she had absolutely no idea what had really happened.

Everything he had done, first to release her from the burden of her old mother and then to escape from Packer's malign influence, had been done out of love and compassion for his wife. And now, just when it had seemed that he'd at last freed himself from the resulting entanglements, he realized that his love for her held him trapped. He could do one of two things: report Packer's death, or not. Whichever he chose, he would irrevocably forfeit what mattered to him most, Christine's love for him.

In comparison with the loss of that, the prospect of any legally devised punishment seemed to be of little consequence. He was too exhausted, mentally and emotionally, to withstand police questioning or to care any longer what happened to him. When he made his final appeal to Christine, it was not for his own sake but for hers. Better for her that she should despise him as a coward than that she should find out exactly how her mother came to die.

'But Chrissie, you don't know the half of it. I can't explain, but if we involve the police, it'll bring us nothing but unhappiness. Please, *please*, say you'll support me – for your sake as well as mine.'

She stood for a few moments, looking at him, saying nothing. Then she gave him a sad, fond smile. 'Of course I'll support you, Dee. Don't worry – everything will be all right.'

She began to walk towards him. He held out his hands to her, but she walked straight past him to the telephone.

'Breckham Market police?' he heard her say. 'My husband wants to report a fatal accident.'

FOR THE BEST IN PAPERBACKS, LOOK FOR THE 🐧

In every corner of the world, on every subject under the sun, Penguin represents quality and variety—the very best in publishing today.

For complete information about books available from Penguin—including Pelicans, Puffins, Peregrines, and Penguin Classics—and how to order them, write to us at the appropriate address below. Please note that for copyright reasons the selection of books varies from country to country.

In the United Kingdom: For a complete list of books available from Penguin in the U.K., please write to *Dept E.P., Penguin Books Ltd, Harmondsworth, Middlesex, UB7 0DA*.

In the United States: For a complete list of books available from Penguin in the U.S., please write to *Dept BA, Penguin*, Box 120, Bergenfield, New Jersey 07621-0120.

In Canada: For a complete list of books available from Penguin in Canada, please write to *Penguin Books Ltd, 2801 John Street, Markham, Ontario L3R 1B4*.

In Australia: For a complete list of books available from Penguin in Australia, please write to the *Marketing Department, Penguin Books Ltd, P.O. Box 257, Ringwood, Victoria 3134*.

In New Zealand: For a complete list of books available from Penguin in New Zealand, please write to the *Marketing Department, Penguin Books (NZ) Ltd, Private Bag, Takapuna, Auckland 9*.

In India: For a complete list of books available from Penguin, please write to *Penguin Overseas Ltd, 706 Eros Apartments, 56 Nehru Place, New Delhi, 110019*.

In Holland: For a complete list of books available from Penguin in Holland, please write to *Penguin Books Nederland B.V., Postbus 195, NL-1380AD Weesp, Netherlands*.

In Germany: For a complete list of books available from Penguin, please write to *Penguin Books Ltd, Friedrichstrasse 10-12, D-6000 Frankfurt Main 1, Federal Republic of Germany*.

In Spain: For a complete list of books available from Penguin in Spain, please write to *Longman, Penguin España, Calle San Nicolas 15, E-28013 Madrid, Spain*.

In Japan: For a complete list of books available from Penguin in Japan, please write to *Longman Penguin Japan Co Ltd, Yamaguchi Building, 2-12-9 Kanda Jimbocho, Chiyoda-Ku, Tokyo 101, Japan*.